FORCELEAP FARM

SUSANNA M. NEWSTEAD

HERESY PUBLISHING

First Published in 2020
by HERESY PUBLISHING
Newbury RG14 5JG
www.heresypublishing.co.uk

Cover design by Charlie Farrow
Editing by Gill Whatmough

ISBN 978-1-909237-04-9

Marlborough and Savernake Forest c.1200 (1)

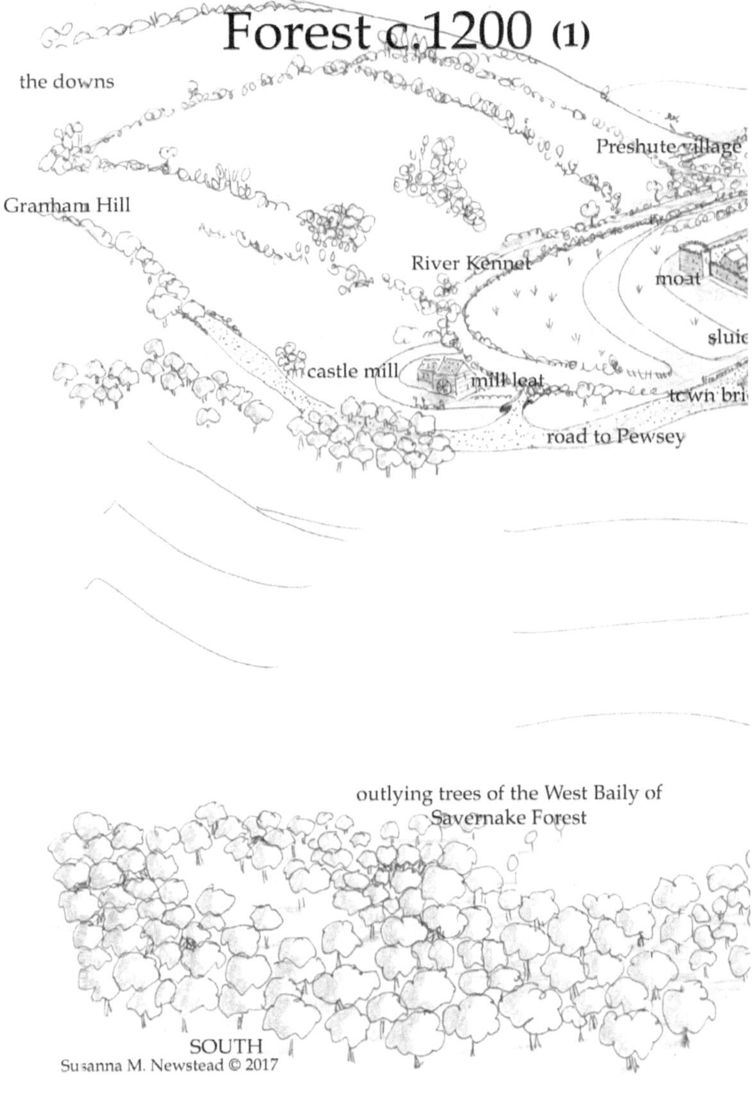

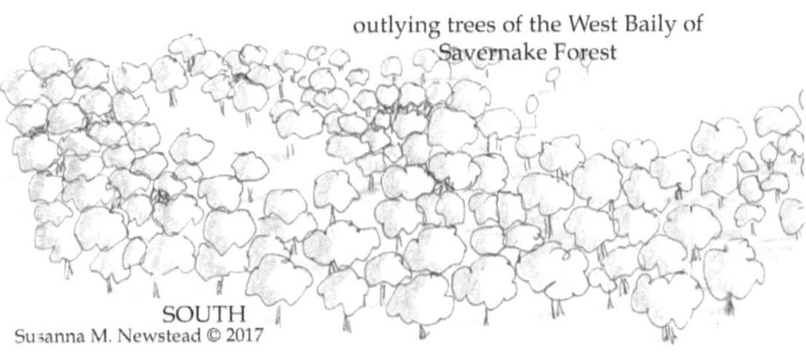

Marlborough Town and the forest c.1200 (2)

Marlborough and the forest
c. 1200 (3)

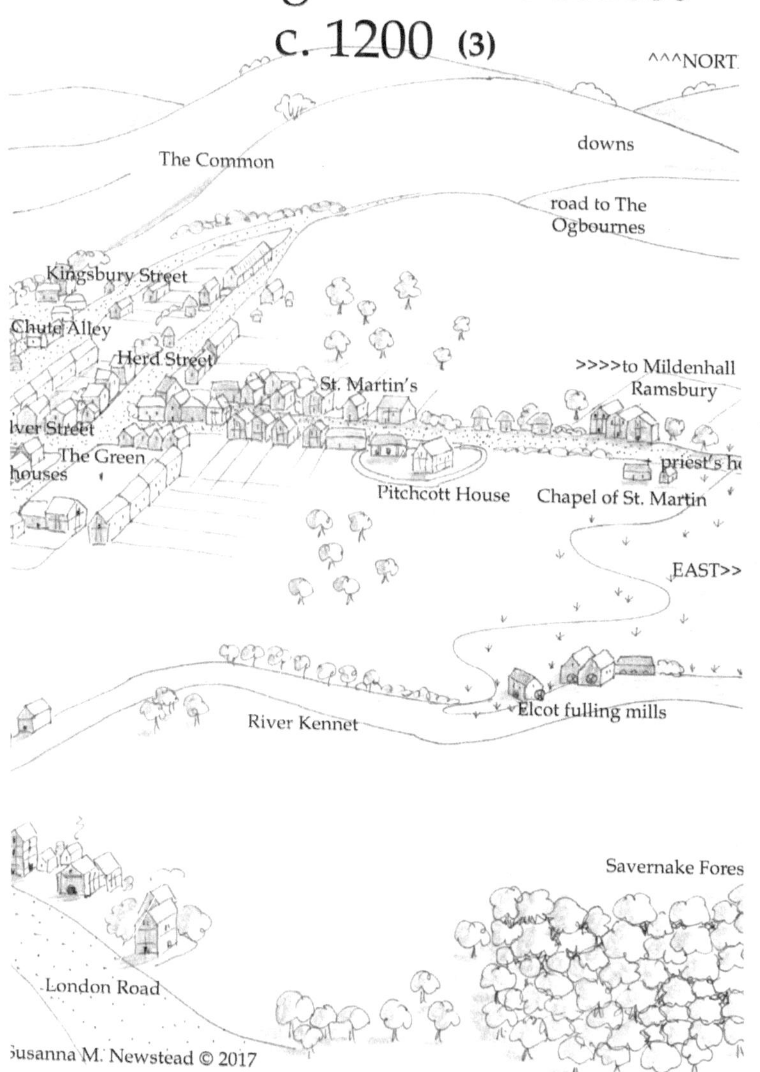

Susanna M. Newstead © 2017

CHAPTER ONE ~ RELEASE

She had honestly never felt better.

It was the day of her husband's funeral when she realised that she had not been this happy for years.

Salt tears of joy and relief ran down her cheeks. 'I suppose they all think that I mourn him and so give me sad and pitying looks.'

The coffin was lowered into the ground; the priest burbled on. Rosalie gave a little strangled cough; 'They have no idea,' she said to herself. 'They all think this show of tears is grief.'

Several faces swept round to her. She turned down her mouth and desperately tried not to smile.

A swift breeze caught the stuff of her veil and she brushed it back with shaking fingers.

The priest's Latin came to an end. There was a shifting of people around the graveside.

'What now?' thought Rosalie. 'What do we do now?'

Her mind left her body and she floated off like the leaves which were fluttering down from the trees along the roadside.

'What do *I* do now? For the first time in thirteen years, I can please myself. I can do as I wish. I can wear, eat, drink, say what I like. I can laugh at what I wish. Oh that one had been so hard. For a girl with a well developed sense of humour, the lack of laughter had been killing.'

The priest was looking directly at her. She thought he looked like a fish; his mouth opening and closing like a landed trout; his large bulging eyes, glassy and yes, oh so ugly. She caught...

"Madam, a word?"

"A word with me?" said Rosalie at last, trying not to giggle.

"A word *from* you."

"Oh...yes...yes.. Thank you Sir Priest. You are all welcome back at the house. Please do follow William, my steward, to the hall. There is food and drink laid on for you all."

The priest nodded. She had done her duty.

William Newbold, the family steward turned dutifully and walked with solemnity slowly down the church path and through the gate, his dark blue robe brushing his heels.

'Dear William,' thought Rosalie. 'If the rest of them were swallowed up forever by a large hole and only William remained, I would shed no tears. Life would be perfect.'

Life was perfect. Now. She only had two men to contend with and they were both at her beck and call.

The journey of not quite a mile was accomplished quickly.

"Thank you, William," she said as she swept through the door of the farmhouse. "Thank you for everything."

"Mistress." William bowed, his twinkling blue eyes, just for a short moment, giving her strength. He knew she was holding the laughter she longed to let out.

She moved in a stately fashion down the room to the table at the head. Her maid, Beatrice removed her cloak and stepped back. Young Adam Page held her chair for her and she sat, tucking a stray hair back into her wimple.

One by one people took their places. Her eyes roved over them all.

Neighbour Nicholas and his haughty wife Nicolaa - she always thought that odd that they had the same name. Her sister-in-law Alfrida and her oh so handsome but ineffectual husband, Edward. Her farm manager, Ancelin Hayward, a tall, brown haired man, dependable and a man of few words. He sat and fiddled at his belt for his spoon nestled in the pouch at his waist and took his eating knife from its scabbard. Her eyes met his. He smiled.

Men from the forest nearby. Those who worked for the warden in various capacities. The most elevated nearest to her and those who laboured with their hands, further away.

Wives, sons, daughters-in-law of the area. They were all there ready to partake of the fruits of the farm.

Roger's burial feast.

The servants came round with steaming bowls of soup. Rosalie nodded her thanks as a young girl slopped some liquid into her bowl.

She picked up her spoon and watched. When all had been served, she took a small amount of the soup and lifted it to her lips.

It was salty. She spluttered a little but swallowed.

"Oh my! I am not going to be able to do this,' she said to herself. She tried again. Again the hiccough.

'Fiddle! This is what comes of keeping in your joy. Your humours get all churned up.'

She broke some bread and took a tiny piece. She chewed and swallowed.

It was like swallowing chalk.

She coughed. Her eyes watered.

'Oh God! Please do not let me disgrace myself.'

She coughed again and took out a small piece of material with which she wiped her eyes.

It was no good. A swift look round showed all the faces turned to her. She gave a great moan and stood, sweeping back the stuff of her dark green kirtle. Well, what else could she do?

"Excuse me," she said hoping she'd got the right amount of anguish into the tone.

She ran down between the tables and through the door. She didn't stop until she had put the wood of the parlour door between her and her guests. Then she ran up to the solar.

She tore off her veil, pulled off her wimple, threw back her head and ...laughed. Laughed and laughed.

Until the tears streamed from her eyes once more.

No, she'd never been as happy as she was today!

*****

She did, at last, manage to compose herself and return to the feast. They were all so solicitous and kind. Only Ancelin and William knew the truth but they kept their own counsel.

People trickled away with platitudes on their lips. It took her all her time not to throw her hands in the air and give praise to God. It was with that thought that she was suddenly brought up short.

'Oh, you *are* a wicked woman, Rosalie Jourdemayne. There are many times you have wished your husband gone...and now he is dead. What must God think of you?' said the little voice in her ear.

Rosalie wandered into Roger's office.

She was hardly ever allowed in this room and when she was, it was usually so that Roger could berate her for some wrong doing.

She sat in his chair. She picked up his pen, always sitting on the table top. She stared at his tally sticks.

What would he think now? Now, if he could return and realise that she could read his parchments, use his pen, reckon his tally sticks. He'd had no idea even after thirteen years of marriage that she was literate. English *and* Latin. And numerate.

Thirteen long, unfulfilled, obedient years.

She stared up at the rafters and addressed God directly. "Thank you Lord. I am sorry if I bothered you too often with my entreaties but thank you for releasing me."

She stood and walked to the window.

"And thank you that we remained childless."

Although she had to chuckle to herself about that one. God wished women to bear children. The priests droned on about one's duty to

God and husband. Well, Rosalie had done her duty to Roger. She had tolerated his feeble attempts at coupling, his selfish ways, his bitter recriminations but she had lain there and allowed him his meagre pleasures. What she had not done is conceive a child. Ha, ha. No. Not at all. She'd made sure of that.

Rosalie had employed every prophylactic known to woman. And it had worked. Not once in thirteen years had she and Roger been able to make a child.

Again she looked to the rafters and addressed God. "I am sorry about that Lord God. But I simply couldn't do it. I am sure you understand. I'll leave it to others."

Feeling just a little guilty, she went to bed, now her bed, and stretched out like a starfish.

No longer was she relegated to the edge of the bed. And if she wanted the dog with her, she could have it snuggling up to her. Oh joy!

She drifted in and out of a luxurious slumber. She felt like a child again. And before she slept properly, she gave a great whoop of joy, like a child!

*****

Upon the next day, Rosalie searched out the cotte which Roger had forbidden her to wear. It was a lovely shade of yellow and he had said he'd hated it. So she'd hidden it; kept it safe, away from the shears with which he had once shredded a beautiful kirtle of pale pink, her favorite colour.

She drew the thin yellow wool languorously over her head and sighed. Cinching it at the waist with a leather belt of dark red, she reached for an linen headcloth. This was the thinnest and finest linen she had been able to buy locally. Again, she had kept the garment secreted away and only wore it when Roger was away from the farm. He had no idea that she had kept back some money from the allowance with which she ran the house, to buy it. She tucked her dark blonde hair into the folds and wound it round, settling it on her shoulders.

Rosalie touched her lips with a little honey and byrony juice and patted a small amount of the dried and ground berry onto her cheeks. Her eyelashes she combed with a tiny brush laden with soot and she was ready to meet her new world.

Her first task was one she wished to complete for herself and no one else. Forceleap Farm business could wait.

She took some money from the chest in the office and tipped it into the purse at her waist.

Roger had never allowed a journey into town unless many tasks were needing to be accomplished there. No one from Forceleap Farm ever went to Marlborough simply for pleasure. Neither to attend the twice weekly market or the fair held in August. Unless there was other business to be done there. Never for *pleasure*. Today, Rosalie was going to Marlborough simply for herself.

She shouted for Beatrice, her maid.

"A cloak Bea and get Fulk to take out the cart. We are going shopping!"

*****

It was a pure unalloyed delight to get out of the farm and go with her maid, her groom and her steward, to Marlborough, that morning.

All right... so this wasn't alone but it was as alone as she dared this close to her husband's demise. She was in mourning after all.

Rosalie knew what she was shopping for. Fulk stopped the cart outside Master Mercer's on the southern side of the wide marketplace and Steward Newbold handed her down from her seat.

Bea clambered down, her round face eager and glowing.

"Are we looking for what I think we are looking for, mistress?"

"We are," said Rosalie confidently.

"And what if we can't find it?"

"Then we shall buy it undyed and get it dyed for us."

"But that will cost..." Rosalie looked at her maid under her raised eyebrows. "The cost is immaterial."

"Oh..how funny...hahaha!" shrieked Bea. "Immaterial!"

Her mistress gave her a sharp look and they both passed into the shop. Master Newbold followed.

Bales of fabric lay on trestles and stacked up against the walls. Two women were already in the shop and were fingering some serviceable dark wool laid out on the cutting table.

"Mistress Jourdemayne. It's a very long time since we saw you here," said Master Mercer, beaming.

Rosalie was in no mood for talking.

"Good day to you. I am in need of some fine, some very fine pink wool in the palest shade you can muster, Master Mercer. Failing that, I will take the best undyed you have and take it to Master Tapiser to have it shaded."

The man took a step back. "Well yes." He scanned the dark blue cloak she was wearing wrapped tightly around her yellow gown and his brow furrowed.

"This is for when I am out of mourning, of course."

His forehead lifted. "Ah well then." Master Mercer delved under a bale of rust red and a roll of green blue wool and pulled hard.

"I keep this..." his voice strained as he lifted the bale to the work surface. "For special orders...like your own."

Rosalie could hardly restrain herself from leaning out to touch the cloth but, although her fingers tensed, she was content to feast her eyes on the blush colour of the wool.

"That, Master Mercer, is perfect. I knew you would have it."

"It isn't the cheapest...such a fine nap..."

"That is just what I wanted."

"Can I interest you in..."

"No..no thank you," she said, "That is what I came for. And that alone."

The shopkeeper took hold of a large pair of shears and expertly measured out three and three quarter yards, cutting it with a flourish.

"May I say, Mistress Jourdemayne, that this pink will set off your complexion to perfection."

'That's enough, you distorted old goat,' she thought. 'Keep your opinions to yourself.'

Then she felt guilty and said, "That's most kind, Master Mercer. Most kind of you to say so."

The smiling salesman folded the cloth and handed it to Steward Newbold who, taking the purse from Rosalie, counted out the coins required to pay for it.

Upon the last two, his eyebrows went up and he threw a glance at his mistress as if to say. "This is an extravagance but I understand why you are paying so much for it."

The transaction complete, they quitted the shop, Bea carrying the cloth.

"Where to now, mistress?" asked Bea, her face shining.

"Home, Bea, we have cutting and sewing to do."

They had not paced three steps from the shop when some lads of the town, chasing a runaway piglet, bowled into the small party of three.

The hogling squealed and ducked under the wheels of the cart. Fulk yelled and jumped down to try to retrieve the animal but the three pursuing boys were tangled in the two ladies, their purchase and the cart. Master Newbold fell against the wall of the shop and was momentarily stunned, sliding down the white limed surface. Shaking his head, the older man cried out.

"Gods! I'm seeing stars!"

Bea fell to her knees and dropped her purchase. Rosalie staggered into two of the boys who fell backwards into the legs of a stranger just at that moment, coming around the corner of the alleyway known as Figgins Lane.

The man was not at all put out. He grabbed the two lads by the necks of their tunics and lifted them as if they'd been made of parchment, settling them on their feet.

"Now boys. That's no way to treat such a fine pair of ladies. Apologise this instant." The lads mumbled something.

Rosalie had lost the folds of her head cloth and she hastily fiddled for it and rewrapped her hair, tucking in the curls which fell over her forehead. She struggled to rise, her shoe having caught in her hem. A strong arm came out and grasped her own.

"Forgive me, madam."

"Oh." Rosalie stumbled and Master Steward glared at the newcomer, righting his mistress and then brushing himself down, he stood.

"Thank you." Rosalie looked behind her for Bea who was rubbing her knees, tears in her eyes.

"You hurt, Bea?"

"No, mistress but your cloth..."

The pink cloth lay on the ground, trampled by a pig with the mud of the road seeping into it.

The stranger swept it up immediately. "Oh." He tried to brush it off with his hand.

"No, please. It's best to let it dry and then it will brush off," said Rosalie. She looked around for her groom.

Fulk had now recovered the squealing hogling and was handing it back to the three lads.

The stranger stood up tall, "Then allow me to refold it and give it back to you."

Bea nodded and took it with an amused expression.

Fulk handed his mistress back up onto the seat of the cart. Rosalie sat stiff and just managed to say, "Thank you, sir," before it lurched off. She did not see the charming smile which crossed the lips of the stranger.

But she did look back, when they had been going a heartbeat or two, just once, to see him staring after them, for quite some time.

*****

The day continued with farm business and decisions to be made about the breeding stock of cattle.

Forceleap Farm had always been a place for cattle. Long back into the days of the Conqueror, the beef cattle had been famous in the area and the skins produced for the tanning trade, excellent. Forceleap was mentioned in that great book commissioned by William the First, The Great Survey. The lush meadows of the Kennet valley allowed good grass for the beasts and the short herb and flower strewn chalk downs were perfect for sheep. Roger's father had enlarged the farm area by renting greater acreage and by buying up the unusual cattle known as long horned, from their Templar neighbours who bred them, at Lockeridge. These beautiful and docile creatures wore magnificent horns on their heads and struck fear into many who saw them. It was said that they resembled the devils of the domain which lies under our feet but those in the know, did not fear them. To those who farmed them, they were more like the denizens of Heaven.

Roger Jourdemayne had farmed these beautiful beasts, both as draught animals and for meat. His father had seen the potential in them and had invested heavily. Forcelap Farm was now a prosperous place and the family who owned it, wealthy.

With the death of her husband and with no male heir or family member to inherit, and no man to tell her what to do, Forceleap had come to Rosalie. She was, at last, a relatively affluent widow.

She turned the word over in her mouth…"Widow."

She spread out the pink wool now cleansed of its pig and mud, on the hall trestle. "Widow."

Bea handed her the shears.

"Widow Jourdemayne."

"Pardon, Mistress Jourdemayne?"

"Oh nothing, Bea. I'm just playing, in my head, with the idea of being a widow. It's all so new to me."

"Oh…no…don't dwell on it mistress. I am sure you will find another man very soon. You are such a handsome looking woman… for your age."

Rosalie tutted and cut, rather viciously. "Thirty is no age, young lady."

"Ah no, my ma was thirty when she had our John. He was number six."

Rosalie shuddered.

"And then she had me, number...er...number..."

"Seven, Bea."

"Ah yes, seven. An' I was the last"

"Oh? Why was that?"

"Well... our Arnold, he died when he was about three months; he was number four and... our Edie... was number...number..whatever and..."

"Five"

"And John and then me and then she died."

'I'm not surprised,' said Rosalie to herself. 'Worn out I expect.'

"Well, I have no intention of remarrying."

Bea gave an embarrassed giggle. "Aw no...mistress, you don't mean that."

"I do. Indeed, I do."

The girl squirmed. "Well...you know...what about... about...?"

"About what?"

Snip. Turn the corner. Crunch, went the shears.

"You know...thingy..."

"Thingy?"

'Oh God! She means sexual congress!' the little devil in Rosalie's brain said.

"If you mean sexual congress, Beatrice, then say so."

"Yes madam. Yes...*that*."

"Do you manage to go without, young lady?"

"I...I..."

"Well you should. You are a maiden. Unmarried and as far as I know you have no young man." She stopped cutting and looked up at her maid servant. She was a plain girl with mousy hair, teeth like a beaver and a face full of spots.

'Oh Jesu. I'd not be fifteen again for all the world,' said Rosalie under her breath.

"Have you?"

"Er...no but..."

"BUT Miss?" Rosalie waved the shears in the air. "I hope you *are* a maid."

"Oh I am...I am but..."

"There should be no buts. Buts are large barrels in which we keep water."

Bea gaped. "If you can do without, then so can I," said Rosalie.

"Well..." Beatrice swished her skirt from side to side. "I do like John. John Sommer."

"John who is one of my tenants and pays rent in the summer?"

"He has lovely eyes... and a big..."

Rosalie raised her eyes to her wayward servant. "Big...what? Big...pig...?"

"*Yes,* he does...He has bigger pigs than..."

"This conversation is at an end, Bea."

"But madam, no one should have to go without...*it*...for a long while. It's very bad for the body."

'Snip round the armhole. Don't look at her.'

"It's also very bad for the body to bear a child every year until you are worn out and you die."

"Yes, madam."

The rest of the cotte of pink wool was cut out in silence.

"Right, you sew one long side seam. I'll do the other."

Thread was procured and they sat at the table to sew.

"Mistress Jourdemayne?"

"Yes Bea?"

"Did you know that man in town today?"

"No. How would I know him?"

"Oh...I don't know. It was the way he looked at you."

"Looks cost nothing to either party, Bea." Rosalie bit off another piece of thread and pushed it through the eye of the steel needle.

"It was like he knew who you were."

"He may have known me but I didn't know him and that is the way it is going to stay."

"Yes, madam."

"He had a very big…"

"Pig…Bea?"

"Sword, madam."

Rosalie looked at her maid under her eyelashes for a whole three heartbeats.

Bea shrugged. "Really - *he did.* A long one." She flushed to the roots of her hair. "A soldier from the castle, I expect."

"Maybe."

They carried on sewing.

*****

The cotte was finished in no time and Rosalie wore it upon the next day. It made her feel fresh and new. And she *loved* the colour.

She was very careful to wear her dark cloak over it and only those closest to her got to see it.

But to Rosalie, it had become a symbol of her new found freedom.

Ah…but not freedom from daily chores about the house. So that she would not soil her new creation, she tucked an apron around her waist and began to chop up some vegetables for a soup.

"Ah…no…" she said out loud. "Not soup."

She swept away the vegetables and turned to the shelf behind her. Apples. Lots of apples. She called to Bea who came running.

"Peel and core these will you please Bea?"

"What for…? We never…"

"No, we haven't until now, but now… now we shall eat pie."

"What? Pastry pie…pie with apples?"

"Yes indeed."

"But the master forbade us…"

"He is not here now to forbid anything."

Bea's face split into a cheeky grin. "No he isn't. The miserable old toad of a skinflint."

Rosalie affected not to have heard her.

"I will make the pastry."

"Oh mistress, you really mean we shall eat..apple pie?"

"We shall Bea. With cream. I'll go up to Mistress Weare at Kennet and buy some." This lady was one of the foremost dairymaids in the area.

"Buy some?"

"Well, until we can do it for ourselves, we shall buy it."

"Oh Lord." The girl grinned inanely. "Life is so much better with you in charge, mistress."

"I am glad to hear it."

"So we shall make cream?"

"We want to eat it. We have the cows with the milk, we shall make it."

As Rosalie made the mixture for the coffin which would contain the fruit, she thought back upon all the things which her husband had forbidden her on the farm over the years.

She had not been allowed candles once it had gone dark. She'd had to retire to bed. Oh Roger might stay up all night if he wished but Rosalie must be in bed with the going down of the sun.

Well now, she would stay up all night if she wished and ruin her eyesight by the light of several candles, sewing everything she had ever wanted to sew.

And chilblains would be a thing of the past. Warmth. She would have warmth from a fire whenever she wished it. She stretched out her fingers, now cleansed of the pastry. The chilblains were receding. 'Eight short days he's been gone and they are fading, like Roger himself,' she said under her breath.

She caught sight of her arm as she pulled down the sleeve of her new pink cotte. No more bruises. She would no longer have to hide them.

Oh he never marked her where it could easily be seen and woe betide her if she was ever caught with no wimple or headcloth. The bruises he'd inflicted on her throat were always to be covered. She wondered what they looked like now. Eight days later. Eight days ago had been the last time he had taken his fists to her. She would buy herself a mirror at the cutler's in Marlborough; a polished steel mirror so that she could look and make sure that there were no lasting marks. He could not tell her that she could not have a mirror now. Nor cosmetics. Nor sweetmeats. Nor sing. Oh, she'd loved singing as a girl. She hadn't sung in thirteen years.

No, that was a lie.

She had sung in the first month she was married, at her tasks in the hall. Sweeping, dusting, cleaning, tidying.

Roger had marched into the hall and told her that such expression was forbidden; that it was a tool of the devil. Evil and debased. Lilith had sung; that wanton night hag, the first wife of Adam who had defied him and was banished from the Garden for her lack of submission.

Rosalie had gently argued her case.

She never argued in such a way again. It wasn't worth the pain.

She went out into the yard, looked up at the sky and filled her lungs.

Could she still do it, after so long? Would her voice obey her?

Tentatively she hummed and then opened her mouth.

*   *"Mirie it is while sumer y-last*

    With fugheles song." She closed her eyes. *"Oc nu necheth windes blast*

and weder strong."

She sensed that Bea had come out after her and was listening.

She sang as loud as she could.

*   *"Ej! Ej! what this nicht is long,*

    And ich with wel michel wrong

    Soregh and murne and fast."

"Oh madam. You have a lovely voice. Why have you never sung before?" said Bea with wonder in her tone.

* Translation in Author's Note page 250

Rosalie turned. "Because I've had nothing to sing about."

*****

That night Rosalie lay in bed and thought about the tasks which would now be hers; decisions about the farm.

'I will learn from Ancelin Hayward, everything I can learn. I'll follow him in his daily routine, for a few weeks in order to understand what he does and how the farm works.' She was an intelligent woman, with a retentive memory. She didn't think she'd have a problem comprehending. All the hard work was done by the lesser men of the farm; she didn't need to get her hands dirty.

So ten days after the death of her husband, Rosalie followed like the little shadow of a faithful dog, the work of her farm manager, asking questions and writing down the answers on a waxed tablet. Ancelin simply smiled and did what he normally did. If he explained something, he was calm and succinct and if she asked a stupid question, he showed no idea of its stupidity. Afterwards she'd go into the office and write everything down on parchment, making what she liked to call her little manual of husbandry.

'Or maybe it should be called 'wifedry'...ah no...a little manual of widowdry,' she said to herself, chuckling.

It was on the fourteenth day after Roger's death that Rosalie received her first visitor. It was a little presumptuous, thought Rosalie, for she was allowed time to grieve alone after the funeral and fourteen days were not long. But she received her guest in the hall, in her dark clothing and put on a solemn face though it cost her dear. All afternoon she had indigestion.

"Madam." The man bowed low and swept off his ridiculous hat which had been perched on his head like an upside down piss pot.

His bald crown faced her and it took all her willpower not to giggle, for the hair left on his head looked to her, for all the world like the hair on her dog's behind. She searched out her dog, Dyamant, who was at that moment standing just to her left swishing her long curved tail to and fro.

'Yes! He has dog rump hair!'

The man straightened. "Please allow me to convey my condolences on the death of your husband Roger. He will be sorely missed."

She nodded slowly.

"Master Pottinger. Welcome and thank you. Will you take ale?"

Bea scurried to the pot board and poured the man ale. Rosalie sat in her chair and bade him sit a few feet away from her.

"I hope I find you well in body...if not completely so in mind?"

"Both mind and body are completely well, thank you, Master Pottinger."

"Ah...yes. Roger always said you were a strong minded woman."

She didn't answer him but the devil on her shoulder said. 'Quite right, Roger Jourdemayne. Quite right.'

"And that little bothers you. You are dealing with his death in a most commendable way."

"Commendable?"

Merely..." He made his hand into a fist and moved it as if he were striking a small object. "You are keeping yourself...together."

"You mean I am not falling apart." She smiled an unfriendly smile.

"Well...yes. It's good to see."

Rosalie sighed. "Master Pottinger, what can I do for you?"

"Mistress Jourdemayne. You see before you one who has admired you from afar for many years."

"Really?"

"And were you not the wife of my friend Roger, well, I would have declared my intentions a long time ago."

"And now Roger is gone?"

"Madam. Might I say how much I admire and revere you?"

'You admire and revere my money. You admire Forceleap Farm,' said the voice in Rosalie's head.

"That is most kind."

The man swallowed some ale and the Adam's apple in his scrawny neck bobbed up and down like the dipper birds she'd seen in the river Kennet.

"And if you should ever..." he laid his hand on his breast where lay his heart, 'ever...think to marry again, I hope that you would consider me a worthy suitor."

Rosalie sat more upright.

"Your farm lies where, sir?"

"Over towards Mildenhall. Thirty virgates of good..."

"Ah yes. By the river. I remember Roger saying it."

"It is a beautiful spot. With the forest rising on the hillside above."

"I'm sure."

"Our two farms..."

"I have no intention of marrying again, sir. In fact I am considering..."

"Oh no mistress, please, that would be a waste!"

"Pardon? A waste?"

"To take the veil. I know that you grieve deeply for my good friend Roger. He always said how much he knew you adored him, but to shut yourself away in your grief..."

"I have no intention of taking the veil but I am considering taking *a vow.*"

"A vow?"

"Of celibacy."

The man's face crumbled like an old stone wall kicked by a carthorse.

His mouth opened and shut.

'Ah another landed fish,' thought Rosalie with an internal chuckle.

"I am sorry."

"Ah well...if you should reconsider."

"You will be the first to know, sir."

The Adam's apple bobbled again. Thrice, as he drained the pot.

He stood.

He bowed.

Bea jumped up to accompany him to the door.

He bowed once more at the exit.

"Good day, madam."

Now his hair stuck out at the side like the straw figures used to scare birds, called hodmedod, which Rosalie had seen in her native Berkshire as a child. She could not help but chuckle at the comparison.

He was gone.

Bea came back in, a huge grin on her face.

"Oh mistress that was…"

"Amusing Bea. The first of many I think."

"Oh no...really?"

"Once word gets round that Roger is dead and his widow is in charge… there will be other flies coming to the body."

"Bees to the honeypot."

'Ah no,' thought Rosalie, 'flies to the dead corpse.'

*****

The second fly came four days later.

"Master Dankworth, how kind of you to come and see me."

She'd wondered how long it would take for this particular fly to smell the decay of rotten flesh. And the sweet smell of Forceleap Farm without a master.

Master Ralph Dankworth was a neighbour who farmed quite close to the ancient circle of stones called Avebury. He had the most evil eyes Rosalie had ever seen and many's the time she had fantasised that he was one of the devil's henchman.

Those evil eyes, cold, pale and blue, fixed on her now.

"I have to come to pay my respects. I hope that I have left a suitable amount of time. One doesn't know quite what to do in circumstances like this. Come quickly and offer succour to the bereaved or wait until..."

"Until the widow is floundering around, deep in the mud of farm business?"

The man stopped. He cleared his throat.

"I am sure...."

"Good...I am glad you are sure. It makes it so much easier to say that I do not flounder, nor do I need succour."

Ancelin Hayward, who was standing close by his mistress, also cleared his throat.

"Mistress Jourdemayne is a very capable woman, sir. I have every faith in her ability to run this farm with the same...nay perhaps even greater aplomb than did her husband."

'Thank you Ancelin,' said Rosalie's devil. 'I now know what you thought of my husband. I heretofore could only guess but that has just set it straight in my mind.'

She turned to her farm manager. "Thank you Ancelin. As I have every faith in your ability to set me straight should I wander from the path."

"I see that the two of you have the whole state of affairs under control."

Ancelin looked at Rosalie.

"I think we can safely say that, all things running smoothly, Forcelap Farm is in good hands."

"But... and here I mean no disparagement, a woman running such an enterprise...how would the rest of the county view..."

Rosalie stood up. "Master Dankworth. My sex is not the issue here."

"Oh but madam, a good farm manager is invaluable, that I will say. But to deal with equals one must.."

"Be a man?"

The evil eyes narrowed and he waved his hands out to his side in a gesture of finality.

"Then..." She stepped away from her chair. "Think of me, sir, as a man."

Dankworth laughed. His eyes roved up and down her dark green body. "Madam it is precisely because you are such a lovely *woman* that I am here."

"Ah… and it has nothing to do with the farm. It's me you desire."

"Ah..well put like that…"

"No sir. No. I have sworn not to remarry."

Ancelin looked quickly at her and then composed his face.

"Mistress Jourdemayne is not looking for a husband," he said.

Dankworth looked from one to the other.

"Ahhh…I see…the manager takes the place of the husband. Well, it's not unknown, is it?"

Ancelin was about to remonstrate but Rosalie's little devil screamed in her ear. And she spoke loudly to Master Dankworth.

"I shall shortly be taking a vow of celibacy before a priest. Marriage is out of the question."

Ralph Dankworth's face went puce.

"I wish you joy madam," he said and turned tail.

"A vow? Of celibacy?" Ancelin folded his arms.

"It is something I have been contemplating."

"Why?"

"It's precisely for reasons like Master Ralph Dankworth, Master Hayward. If I am not available, then neither is Forceleap farm."

A little twitching smile crossed the lips of Ancelin the manager.

"I hope you know what you're doing."

*****

It was at church the following Sunday that Rosalie had her third encounter.

The mass was over. A stiff wind was blowing and Rosalie, leaving the church, looked up at the scudding clouds racing behind the church tower. She caught sight of the mass dial scratched onto the wall above the porch. It had lost it's gnomon.

She peered into the grass and spotted it; bending down to retrieve it, she came face to boot with a man.

"Mistress Jourdemayne."

She took her time picking up the piece of metal with an ungloved hand.

Rising, she said. "Sir Hugh, how pleasant to see you."

Now, in this instance, she meant it. Sir Hugh of Yatesbury was a handsome man in his middle twenties, with perfect skin, perfect teeth and a perfect sense of dress. He was good to look upon.

She smiled at him. "I am so sorry to hear about the death of your mother, sir."

"My thanks. As was I to hear about Master Roger. It must have been quite sudden."

"He did not suffer long."

"That is always good to know." The man crossed himself. "Shall we walk a little about the churchyard?"

Rosalie turned to nod to Bea who knew to follow out of earshot.

'Out of earshot, my fiddle faddle,' said Rosalie to herself, looking back again.

"So what took him off...if I might be so bold as to ask?"

"Yes, you are right."

"Pardon?"

"Your tone implies that you think he was in general good health. He was. And it took only one day for him to be taken by God."

'By the devil,' said her own little devil.

"Ah. Would that we could all go so quickly and easily."

He walked purposefully over the wet grass.

"In his sleep?"

"The very same."

A smile touched his handsome, tanned face. "God was kind to Master Roger."

"You have the right of it, sir. He was but fifty eight."

"What are your plans now?"

"Oh...carry on much as we have been doing."

The man was quite tall and Rosalie quite short; he looked down at her. "I had heard you were making sterling work of Forceleap Farm, madam."

"That's kind of you. I am compelled to learn quickly."

The man nodded his head. "And I have no doubt that you are up to the task."

"With the help of all my staff, I can see no reason why we cannot carry Forceleap Farm on to the next level of prosperity."

"Oh? You have plans."

She put her fingers to her lips. "As yet unformed but…"

"Well done. Well done indeed." His handsome face creased into a smile. "Should you be thinking of expanding…our properties boundary each other. Might it be sensible…"

"For you to purchase Forceleap?"

"Ah no..I was thinking more of…"

"For me to purchase Pennyhooks Farm? Alas no."

"No, madam for us to join together, the two farms. To *marry* them together."

She suddenly had a ridiculous vision of two fields being married in the church porch.

She looked over to that stone edifice.

"I doubt we would get the two properties to come to church, Sir Hugh. Nor would there be the space."

It took him a while to understand her joke.

'Oh he is so handsome but so very much the dullard,' said Rosalie's disembodied voice.

"Ah I see… oh yes… a joke. Ah no…I meant…"

"I know what you meant, Sir Hugh. And I am sorry to have to tell you that Forceleap will marry no one."

"But…"

"I am about to take a vow of celibacy."

Sir Hugh's fine features creased into disappointment.

"Oh Madam, that breaks my heart."

She tapped his breast, where lay that heart, rather flirtatiously. "There. T'is mended."

"There is no going back?"

"No."

"Oh what a waste."

She shrugged.

"I cannot prevail upon you to become Lady Rosalie Yatesbury of Pennyhooks?"

"Even such a title cannot tempt me." 'How ridiculous,' she said inside her head.

"Then…" said the poor man. "I shall go home to weep into my wine."

"Aw…I am sure you'll recover."

He laughed then, bowed and disappeared into the throng of church goers.

Rosalie returned the gnomon of the mass dial to the priest.

*****

But for his height and breadth, Master William Newbold was the sort of man whom you would easily pass by. He walked as if the world had no real place for him, quietly, and with a sense that if he drew attention to himself, something which he could not manage would overtake him.

Nevertheless he ran the farm house and buildings, the accounting and the house servants, of which there were few, with a discreet efficiency.

He was passing from that time of middle into old age and his face had not yet decided which state it was to reflect. He was a free man and a lifelong bachelor.

William Newbold was balding but managed a dark beard upon his chin with very little grey in it. His eyes which were a twinkling blue of youth, saw everything but his mouth, which was surrounded with tiny lines, spoke in a matter of fact way so that it was impossible to dispute what he said. And what he saw he rarely spoke about at length.

"The farm is not for sale"

"But Master William - a woman."

"A woman may stand at the head of the household as well as a man."

"In the town maybe...but a place such as Forceleap?"

"Mistress Jourdemayne has two men to aid her. There is no difference were she the inheriting widow of a cordwainer, a potter or a mercer."

"But farming is man's work, sir."

"I would agree with you there, Johnson, so be about it. Or I will have Master Hayward down upon you."

The labourer scoffed and wiped his mouth on his wrist.

"I'll not work for a woman."

"Then off you go and tell that to Master Hayward. You can collect your wages to date and be off."

The man did not seem to realise that Master Newbold had not begged him to stay. And then the words sunk in.

"Go?"

"If you cannot bring yourself to work for a woman, then there is no place for you at Forceleap Farm."

"She should marry."

"She will not."

"Oh she will...never fear. Then we shall have a man in charge again."

"She will not marry."

"How do you know?"

"Because I do. She has told me."

"Aw women! They can't make up their minds. One moment wanting this and the next that."

"If you feel like this Johnson, then you can certainly leave, for you do not know your mistress at all." Newbold turned to leave him.

Johnson shuffled his feet. "I can't go. I have a wife and three childer to feed and if I go, where would I go?"

"Go to the fair in the town or to Devizes and hire your arm to another man," said Newbold. "Farm workers are always needed."

"But where would I live?"

"You'd give up a good house on the farmlands because you can't work for a woman? I'd go home and discuss it with your wife, if I were you. I'm sure she'll have a sensible opinion on the matter."

Master Newbold walked away and back into the farmyard. He caught sight of his mistress watching him from the door of the house.

"What was all that about, William?"

"It was a minor disagreement, madam. All sorted now."

"Did I hear you say Ancelin's name?"

"Nothing with which Master Hayward and I cannot deal. It's a labouring matter."

"Oh? And I am not to understand labouring matters?"

William sighed. "The man will not work for a woman."

Rosalie dropped her hands to her sides. "And do any of the other men feel this way?"

"No one...as yet... has said anything. Master Hayward has mentioned nothing to me."

"If they will not work for me, who will they work for?"

"Anyone in the vicinity who will hire them. Or if you take a man to husband, him."

Rosalie folded her hands at her waist again.

"William, will you keep your hands upon the reins and your ear to the air. I will talk to Ancelin and ask him to do the same."

Their conversation was interrupted by a man coming around the hedge of the farm yard, swinging his hands and in one of them, a package tied up in hessian with string.

He stopped, stared and then made for the steward.

"Good day, master. I have a package from the town. For Forceleap Farm."

"This is Forceleap."

The man held out the package to William. Rosalie extended her hand to take it.

The man withdrew the package from her hand's distance.

"For the farmer."

"I am the farmer," said Rosalie leaning forward and wrenching the package from him. "And I know from whence this has come."

The man relinquished it with a curse.

"Go back and give Master Lorimer my thanks," and she turned and marched into the house.

*****

"Oooh Mistress Jourdemayne..."

Rosalie undid the package carefully and snipped the string with her black metal sewing snips.

Bea leaned forward to wrap the string but Rosalie stayed her hand.

"There is no need to be so parsimonious now. The master may have kept every tiny bit but I am not so mean."

The hessian in which it was wrapped *would* be kept though. With Bea at her shoulder, Rosalie removed the wrapping.

Into the light came a round object about six inches in diameter. Upon the metal back was a pattern of dots and dashes in no particular order but it was still pleasing to the eye.

Rosalie turned the object round.

"Oh!" Bea leapt back crossing herself, "Saints preserve us."

Rosalie chuckled. "Are you frightened of yourself, you silly girl?"

"What is that...me?"

"It is."

Bea narrowed her eyes and peered at the polished plate again.

"And this is a mirror?"

"It is. This one is polished steel. Master Lorimer in town made it for me."

"Oooh." Bea moved her head to right and left. "I ain't never seen myself before except in water. And that's moving all the time."

Rosalie chuckled. "With this, you can look at every bit of you."

"Lord...I don't think I want to do that."

Bea picked up a lock of her hair. "Ooh I have got nice hair, haven't I?"

"You have."

Rosalie turned the mirror on her own face. Framed by a white wimple, a serious looking young woman looked back at her.

"Come, let's go to our room and we can take off this head covering and look properly."

They ran giggling up the hall, through the parlour door and upstairs to what they fondly called the solar which served as their bedroom.

Once there, Bea undid the veil pins and pulled off the wimple from Rosalie's neck, leaving her hair in the crespinette or caul, piled onto her head.

"I know I never have required you to help me with dressing, Bea and so you will never have seen what you are about to see now. You are always up and away before I rise."

"Oh..mistress, I know what we look like under our clothes."

"Ah no...that isn't what I mean."

Rosalie tentatively pulled the dress from her neck and undid the brooch which kept the neckline from falling over her shoulders. She pulled down her shift. Her neck and shoulders came into view.

She took up her mirror and peered into it. It was not easy to see.

"Maybe if we polish it a little more..."

Bea was staring at Rosalie as if she had suddenly become a beast with two heads.

"Oh mistress."

"Is it really that bad, Bea?"

Her servant reached out and touched her shoulder. "The bruises are fading. Almost gone. But..."

"Have I scars?"

Bea didn't answer.

"Have I scars, Bea? I can feel something but until now I have seen nothing."

Now her eyes had become accustomed to the slightly distorted and misty image, she recognised her own face, her dark blonde hair pulled over her forehead to her ears and her pale blue eyes. Her mother had always said that her eyes were a beautiful blue and her best feature.

She wasn't wrong.

She smiled. The face smiled back.

Bea took a deep breath, "Right, you have a scar here..." she touched Rosalie to the side of her neck. "It looks like a knife has pricked you. It might go in time."

Rosalie nodded.

"And there are lots of red marks on your shoulders. What are those... oh!" She took in a surprised breath. "They are..."

"Burn marks," added her mistress, "Charcoal mostly. Bits of red hot wood."

"The bastard," said Bea without restraint.

"They won't fade will they?"

Bea took her lip in her teeth and shook her head.

"No...they might just be less red and go whitish but...they'll always be there."

"It's alright."

"The evil bastard."

Mistress Rosalie Jourdemayne put down her new mirror, put her head into her hands and wept. Afterwards she said with relief,

"It's over now."

CHAPTER TWO ~ THE VOW

Next day, Rosalie called for the cart again and they jogged along the mile to the church in the village. It was a sweet little church of Saxon origin with clunch courses and flint stone between. The thatch was a little dilapidated but there were no holes that she had detected, at least, it had never rained on her at mass.

It sat on the banks of the River Kennet where the water split into several tributaries and where it spilled into one of the small leats which fed the castle moat. She could see the keep of the castle not half a mile away; its white bulk rising from Myrddyn's mound, the magical hill around which the castle had been built.

Preshute was a small village and not quite a suburb to the town of Marlborough but close enough to be influenced by it. It housed the nearest church to Forceleap Farm. If Rosalie desired to worship elsewhere she must travel to Avebury church which was set in the middle of an unfathomable stone circle of great age. The church there was bigger and more affluent but somehow, Rosalie couldn't abide it. She always felt that there was an unseen malevolent presence there. Her rational mind told her that it was nonsense. This was God's building, how could there be anything evil there? Her inner voice said, 'Do not go there. Preshute is a friendly little place. Stick with what you know.'

Besides she had been married in Avebury church. To go back into it would turf out all manner of horrible memories from the deep chest of her mind where she had locked them.

She approached the building and was glad to see that the gnomon of the mass dial was back in its place.

The priest greeted her at the door.

"Mistress Jourdemayne, welcome. Do come in and we shall discuss things in the priest's room."

This was a grand name for a miniscule space; a small part of the tiny church set aside for the robes and holy oils used in the services. A curtain gave them privacy from the main body of the church. Bea stood behind her mistress, looking around at the paraphernalia of the Godly Father Robertus.

"You wish to discuss the taking of a vow?"

"I do."

"As you know, the church encourages women to take vows of chastity rather than remarry."

"I have no desire to remarry."

"Chaste widowhood occupies a position in the three grades of chastity, superior to marriage, though inferior to that of virginity."

"Yes. I know."

"It is the task of the church to care for widows and orphans to prevent their remarriage to pagans."

"I beg your pardon, father?"

The priest shrugged his shoulders. "It all stems from a time when there were many pagans in the community and our good women had to be protected from them."

'Lord,' said Rosalie's little devil. 'Pagans! Have we pagans in Wiltshire now? If so, where are they? I will go and make their acquaintance.'

"Surely there is no fear of a widow fornicating with a pagan nowadays, sir?"

The priest did not like the word 'fornicating'...coming so blatantly from the lips of a woman.

His face drew into itself, like he had just sucked on a bitter gall. His fish eyes bulged as if he'd been squeezed at the neck.

"Whilst chaste widowhood is regarded as preferable to remarriage which is a form of bigamy, it is regarded as preferable to...*for-ni-cation*."

Bea could not help but give a suppressed laugh.

Rosalie turned and rather than give her maid an evil expression, she smiled at her with no warmth in the smile, showing her teeth.

Bea looked up to the roof.

'And the frailty of the flesh of widows in particular, finds Biblical expression. To quote from the first epistle of St. Paul to Timothy:

'Vidua elgiatur non minus sexaginta annorum quae fuerit unius viri uxor..'

"Let a widow be chosen of no less than threescore years of age who has been the wife to one man."

Rosalie smiled, "Yes I know that one. But father, I am but thirty and desire to take a vow. I also know the rest of it, 'Adulscentiores autem viduas devita cum enim luxuriatae fuerint in Christo nubere voluent."

The priest stared at her and she watched as his face went purple.

"Which I think means...and please correct me if I am wrong for my Latin is obviously not as good as yours... 'But the younger widows avoid. For when they have grown wanton in Christ, they will marry.'"

Father Robertus made a strangled sound like one cat calling another out when a mate was being fought over.

"I hoped you'd make an exception for me. I know of course," went on Rosalie, "that chaste widows must live secluded and privy lives. I have my work at Forceleap Farm to engage me. I ask for no more." She smiled sweetly.

"Well..." Father Robertus grimaced. "Let us leave it a little longer. You must be allowed time to think about it."

"I have been thinking about it and it's what I desire."

"Nevertheless. It's not something you enter into...lightly. You are as yet a handsome and sprightly woman."

'Oh no, not him as well!' said her inner voice. 'God save me from priests deprived of for-ni-cation…' She repeated the word in her mind louder and louder until she was afraid she might actually say it. 'And from avaricious agriculturalists.' She didn't mention Sir Hugh, to herself. Sir Hugh was all right."

"I have no desire to remarry."

"It is very early after Master Roger's death, you must think about it. Give yourself time. That is my advice."

Rosalie stood and angrily shook out the material of her skirt. "I have not come all this way to be sent home like a green girl!"

She turned and took hold of the material of the curtain which was stretched on a pole between the two pillars at the western end of the church and yanked it to the side.

"I think I will worship in Avebury from now on."

The pole gave a clunk and fell to the ground with a rattle, the material of the curtain slid after it.

She stomped off and at the last moment felt guilty and poked her head around the pillar.

"Sorry."

*****

Bea followed sheepishly. "I have never liked him. He's creepy."

Rosalie took in a deep breath.

"Well, there are further churches. This is just the nearest."

The priest had followed them out and stood in the porch looking at them with a sort of sad expression which Rosalie thought was probably pity.

She looked up at the sky and caught sight once more of the mass dial on the church wall.

"I see that the gnomon has been replaced, father."

"Yes..yes.." The man rubbed the side of his nose.

"No sooner had you given it to me than Sir Maurice FitzAlan came and being a taller man and an adventurous one - I am not inclined to climb ladders - he put it back."

"Ah."

"He is of course the captain of the guard of the castle, so we see a little of him here, when he is inclined to worship. He sometimes goes to the garrison chapel but he tells me, he likes it here better."

"Oh." Rosalie was not really listening. She was planning a visit to the town. To the church of St. Mary at the far end of the long High Street. Maybe they would listen to her.

She hadn't come this far to be thwarted by another man!

"I shall go and...pray over my husband's grave. Yes. Then we haven't had a wasted journey."

She hurried along the banked up side of the graveyard and made for the eastern end.

"Come on Bea."

"But mistress...why do you want to...?"

"Listen to me, Roger Jourdemayne, wherever you are. You must have some influence. I want to make a vow. Do something about it...or I will rescind all the masses I have paid for, for the repose of your soul," said Rosalie out loud.

There was a strangled laugh. She turned abruptly hoping that the priest hadn't followed her.

It was the young man whom she had met in town. The man who had retrieved her pink wool and lifted her from the ground.

He was tallish, blond, and his hair was long, swept back and worn in a queue. He looked as if he didn't smile very often, for even though he was obviously amused, there was no laughter or smile beyond the strangled noise he'd made. He was tanned and even featured with brows, eyelashes and eyes which would not have disgraced a girl.

"Mistress. Forgive me."

"Do you make a habit of eavesdropping on those communing with their dead loved ones, sir?"

"No. Not at all."

"Or following a young woman around?"

"I am here with..." he picked up a small bucket, "a little lime mortar with which to secure the gnomon of the mass dial. I promised the Father I would mend it. I have access to a little of the masons' mortar... being resident in the castle...you see."

"Where there is a great amount of building going on."

"Exactly."

The man bowed. "Sir Maurice FitzAlan. Middle son of the FitzAlans of Chalfield."

"Rosalie Jourdemayne." She bobbed a very small curtsey.

"Of Forceleap Farm."

Her little devil murmured in her ear and she said,

"Widow."

Bea sidled up to her and whispered in her ear.

"See. I told you he had a big one," she said.

Rosalie looked carefully at Sir Maurice. "How can you tell...? Oh! Oh yes."

"*Sword*, mistress."

*****

Rosalie nodded and moved off down the bank. Sir Maurice stretched out his hand to help her descend. She didn't take it.

"We are going into town now," she said, "To the church of St. Mary."

"Might I walk with you, madam?"

Rosalie gave him a disparaging look. "We shall take the cart." She indicated Fulk with the cart sitting at the end of the path.

"I think we can manage, thank you. And..." She nodded to his bucket. "Do you not have a gnomon to replace?"

"If you will wait a while I..."

"No, I'm sorry we can't wait," and she bustled along the uneven path like a charging goose.

It was her undoing.

She tripped on her long cotte and her ankle turned on a stone.

She went down ungracefully with a shriek, on the gravel of the path. Fulk, seeing her approach the cart, had jumped down in order to help her up to it and he now ran to recover his mistress who was a lump of tangled green and dark blue cloth at the beginning of the pathway.

Sir Maurice came up quickly behind.

"Mistress, are you hurt."

"No..no.." said Rosalie weakly, attempting to roll onto her knees to rise but somehow her wrist would not bear her weight.

She put her foot beneath her just as the soldier reached her to take her by the arm.

"I can manage thank you." She tried to shake him off but he did not relinquish his grip.

"Argh!"

"You *are* hurt, madam," he said.

"It's nothing," she replied.

"Ouch." Her ankle was very painful and her wrist was throbbing nastily.

She looked at her palm. It was a gouged mass of little scratches filled with tiny pieces of gravel, where she had put out her hand to save herself.

"Lean on me mistress."

"Thank you Fulk."

The young lad offered his shoulder. It was the shoulder of a thirteen year old boy; bony, underdeveloped and about as muscled as a stalk of corn.

"Oh mistress let me look at your ankle. You might have broken it."

"If I *had* broken it, Bea, I would be yelling and blaspheming like a sailor!" she had once seen a man break his wrist. It had been an interesting experience...for her at any rate. And for her vocabulary.

A shiver of a smile passed over Sir Maurice's face, soon stilled.

He took her gently from the shoulder of her angular cart boy and picked her up with ease, arms under her knees and shoulders.

"It seems that I am destined to rescue you from misfortune again, madam."

"That sir, is simply not true."

She glared at him as he strode down the path, her face inches from his own. "I demand that you put me down this instant."

He did. He dropped her from a height of about three feet onto the bed of the cart.

"Ouch!" Now she'd have bruises on her rump too.

She was so surprised and not a little embarrassed, uncharacteristically, she managed to say nothing.

"Now, Mistress Ungrateful, if you will forgive me, I have a gnomon to mend." He bowed.

She righted herself and rubbed her sore side as she watched him jog down the path.

'Insolent peasant!' said her inner voice.

Fulk grinned.

"Where to now mistress?"

"Home please, Fulk."

The church of St. Mary would have to wait.

*****

"Beatrice!" shouted Rosalie from her bed where she lay with her leg propped up on a cushion.

The maid came running.

"I think we have left some gravel in my palm. Can you have another look?"

"Madam, you said that you'd had enough of the probing and prodding. So I..."

"Yes, I know. But it hurts when I squeeze my hand."

"All right. Just wait while I get the tweezers."

Rosalie undid the linen bandage which Bea had wrapped around her palm and peered at her injury.

Her wrist and ankle were as nothing compared to her damaged

pride. Her self esteem had taken a tumble along with her leg. It hurt painfully to recall the look on Sir Maurice's face when he dumped her in the cart.

'Noble he may be but he's no gentleman,' said her inner voice. 'What do you expect from a man who wears such a long sword?'

"Ach faddle!"

Bea then spent a good few moments probing the wound on Rosalie's palm picking out tiny pieces of gravel.

Rosalie gritted her teeth and squeezed out tears from her tightly shut eyes, in silence.

'Serves you right,' said her devil. 'You were rude to him.'

"I was not rude. I merely made sure that he was aware that I am not the sort of woman who goes all mawkish when encountering a man with a handsome visage and well muscled arms."

'Ah well, have it your own way. You usually do.'

Rosalie squirmed and not just in pain.

"Thank you Bea, that is much more comfortable."

Her maid tucked the bedclothes tighter, even though Rosalie was perched on top of them.

"Anything else?"

"Correspondence? Anything which either William or Ancelin has left for me to see?"

"Just one bit of parchment."

"Is it sealed?"

"Yes."

"It's called a letter, Bea."

"Alright. A letter."

"Whose seal?"

"I don't know, do I? It's a bird."

"A bird?"

"With its wings spread out."

"Hmm. Well, let's have a look then."

The missive was short and to the point. She spoke aloud.

"To The Most Estimable Mistress Rosalie Jourdemayne, Widow, Greetings. I, Odo of Marlborough, your humble friend, trust that you are in good health."

"Well he obviously knows Roger is no more but doesn't know what has befallen me of late...thank goodness. The whole town will know soon, no doubt."

"Ah...no madam, I doubt that Sir Maurice would tell anyone anything. He *is* a knight. He *is* sworn to be kind to orphans and...widows."

Rosalie sighed. "Oh forgive me Bea, I am distempered. I am fed up of fending off hopeful suitors from far and wide. I expect this is another one."

"Who is Odo of Marlborough?"

Rosalie searched her memory.

"Another friend of Roger's I expect."

Rosalie examined the seal. "I don't recognise it."

She shuffled herself further up the bed.

"He wishes me all the best things the world has to offer and the protection of God and all his angels." She looked up with an amused expression. "Asked God has he?"

"Oh mistress..." giggled Bea.

"I am writing...ah, at last... to invite you to a gathering at my humble house upon the London Road in the town of Marlborough."

"The man must be wealthy. Only those with money live out on that road," she said.

"Ooh, is it a feast?"

"A gathering, upon the occasion of my daughter, Edith, becoming of age."

"Oh...do rich folks give feasts when their daughters reach... reach... becoming of age?"

"Twelve, Bea, normally."

Rosalie read on, "And her betrothal to Master Florentin of Hungerford."

"So she is to be married too?"

"It looks as if they are combining the celebrations and holding a party."

"A what mistress?"

"A festivity."

"To which you are invited?"

"Yes. Upon the third day after the Assumption of the Blessed Virgin Mary"

"When's that?"

Rosalie looked up at the rafters, "About four days away. I can't go."

"But mistress...a feast!"

"Why do I have to go? I don't know the man, nor the girl...nor for that matter her betrothed. Why have they invited me? And anyway, I am in mourning."

"There is no fixed time for mourning...you know that. But a feast? And you get a chance to wear your best wool cotte. And your silk headdress. And your silver filet. And that lovely brooch with the two..."

Rosalie tapped the letter on her lips.

"I will think about it."

"Not for too long, madam. Your reply has to be written and get back to them. And I'm sure your ankle will be much better by then."

"No, I can't go. I can't be seen hobbling about on a stick. They'll all think I am an old woman!"

"You'll have to rest it and then practice walking on it. Even if it still hurts."

"Oh Bea."

"Madam, you are a great lady of the area..."

"I am not a Lady Millicent Mortemer, nor a Countess of Salisbury..." said Rosalie archly. "Not even my friend Lydia, Lady Belvoir."

"No, but you are a wealthy widow of property and land and a force to be reckoned with. Isn't that what you are always saying? A force to be reckoned with...now."

"In my small way. Yes. I am no longer a woman beholden to any man."

Bea planted her hands on her waist, "Then show them!"

*****

The letter was written. William wrote to her dictation though it was possible for her to write her own letter, it looked better in a clerkly hand.

"Are you sure, mistress, that you want to go?"

"No. Not at all but it seems to me that if I am to slough off the reputation which at the present moment seems to attach to me, that I am a mewling girl ripe for the picking and cannot say boo to a goose, let alone run Forceleap Farm, I must be seen there."

"Everyone who is anyone in the locality will be there."

"I can appear and then disappear can't I? I don't have to stay long. Just long enough to make people understand that Forceleap is mine. Mine alone. And that no one - especially a man is getting their hands on it."

"There are a few in the community who have cause to regret that opinion of you," said William with a grin.

"Ah...yes..." Rosalie patted her head cloth in place. "You mean, Clifford of Ramsbury?"

William chuckled. "His face, madam, when you told him that you would not marry a man who had had five wives already and survived them all."

"Ah yes. Well."

"And that you were sorry that you could never be number six. For it might be that he might not survive to marry number seven."

"Oh William. He was all over me, like a shower of cold rain but less pleasant."

"Well the water you tipped on *him* certainly dulled his ardour."

Rosalie chuckled. "I have not thanked you for arriving when you did. It was timely. He had his hand upon my..."

William coughed. "I am glad to be of service, madam."

He turned and took up the replying letter. "So I am to send it, am I?"

"Oh alright. Get Adam out on the cart horse and get him to deliver it."

William reached the door. "But madam. A quiet and friendly word of warning. Whilst I appreciate your wish to remain a widow, you must be careful how you go about refusing all offers of matrimony. Firmness and determination, must be matched with kindness and empathy, lest you be branded a harridan, a shrew, a virago…"

"A what William?"

"It is a word in the Bible, madam, meaning a termagant and a vixen of a woman."

"Oh…"

"I know you as a feminine lady of good humour and kindness…grace and good manners…"

"You don't think that those virtues might be misinterpreted by some, as weakness?"

William made a moue. "Perhaps."

"What would you do?"

William smiled a sweet smile. "I would judge every man as I would wish to be judged whether or not his manners were a match to mine own. I would weigh up every behaviour and act accordingly."

"So, not assume every man is the same? Every man is out for Forceleap?"

"Indeed."

"And if the good man had his hand upon your breast?" Her face took on a mischievous expression.

"Then I would kick him in the cods, madam."

*****

The celebration was in full swing. The young girl whose birthday and betrothal they were all recognising, sat with a fixed smile at the head of the table, a garland of flowers upon her head. The young man who was her betrothed sat beside her, a shy, slightly tipsy, seventeen year old, who stuffed sweetmeats into his mouth one after the other.

Rosalie, sitting at the second table, looked around the room. She caught the eye of her friend Lydia Belvoir, and her husband the Lord Aumary, on the high table. Her eyes moved on. She spotted the ancient lady Millicent, Lady Mortemer.

'Oh Lord preserve us,' said Rosalie's little devil. 'What has she done to her face?'

"Too many cosmetics for her age. That's what. She's as white as a sheet."

Rosalie had no idea she had spoken aloud.

"There, I must agree with you, mistress," said an amused voice.

"What..pardon?"

'I must stop speaking my private thoughts out aloud,' said Rosalie to herself.

She turned but the large silk veil which she had decided to wear that day precluded any sight of her dining companion.

She blew the silk away with the corner of her mouth.

"I'm sorry sir, I have not had the pleasure…"

The man bowed from the waist. "Yes, manners were a little lacking, were they not when we were first seated together here? We should have been introduced by the steward."

"He *was* very busy."

"Henry Godechepe, merchant of Marlborough town. Though I do not have a house there now. I have a farm out at Boreham. I made my money in wine."

"Oh yes… I know of you. I am Rosalie, widow of Roger Jourdemayne of Forceleap Farm."

"Roger's wife." The man stared at Rosalie. "I heard he had died suddenly. I am so sorry for your loss."

"Rosalie gave a little smile, not too friendly or happy. "Thank you. That is most kind."

"Well…Roger!" The man fiddled with the spoon sitting on the tablecloth before him. "How did he manage to keep you such a secret?"

"Whilst Roger was alive, sir, I did not get out much." 'Oh why did you say that?' said her little voice.

The man seemed to understand.

"Ah he kept you away from prying eyes heh?"

Rosalie had no wish to give him the impression that she had been under Roger's thumb but again the man seemed to read her mind."

"I understand. I know what he was like."

Again her little devil said, 'You have no idea, sir.'

"He was a very private man, sir."

The man laughed. "Aye... very private. But then I am sure you know this."

"I beg your pardon...I...I do not quite...understand."

"Oh no, forget it,' said Henry Godechepe. "So, how do you know the family?"

"Indeed, I do not. It was for the reason of my husband, I expect, that I obtained the invitation."

"I am Odo's confidant, carousing and drinking companion," said Henry. "Forgive me if I am blunt. But I am also the little chit's Godfather."

"The little lass who..."

"Emma, yes."

"Has the man no wife?"

"Alas, no. Sabina died last year. It was awful. Childbirth. One moment she was hale and hearty and the next..."

He turned to her and leaned back "Like your Roger."

The servitors then came about with food and they found themselves sharing a bowl together and a goblet of fine white wine. All conversation was then about the fare on offer.

In a gap in between the removes, Henry started up a conversation about grass and acreage and cattle. And his own sheep.

"I'm right aren't I? You farm mostly cattle at Forceleap?"

"We do but we have some arable with which to stable our beasts and up on the hills, some sheep cropping the downs."

Rosalie went on to explain how it all worked and how many furlongs of each held how much produce and how many cattle.

"I am impressed, madam." He truly looked it. "I don't think I know any other woman who knows as much about her farm as do you."

"Do you know any other women farmers, Master Godechepe? I should like to speak with them."

"I believe there is one lady out at Ashdown… but that is in another county."

"My county sir. I was born in Berkshire."

"Oh, whereabouts?"

"Wantage, sir."

"Ah, the home of our Great King Alfred of Wessex."

"You know our history, sir."

"I am very fond of it."

They looked at each other for a moment, until a plate was forced between them, with an, "Excuse me. If I may…"

Then they turned the conversation to food once more.

Rosalie ate sparingly and turned over in her mind, a picture of the face of her neighbour, Master Godechepe.

A high forehead. She seemed to remember somewhere, someone telling her that this was a sign of intelligence. The man had hazel brown eyes which crinkled at the edges. His voice was quiet and restrained and there was a faint accent which she could not fathom. No, she didn't think he was foreign. His English was perfect.

He was of a middling height and well made. Prosperous but not running to fat; he wore a burgundy red cotte with a band of brown embroidery at the neck and brown hose and boots. He seemed to be about forty.

He was speaking and she wasn't listening.

"I beg your pardon, sir."

"Yes, the noise in here is prodigious…and I know and I am quietly spoken. I said that I have long been fascinated by the name Forceleap. Have you any idea where the name originated?"

Rosalie smiled.

"It is a Saxon foundation, Master Godechepe. It is mentioned in the chronicle compiled by those people. And in the King William's Great Book of the eleventh century. It must have belonged to a man who owned four leas...four fields or meadows. Now, of course, the place is much bigger. But there is also a story about Forceleap Farm which is, I'm sure just legend."

"Oh madam. You have my full attention." He swivelled his backside on the seat, to face her. All food was forgotten. It was cold anyway.

"Well... a very, very long time ago, when the whole country was covered in woodland."

"Oh...was it?"

"Very much of it. Dense woodland like parts of Savernake."

"Ah I see."

"Forceleap was within the forest, though it was not completely a thing of trees, it was meadows and commons and in this area grazed many deer."

"As happens now."

"Yes, sometimes the deer escape the forest and start to graze on the fields of farms nearby."

"You are not allowed to stop them are you?"

"We cannot shoot them, no. But we can drive them back."

"Ah..."

"And in order to prevent them from leaping into our lands again, there are defences which keep them in the park, where Sir Aumary Belvoir, the warden, requires them to stay."

"Oh?"

"The warden of Savernake, Sir Aumary Belvoir, Lord of Durley, you must know him. He builds something called deerleaps."

"Ah yes. I am sure I have seen these. Fences all around the deerpark except for one or two dips, with a ring of ditches to the inside...?"

"That's right. The deer can only leap one way. You might say they are ...forced to leap."

"They are, I believe about eight feet high on the inside?"

"Just so. And our farm has several of these."

"So, from four leas to Forceleap."

"And it is said that in those far off days, a grieving widow, feeling her life unbearable without her beloved, threw herself from the top of one of these great leaps and dashed out her brains."

Henry Godechepe looked carefully at Rosalie.

"Madam...?"

"Oh no, Master Godechepe, I have no intention of proving the legend's truth."

"I am pleased to hear it."

More food arrived.

Their next conversation was about meat.

"You raise the cattle which the Templars brought here from their lands in the north, don't you?"

"We do. Long horned. They are larger creatures than the normal beasts and are excellent draught animals and good for their meat."

"Is this their meat?" He prodded a cold piece of beef which he had tried to cut up for them to eat.

Rosalie examined the gravy covered morsel of meat.

"Ah no...sadly...this is..." she put her head close to his, "far inferior meat."

She prodded it with her knife. "The intramuscular fat or marbling throughout the meat of the long horned is largely responsible for the succulence, tenderness and flavour of our beef."

"I must seek out some of this excellent beef."

"Master Fleshmonger in the town is one who takes our produce, sir. Try there."

"I will Mistress Jourdemayne. I will." And he toasted her with the goblet.

*****

The dancing was about to begin.

Rosalie moved to the edge of the room and found a seat.

"Mistress, will you do me the honour of joining me in a roundelay?"

"Oh Master Godechepe, I am so sorry. I have an injury to my ankle sustained just four days ago and whilst it is mending, it is still painful. I should not aggravate it."

"Oh, I am sorry to hear it."

He sat down beside her. "Then I too shall sit the dances out."

"Oh no...please, do not absent yourself on my account. I have friends seated about the hall with whom I can chatter..." It was not entirely true. "I will be perfectly fine."

"Well if you insist. I shall go and see if my sister will dance with me."

He bowed and picked his way through the dancers who were forming up in the centre of the room, removed of its dining trestles.

Now she had a chance to look at him carefully without him knowing. She saw him reach an older lady wearing a tall stiff linen crown and a barbette. Her cotte was a costly mixture of linen and silk and the lustre of it shone in the candlelight.

The woman tried to say no, but he pulled her up and she was pressured to join the dance. She laughed coquettishly. The music began. Rosalie tapped her good foot. She loved this music, cheery, bouncy, happy.

Everyone was enjoying themselves. It was good to see.

She noticed a man staring at her.

'Oh no. It is that odious little man, Master Dankworth.'

She averted her gaze and tried to blend into the background but it was quite difficult dressed as she was in pink.

He stood before her.

"Madam...you are not dancing."

"I do not wish to dance, sir."

"Oh...like you do not wish to marry."

She ignored him and looked past him to the dancers threading their way in a circle.

"Then you must dance with me."

"I am so sorry, but as I just told Master Godechepe not a moment ago, when he asked me, I have an injury to my ankle and am unable to tread the dance."

"Ohh! How inconvenient."

"It is, for I do like to dance."

The man made a grab for her arm.

"Then you shall dance with me and I will lift you so that your feet do not touch the ground."

Dankworth caught Rosalie by the middle and hugged him to her.

"This is most improper, sir. Let me go."

He lifted her, as lightly as one might lift a piece of chaff and swung her into the circle. She tried to put her foot to the ground.

Then in desperation, she swung her good foot at his shin. It made contact.

A voice almost in her ear said at a whisper.

"Unhand the lady, sir. She has no wish to dance. She has an injury to her foot. I can confirm this for I was with her when she sustained it."

"Sir Maurice!" said Rosalie, hopping on one foot. The dancers reeled on around them.

"GO!"

Dankworth sneered and moved off.

"And yet again, madam, it seems it is my role to keep you from harm."

This time, Rosalie smiled. "Thank you. The man would not take no for an answer."

"I saw what he did. It was unforgivable."

Maurice offered her his arm and she hobbled to the edge of the room again.

"He is a horridly persistent man," she said. "I do not wish to set eyes on him ever again."

"Difficult for you, for he farms very close to your lands."

"Oh...you know Forceleap, sir?"

He did not answer but bowed and said, "Might I call upon you at home, mistress, someday soon? Just to make sure that your foot is mending."

Rosalie saw Master Godechepe returning to her across the floor.

"Please do, Sir Maurice."

Godechepe's eyebrow lifted at one corner.

CHAPTER THREE ~ THE FLOOD

The rains came down solidly for the next three days. Rosalie stayed in, resting her ankle and poring over the farm books and tally sticks.

It was then she realised just how very wealthy she was, for not only did Forceleap Farm have furlongs and furlongs of good agricultural land, wonderful cattle and abundant sheep, Roger had also bought up some properties in the town and the larger villages and rented them out. This gave her an income every quarter day which could keep her in excellent wool cottes and fancy mirrors for a whole year.

She took up her stick and wandered into the hall, looking up at the wall, the windows and the roof. Might she perhaps beautify the place a little with painted cloths for the walls? It would certainly prevent the draughts swirling around the knees of a winter's evening. She looked at the central hearth. Maybe build a new fire too? She could afford it.

It had been a lean year and still Rosalie's business thrived.

The winter of 1204-5 had been dire. Snow and ice had locked up the countryside for months. Livestock and people had died. It was only through the skill of her farm manager, Ancelin, and her other staff that her own animals had survived and bred; that her own workers had survived. And she grudgingly had to give some credit to her husband Roger.

Things had been lean for many that year and into the next, for with the ice hard ground, planting was impossible and was delayed for months. People and livestock starved.

Eventually spring came and summer followed. The swallows nested in the barns at Forceleap; the swifts screamed overhead at their banquet of high flying insects and the spotted flycatcher, who always came to the ivy on the wall of the garth, nested again and brought forth his young.

Then came the rain. Days of it.

Rosalie was still standing in the hall contemplating plastering and painting it with pattern and colour when the young lad who looked after the farm carts and other wains, came running up.

"Mistress, mistress!"

"There is no need to shout Fulk."

"No, madam…"

"What?"

"The rain has flooded the bottom meadow."

"What do you mean, bottom meadow? Fyfield? We have no river there in that meadow. It flows from Swallowhead Springs… "

"No…just a flood, out of nowhere. The cows are there and pinned in the western corner."

"But how can the water get there Fulk?"

Now Ancelin's capable tones broke in over the excited young man's voice.

"I suspect we have a spring we did not know about, somewhere there."

"A spring?"

"The river Kennet rises close by. Who knows what else…"

"Why now?"

"You know, m'am, that the river disappears in dry years and the bed is dry. The reverse, I'm sure, can happen in very wet years. The water rises and the spring gushes forth. It's flooded Fyfield."

"But I have never…"

"No, something, somewhere in the surrounding countryside must have changed."

"Then Hayward, what do we do?"

"We all go out and lead the cattle to safety."

Rosalie bit her lip, put her foot to the ground more sturdily and pushed, testing it. A pain shot across her ankle. Her inner voice said, 'It will serve.'

"Right! Every able body, out to Fyfield meadow. I will ride there on Goliath and meet you there."

"Madam…? Goliath?" said Fulk and Ancelin together.

This was her husband's stallion.

"I can manage him."

The men looked at each other.

"Go on Fulk. Saddle him for me. The cattle will not wait for the sun to shine and dry up the water."

"Yes mistress."

"Mistress Rosalie, we can manage…" started Ancelin.

"I have no doubt you can," she said, forestalling his objections. "But I would see for myself what is happening and what has changed, if anything and why. And if I must, I will lead the cows to dry land myself."

*****

The party of men ran along the road which was a good few feet higher than the meadow.

"See m'am, the cows have backed into the dry corner of the field but they'll soon be overwhelmed. There's no way back." Fourteen cows had huddled together on a hummocky piece of ground no larger than about twenty feet. With the hedge to the side of them and another large pool of water to their back, they had nowhere to go.

Rosalie chewed the side of her mouth. "How deep do we think the water is there?"

Alfred Hadden hissed through his teeth. "There's an unseen dip there it's gotta be about six feet or more."

"Why won't they walk through it?" asked Rosalie.

Ancelin answered her. "Cows are prey animals, which means in the wild they would be chased by other animals to bring them down to eat. So they have an inherent fear of unusual objects, situations, noises, sudden movements and smells. This water isn't usually in their field. They've instinctively and intuitively backed away as the waters rose but they're now doing something we call baulking."

"Oh?"

"Which is when the animal flinches and ceases movement."

"We can't get them to move?"

"We can try but sometimes even with someone leading them, they baulk."

Rosalie narrowed her eyes and fixed them on the small huddle of cows.

"Can we take up the hedge, further up?"

Ancelin shielded his eyes from the glare of the water and rain. "Aye, we might do it and lead them uphill and across."

"The water only seems to be a couple of feet deep there, we might get them through with coaxing."

Master Hayward bellowed up to the men milling around on the road close to the next field.

"Tools to grub up the hedge just there, Cotterill. Take out the hedge! Gently and quietly mind." He pointed.

"We must go down there and keep them calm whilst the men do this, I think," said Rosalie, pulling her cotte up over her belt until it was pouched all around her waist. She sat on the slope and pulled off her shoes and hose. Then, standing she took the hem of her dress and pulled it up to tuck it in her belt. The white of her linen shift became visible and a foot and twelve or more inches of her leg.

She squirmed a little. "Sorry Hayward...needs must." And she strode off barefoot down the hill.

Crooning indecipherable words to the beasts, Rosalie came to the water's edge. The cows looked up. This was another strange object in their field. Another thing they didn't recognise. Ancelin Hayward came up behind her.

"They know me but you are a stranger...wait."

He pulled off his working tunic, a padded jacket which was worn over a shirt or cotte and tossed it to her.

"That smells of me. Put it on. They'll be more biddable then. They have a keen sense of smell."

Rosalie nodded and caught the garment before it hit the water. It smelled musty and damp. But there was another aroma there too which was quite pleasant. She struggled into it.

'Bosoms are such a waste of space,' she said to herself. 'If I was straight up and down, like a man, I'd have no trouble with this.'

Eventually she managed to get it on and three or four more cattle men came up to her elbow. One of them pulled it down at the hem at her back.

"Right into the water we go. Gently now. We have no idea what is under our feet," said her farm manager.

"There are a few rocks here mistress, outliers of the sarsens, be careful," said Warin Logge.

Rosalie lifted her hem higher and waded carefully into the water. At its very edge, she could see the grass, and the chalk mud began to squelch between her toes. It was a shock however when she reached the water that was deeper. How cold it was.

She waded on. The water came up to her shin and beyond. She pulled her cotte higher. Soon the water would be over her knee. She thought about tearing off her hem with the little knife which hung from her belt, but no. She'd put up with the waterlogging.

Her little voice said 'It will dry. And if it is ruined, you can buy another.'

She heard Ancelin, wading a little away from her, say "Vision is their dominant sense. They'll see you and be restless initially. In order to get the best possible vision, cattle will lower their head and face the thing of interest front on. Don't be worried if they do that."

"Thank you for telling me."

"The cow sees well at the front but although they can see to the side, it's less clear. It's always best to approach from the side."

"I will bear that in mind."

The water was now over her knees and lapping her cotte. Ancelin was slightly ahead of her and the cowman to her right, was four feet ahead and wading in water which came to his upper thigh.

Rosalie could hear a crunching and snapping as the men, deputed to make a hole in the hedge, went about their work.

The cows were getting restless. They were unsure of the noises close by them.

"No quick movement now, mistress, no high pitched noises," said Ancelin. "They don't like it."

"I promise not to sing to them," said Rosalie with a grin as the water rose to her lower stomach.

"Oh it's hard to walk in all this sodden material."

"Not far now, though we shall have to scale the drop."

Two of the cows lowered their heads and Rosalie could see how intimidating this might be, if she didn't know that they were merely getting a good look at her.

"Now then ol' girl. See it's only me." She waded sideways a little to come up against one of the beast's flanks.

The wicked curved horns gleamed in the wet.

Suddenly she struck a rock beneath the water and overbalanced. Her poor ankle could not hold her and she went down in four feet of water.

Disorientated for a heartbeat she spluttered but with a hand from Ancelin, recovered.

"Bad ankle let me down." She shook her head and her head cloth came undone. Quickly she grasped it and tied it tightly around her neck in a knot. It wasn't how they were supposed to be worn but at that moment no one was going to care.

Now she was almost completely wet. She forged on grimacing at the pain in her ankle.

Two men had reached the dry ground and scrambled up the beetling slope. The cows made frightened noises but were soon reassured.

"Fear will make them prone to flight…" said her manager.

"Even with all the water around?"

"They'll panic and maybe slip on the mud; we can't risk them breaking a leg. We must do everything slowly and calmly," said Hayward.

"Even if they don't?"

"More so if they don't."

"They aren't aggressive are they?"

"Not usually. No."

Rosalie eyed the nearest large horn to her face and ploughed on. A hand came out to help her up the steep bank.

'Oh good...I had visions of the water being over your head in a moment.' said her little voice.

"Can you swim madam?" said one of the cheeky cowmen, Alfred Hadden.

"No. Are you offering to teach me?"

The man laughed and set her down on the drier ground. She dripped and ran water from every thread.

Now she had ceased to struggle, she began to chill.

"How are they doing with the hedge?"

"Quite well," said Ancelin, wiping the rain from his face. "Not long and we can start to lead the main cow up the hill."

"Which is the main cow?"

"This one."

Ancelin was standing beside a beautiful beast of glorious markings; blotched with brown and white, with a delightful white face.

"He stroked her cheek. "This one's Perle. She's a good girl. Easy calver. Sweet temper. Good mother. Aren't you gal?"

"Where are the calves?"

"A couple are there."

Rosalie turned to see that the smaller beasts had drawn up tight against the thick hedge. They were a few months old now.

"The others got separated and we have taken them into the field on the other side of the road."

"These girls will be happy to see their children again."

"Aye they will."

Ancelin clicked his tongue. "C'mon girl...let's get you over here."

He tugged on her ear and laid his face on her cheek. She followed him docilely.

"Try the same thing though if you've no wish to get so close..."

"No, I'll do as you do. Which one shall I take?"

"There, take Ella, she's easy."

Rosalie approached the cow from the side. She reached out and stroked the harsh coat. "There Ella, see. My name is Rosie. I am here to help you." She clicked her tongue as her manager had done.

Ella swivelled a brown eye to Rosalie's face. The look said "I won't hurt you. Just point me in the right direction. I trust you."

Suddenly one of the men making the hole in the hedge gave a mighty thwack to the trunk of a hawthorn bush and it shook and then tumbled with a rattle and a settling of leaves.

Ella backed and turned her side into Rosalie. Her grip on the cow's ear was gone.

Ancelin leapt back and recovered the cow, to prevent it slipping, softly mumbling in its ear.

But Rosalie had fallen back into the water.

*****

She spluttered and coughed and despite the words of her manager, she moved quickly and made noise.

"Here...take my hand," said Alfred Hadden. He reached out over the lip of the chalky wet defile but she couldn't reach. Her hand splashed into water and nothing else. Hadden speedily laid down on the grass, his feet between the legs of a cow…"Here!"

"Jesus," said one of the other men. "The water's really deep there."

Rosalie was taking in gulps of air and, sadly, water. She began to feel cold and light headed.

A hand grabbed her wrist and she let the man pull her, making no effort to help until she had reached the slippery side of the defile. Then she scrambled, digging in her toes.

"Idiot Cotterill!" yelled Ancelin."I said quietly!"

"Sorry, sir."

Ancelin pulled Rosalie up by her arms. Her head cloth was gone and her blonde hair, loose from its crespinette, came tumbling across her shoulders.

Ancelin, holding her against his knee, brushed the hair from her face.

"Mistress Rosalie, can you hear me?"

"Hmmm," she mumbled and then coughed as a rush of water came from her mouth. Her eyelashes flickered.

Then she realised that folk were staring down at her and her eyes snapped open. She struggled to rise, trying to pull up and cover her neck with the sodden jerkin which Ancelin had given her.

"Here." Someone wrapped another jerkin around her. She'd begun to shiver.

"Get her through the hole!" shouted Ancelin, "Take her home in the cart."

"I'll get Goliath back to Forceleap…" said Hadden.

Rosalie struggled against the hands of her manager.

"Madam…please…just rest. I'll lift you. We'll get you through the hole in the hedge." She was still trying to cover the scars and marks on her neck with the jerkin.

Ancelin saw what she was trying to do and pulled a fold across her body.

"We shall find your head cloth, hose and shoes and get you home as soon as we can."

"I can ride."

"You cannot, your ankle has swollen again. Goliath will go home without you. Hadden will take you in the cart. Rest easy."

She took a deep breath and coughed again and coughed so hard that she was almost sick.

Her stomach felt churned up. "Have I swallowed mud?"

Ancelin Hayward smiled. "No..not mud."

He didn't like to tell her what was churned up in the water of that temporary pond.

He lifted her and passed her to Hadden, through the hole in the hedge.

"Keep cutting...we need more space," he told the men demolishing the greenery.

Then he went back to his cows, to croon and talk to them once more, to settle and calm them.

"Ay...Hesper, there, Darla." He gentled one cow on the rump. "There Rosalie."

His mistress looked back at him as she disappeared into the hedge, cradled in the arms of a cowman.

Her little voice said, 'Cheek! He's called a cow after you!'

*****

She was really shivering when she at last was helped into the house. Martin Cowland bellowed like a bull into the hall,

"Beatrice Farley! Where are you? Your mistress needs you."

He set Rosalie down by the fire.

"Heavens. What has happened?" said Bea as she ran into the room.

"Warm clothes. Maybe broth. Something warm at any rate to drink."

Rosalie was shrinking into herself.

"Leave me. I'll get myself to my room. Thank you." Martin threw up his hands and marched out, saying something about telling Master Ancelin.

Bea helped Rosalie to stand and she hobbled up the steps, leaning on the arm of her servant.

All wet clothes were pulled from her and she was wrapped in a blanket and chafed until she was dry and warm. Bea began to dry Rosalie's hair and once it was less soaked, she brushed it and left it loose to dry further.

Whilst all this was happening, Rosalie was trying to tell Bea what had transpired.

"You should leave the cows to the cowmen, madam. That's what you pay them for."

"I want to understand them, Bea, to know them."

"It's man's work."

"Knowing and working with cows?"

"Aye."

"And dairymaids? Are they all men?"

Bea scoffed. "Some are yes."

"If it wasn't for my idea then it's possible they would have foundered. I needed to be there."

"You didn't need to get up close."

"They are my cows. I want to understand them."

"Why, for Heaven's sake?"

"Because they are mine."

Bea stopped brushing.

"Oh, I understand. You want to do everything that Master Roger did. You are proving to him, even though he's dead, that you are as good as he was."

Rosalie gave her servant a venomous look.

"Why can't a woman do as well as a man?"

"We can...in fact...we can do better."

Rosalie looked round at her.

"It's just that men won't let us."

She thought back to her adventure today. She brought Ancelin to mind. He hadn't stopped her. He'd done his best to educate her, help her. He hadn't discouraged her.

"Not all men."

Bea helped her to the bed and into a clean shift. Then the ankle had to be re- examined.

"Aw no.. you've undone all the good you did by resting it the past few days."

"It will mend again."

"I hope it doesn't come back to haunt you when you're old."

"I'm not going to get old."

"Pah!" said Bea with meaning.

Her maid strapped it up and Rosalie screwed up her face as the pain shot through her foot.

"Your feet are as cold as two nuns at a wedding."

"What?" laughed Rosalie.

"Cold...icy."

"Then find me a heated stone."

Bea sighed.

She went to a chest in the solar and took out two large stones which were covered in wool. She removed the woollen casings.

"I'll be a moment."

The maid left the room to place the stones next to the flames of the open fire downstairs. She walked round and round until she considered the stones hot enough, put them into their woollen covers, made an apron of her cotte and carried them upstairs. She placed them at Rosalie's feet.

She looked up. Rosalie was asleep.

*****

"Have we managed to get all the cattle away safely?"

"We have."

"Is it still raining?"

"Sadly it is."

"Then we need to check on all the other cows."

"Being done."

"I want reports of all the fields. How many are inundated. What's the state of the crops?"

"I am gathering information now."

"Bring it to me when you have it."

A slight smile crossed the lips of the farm manager.

"Aye ma'am."

Rosalie wriggled herself further up the bed.

"Thank you for your help."

"It's my job."

She looked carefully at him. How long had she known him? Ten years? She had had much more to do with William, of course in her younger days. Roger had dealt with Ancelin. How old did she think he was? Thirty five, forty? Where did he hail from? She didn't know.

"So what do you think happened, Master Hayward?"

The man stood upright and folded his arms across his chest.

"The water rose where there's a spring we had no knowledge of."

"I know that there's a myriad of little springs and trickling runnels on the land."

"And the recent wet weather has swollen the groundwater."

Rosalie chewed her finger end.

"We have had terrible rain before. Why now has this spring decided to burst out?" She cocked her head. "Have we any record of this happening before?"

Ancelin shook his head.

"Oh sit down man, you are giving me a neck ache looking up at you."

Ancelin looked surprised but hooked a stool from under the table and sat.

"We need to ask the old folk. They might remember times when the valley has been badly flooded."

"I am sure that Lord Lillebon won't mind us asking his folk."

"I'll get a man over there tomorrow," he said.

But when Ancelin came to send out a man to Fyfield village and manor, the next day, the way was impassable with flood water.

He called in to see his mistress. She greeted him sitting in a chair and wrapped in a blanket.

"Madam, we are cut off. We can't get to Marlborough and we can't get to Devizes. I don't need to say that we can't pass south over any bridge or ford. We can only go north over the downs."

"The whole way is flooded?" She put down a parchment she had been reading.

"I sent men both ways. Harry could get as far as Avebury and Beckhampton and then only by jagging about and Henry couldn't get beyond the Manton road. All bridges are down and the fords impassable"

"Our beasts?"

"Those on higher ground are fine. Those which were on the lower meadows have been brought in."

Rosalie crossed herself. "Have we lost anyone, any dwellings?"

"Not yet. But there are a few cotts which will be in danger of being swept away."

"Can we get to them?"

"It's doubtful now. It's been raining solidly for four days."

"Five."

Ancelin nodded. "Aye, five. You're right."

"What can we do?"

"Nothing Madam. Sit tight and pray."

*****

It rained for five more days and then the sun came out. Everyone heaved a sigh of relief and started the task of cleaning up. And then on the seventh day, the heavens opened again.

"Bound to!" said Bea as she braided her mistress' hair. Rosalie had always done her own hair when Roger had been alive, mindful of her scars but now she was more relaxed.

"Why?"

"It rained on St. Swithun's day and it will rain for forty days and forty nights now."

"The river will burst its banks."

"It has already."

"Oh…"

"Master Hayward told me."

"I worry for all those people down the river whose houses will be underwater. And the people of the town."

Bea crossed herself. "Makes us glad we are up on the downs in the dry here."

"Yes indeed."

They carried on in silence thinking the unthinkable.

"Where exactly is Master Hayward's property Bea?"

"Oh don't worry mistress, his house is the one on the very edge of the downland village at Kennet. He's safe there."

"And Master Steward lives here so my main people are still able to get about."

"Unlike some."

"Yes." Rosalie turned to Bea. "What about your Master Sommar?"

Bea blushed to the roots of her hair.

"He's not *mine*. I just like him."

"Well, Master Sommar whom you admire?"

Bea shivered her shoulders a little in a kind of embarrassment. "He lives as you know, up off the Herepath."

"Ah…good."

Rosalie's little devil piped up. 'You'd never hear the last of it if the man lived in the river valley.'

"Can you ask Master Hayward to come and see me please, Bea. When you have a moment."

"If I can find him, mistress. He's very busy just now."

"Ask one of the lads to go and find him."

"Yes ma'am."

Ancelin Hayward came into the hall a little while later. Rosalie was sitting by the fire toasting her toes and plying her distaff.

"Master Ancelin. Come sit down. Take some cider. Tell me what's been going on."

The man looked weary. His normally symmetrical oblong face was slumped and grey. His beard was a little unkempt, his hair uncombed. He ran his long and strong fingers through the waves of it.

"Forgive me ma'am, I haven't slept for two nights. We have been busy fetching in the cattle and sheep and moving them to safer ground. When the river burst its banks we had to fetch them even higher up."

"When did that happen?"

"In the early hours of this morning."

Rosalie put down her spinning and took up a beaker. Filling it with cider, she handed it to him.

"Thank you." He sighed. "We can't have the beasts on waterlogged ground. They'll get hoof rot."

"Ah yes."

She had heard of this.

"Have we any casualties besides the meadows?"

Ancelin looked sad and closed his eyes for a brief moment. "Aye. Just one. We have recovered the body."

Rosalie's eyes grew round. She had not meant...people.

"Who, who...?"

"We were out at Audley Down, near Clatford. The river is fierce there now. Master Hadden slipped and fell into the river. We couldn't reach him. It was too fast."

Rosalie closed her eyes. "Oh..no not poor Alfred?"

"He drowned," said Ancelin baldly.

Rosalie pictured the young man who had joked with her out in the field. His round jocular face. His tight muscular body. His strong arms. Not strong enough to fight through the swirling waters to the safety of the bank.

"No...no."

Ancelin crossed himself. "I have never been so glad that a man wasn't married."

"No. I see what you mean."

"To die after a long and productive life, one understands. One accepts God taking a man's soul to him, but..this...he was but four and twenty and as fit as a fighting fox."

"We shall bury him with honour at Preshute."

"He's a Kennet man. He'd like to be laid to rest there, I suppose."

"It will be done."

Ancelin swirled his ale in its pot, looking down at it disconsolately.

"And you, Master Hayward? Where would you like to be buried?"

He took a deep breath and let it out. "I'm a Devizes man, madam, but Preshute would be fine for me. I have none to mourn me in Devizes."

She gave a little smile but said nothing.

Then her little devil said chirpily, 'why ever did you ask him that? Now he thinks that you think he's going to snuffle off.'

He smiled at her.

"Take care Master Hayward."

He rose and wiped his mouth and nose on the back of his hand. "Aye. None of us knows..."

Rosalie thought...'Alfred Hadden didn't know that yesterday would be his last day on earth.'

"Take care. I have no wish to break in a new farm manager. We would miss you enormously."

His visage lightened immediately. "Ah no...it's not... "

"Ten years of experience with my land and cows. Your knowledge and experience would be hard to replace."

His face slumped again. "Aye madam, " he said and with a slight laugh, he left.

'Oh Rosalie Jourdemayne! You have done it again.You just never seem to say the right thing at the right time.'

Bea stepped forward.

"He's such a nice man. Very quiet but he has an answer for everything."

Rosalie turned to look up at her maid. "Does he?"

"Oh yes. I think he's the cleverest man I know. But not like the priest. He doesn't show off."

"What about your Master Sommar?" said Rosalie mischievously.

Bea snorted. "Aw he's pretty to look at but besides cows and sheep… he knows nothing."

"And Master Hayward does?

"Oh yes, mistress."

"Like what?"

"Well, he can count and write and read."

"Yes."

"And he knows about plants and birds and animals."

"Yes."

"And he's been to all sorts of places. Far away places."

"Has he?"

"Oh yes. Like Newbury. And Swinedun. And Chippenham"

"Well, well," said Rosalie.

*****

They could not get to Preshute church the following Sunday, for the ways were impassable but the church at Kennet just a little way from Avebury was possible and so they took Master Alfred Hadden to his home village to bury him. Rosalie paid for a coffin.

After the mass and burial service, they took the body of Forceleap Farm's cow worker to the graveside.

They stood in the churchyard looking down at the grave as they began to back fill it; Rosalie was reminded of the last funeral she had attended and how she had felt on that day. This was the utter antithesis of that time and she shed a true tear for poor Alfred and his widowed mother.

"What will she do now, William?" she said as she watched the weeping old lady led away. "Alfred supported her I know, with money and…"

"Only a sister at home. She spins, I believe, madam."

"Ah."

She thought hard. Her little devil did not dare interrupt her.

"William, might we allow them a little pension? Can we do that? It might make life a little more bearable for them."

William, her steward, looked at her intently.

"You truly wish to do that, madam?"

"Just a little to smooth their path. Am I being too sentimental? Is it not something the local farmers would do for their workers?"

"Some but…"

"Not Roger."

He thought for a moment. "I can arrange it. If they will accept." He nodded his head in their direction. "It will not be for long, I think. The woman is over fifty. And she is not in the best of health, it seems."

"Then do it. I am sure that we can afford it."

He bowed and smiled, "Madam."

She turned to leave and faced the priest. "Thank you Father Augustine. That was beautiful." She pressed coins into his hand.

She began walking up the slight slope of the churchyard path, when there was a crunching of gravel behind her.

"Madam!"

"Master Hayward. You seem a little distempered. Are you alright?"

"I must speak with you."

"Here or might we?"

"Here, for this is where the damage is done."

"I beg your pardon, Hayward?"

He grasped the wool of her sleeve.

"Madam I know why our field was flooded. Why meadows which haven't seen water since the flood of Noah, should flood now."

"What might we see here, Hayward?"

He smiled. She thought it was rather an improper smile considering the circumstances.

"The source of the problem."

"Here?"

"Aye...here. Madam, girdle up your cotte again. We must once more travel the wet grass."

Rosalie lifted her dark kirtle, pulled it into her belt and wrapped her cloak around her.

"Where are we going?"

Just a little way behind the church. Two small fields away to be precise."

Rosalie resigned to getting her feet wet again.

She followed her farm manager and her maid followed her.

"You need not come Bea," she said. "I will be quite safe with Master Hayward."

Bea grimaced. She wasn't following because she was worried about her mistress' honour. She wanted to see for herself what drew them two fields away.

Rosalie struggled to keep up with Master Hayward's swift pace. He was used to marching about the countryside and was confident upon the undulating ground under his feet.

"Wait! Wait!" she cried, "My ankle won't stand much more of this."

Hayward stopped abruptly. She barged into him.

"Oh I am sorry. I forget that you are not Sir Roger. And that you are hurt. I apologise."

Rosalie pulled a face.

'In case you haven't noticed Master Hayward, she's much younger than Roger!' said her little devil. 'And she has lumpy bits!'

"Walk on," said Rosalie as if he were a horse.

Hayward gave her his arm and they walked together to the meadow behind the church at a more sedate pace.

"Look down. What do you see?"

Rosalie raked the scene before her with a critical eye.

"The river. And the little pools into which it splits."

"So you know that here, there are several tributaries of the Kennet. In a good year they all make little runnels alongside the main stream."

"I have looked at the maps that Roger had made."

"So you know that in some years they dry up completely...and..."

"Winterbournes, only flowing in the winter."

"Or wet springs or autumns."

"But they are rarely engulfed by the river."

"They take the overspill."

"But it does flood, even so."

"Now and again, but never to this level." Hayward's eye sparkled. "Look again."

Rosalie gave a grimace of uncertainty.

"The runnels and oxbow cutoffs can be seen as separate rivers. Like they can in the drier weather."

"Yes, meaning?"

"That the main river is taking all the water."

"Why? That should not be."

"Master Hayward...?" she said.

His eyebrow rose up..."Yes..." he said encouragingly.

"I don't understand."

"It shouldn't be."

"No," said Bea suddenly. "Me da used to do that when he wanted to dip his sheep."

Rosalie felt a little slow of mind. "What have your da's sheep to do with it?"

Bea sighed in exasperation.

"Someone has dammed the river's overflows, madam.

CHAPTER FOUR ~ SUITORS, AGAIN

Rosalie took off her sodden clothes once more. She grew hot and angry. "Someone has dammed the leats?"

"Yes they have."

"But why? What possible reason can they have?"

"Who owns that land madam, the other side of Kennet?"

Rosalie threw a clean shift over her head.

"Let me think. That has to be...Master Dankworth's land.

Bea handed her the recently completed pink cotte.

"Why in the name of all the archangels should master Dankworth dam *his* part of the river?"

"It's his land. He farms sheep. Most of them are up on the high ground of the downs,"said Bea

"You mean that his animals are not in danger but he puts others further down the valley, in jeopardy?" .

"Like our cattle."

Rosalie sat with a bump.

"But why?"

She asked that same question to her farm manager a few moments later when she met him in the hall.

"Why would he do that?"

"Master Pottinger farms at Mildenhall, the other side of the town.

Downstream. It's not him."

"Why should that be anything to do with Master Dankworth?" said Rosalie.

"It's known that the man paid you a visit and that he was interested in joining Forceleap Farm to his other properties."

"He asked me to consider him as a suitor, yes, if I were thinking of remarrying. Master Dankworth did the same."

"Both rebuffed."

"I rebuffed Sir Hugh too."

"Ah but his property isn't in the valley."

"No."

Rosalie wrung her hands in her lap. "Master Pottinger is like a wet withy. He's has about as much backbone as a slug."

"That's very unkind,' said Rosalie's little voice. 'But true.' She saw the expression of her little demon in her mind's eye. Smug.

"And his land is unlikely to be really damaged...all except for the mill," she said.

"Ah no. I think that will survive. It's well placed," added Ancelin Hayward. "The person who is most harmed... is you."

"All because I refused his offer of marriage?"

Ancelin shrugged.

"Oh Master Hayward. It's my fault. All my fault that poor Alfred died."

"No. It's not your fault, madam. Alfred went too close to the edge of the river to recover one of the calves. He managed to push it free of the mud and toppled backwards into the flood. It was an act of God."

Rosalie stood and hugged her arms to her body.

"But if the river was not so...raging..."

"It could have happened anyway."

She sat down by the fire again.

"What can we do? How can we bring him to justice?"

Ancelin shook his head. "I doubt we can do anything."

"No. We cannot prove anything."

"No. But we must watch Master Dankworth in future. He's obviously a vindictive man."

*****

The flood gradually receded and the meadows sparkled under just a few inches of water. The way east and west became passable once more. Many bridges had been washed away, for they were only made of wood. Rosalie resolved to rebuild those situated on her land, in stone.

Not two days after the traffic upon the road to Devizes began to flow again, Sir Maurice FitzAlan clopped into the farmyard and dismounted from his great horse.

He bowed graciously.

"Madam. I am pleased to see that you are once again upon two feet."

Rosalie curtsied. "Thank you Sir Maurice. It has been an eventful recovery."

The man followed her into the hall.

"How are things in the town?"

"It has been dire but things are returning to normal.The bridges held when we didn't think they would. A few business properties were damaged but no lives lost. I hear you had a bad time of it here at Forceleap?"

"It was a time for quick thinking and action, Sir Maurice. We lost no livestock though we are sad at the loss of a young life. Master Alfred Hadden was taken in the flood."

The man shook his head. "Drowned saving cattle from the raging river I hear."

"You hear correctly." Rosalie's little devil started to growl. 'And if I have anything to do with it… a certain someone is going to pay.'

"Serving his mistress in the best way he knew."

"I am grateful for the loyalty and selflessness of my staff, Sir Maurice."

"Such a delightful lady warrants much loyalty, madam."

'Oh he's such a flatterer,' said her little devil. 'Don't believe a word of it.'

"I am sure were I so inclined, I too could give my life for you." He smiled shyly.

Rosalie blinked. She blinked again. 'What can this career soldier, who is the second son of a Lord, want with Forceleap Farm?' said her little devil.

She pretended she hadn't heard it.

And she pretended she hadn't heard the compliment.

"Sooo...you are happy with your life at the castle?"

"It suits me. There are few avenues for the second son, save the church and soldiering, madam."

"Not farming?"

Maurice looked into his ale cup. "Aw...no...I don't think I have the temperament for farming. I have little patience you see."

"Oh I cannot believe that." Rosalie examined him under her eyelashes. He really was quite the dashing man.

"You come, you told me, from the north of the county?"

"Chalfield Madam. It's close by the town of Melksham. My brother is in charge there now since my elderly father's illness and my younger brother, Alain is the one content with the farming of the lands."

"I have no brother or sister. I always think it must be nice to have company when you are young."

"It can be...interesting."

He took a sip of the ale. "When did you come to Forceleap, madam?"

"I have been here thirteen years."

"A whole lifetime ago."

"I came from the town of Wantage in the county of Berkshire at the age of seventeen."

"From farming people?"

"Yes indeed. My father farmed for the Earl of Albermarle, sir. Sheep."

"Ah yes. One of King Richard's men...of blessed memory."

Rosalie watched him again.

He seemed ill at ease with the kind of chatter which some people find easy, that inconsequential trading of facts about each other which she had heard called 'small talking.'

He smiled at her again "Have you managed to convince the priest that you wish to make the vow you spoke about..." He faltered. He'd realised that he shouldn't really know about this as he'd been eavesdropping upon a private conversation at the time.

Rosalie wasn't going to upbraid him for that. She'd got off to a bad start with him on that score anyway.

"I haven't had the chance to discuss it further. I had planned on going to Marlborough that day but..."

"Ah yes."

Both of them now stalled. Rosalie because she didn't want to recall the embarrassing incident of her accident and Sir Maurice because he had reacted badly to her rebuff and dropped her in the cart.

"I am glad in a way that..."

"Yes, Sir Maurice?"

"That you have not had a chance..."

"Oh?"

"To make your vow...yet."

"Oh why is that?"

She suddenly recalled William the steward's words. 'Not all men are after Forceleap Farm.'

Surely it couldn't be that Sir Maurice was interested in her...for *herself*? Herself alone?

"Oh Sir Maurice, you cannot mean that you do not wish me to live a holy and celibate life?"

"Good company, madam is so very hard to find, in these parts. I am afraid that if you make this vow, gentlemen callers will no longer be welcome at Forceleap Farm."

"My good sir. There must be many a girl in the town who..."

"I am sure there are. But I do not really get to socialise with them. Living at the castle. And so few are unmarried who are of my age. And forgive me, interesting to me. "

"You are welcome to come here, at any time. But I must remind you that as soon as I am able, I will be making that vow."

"I wish I could dissuade you."

"You are not the first to try to do so."

He smiled a rather disarming smile. "How might you feel in a few years? I would hate to see you ruin your life. You cannot know what is in store."

"As poor Alfred did not."

"Ah...no."

Silence again.

"But madam, might you not wish to remarry at some time and have children?"

The little devil sitting on Rosalie's shoulder piped up loudly then.

'Children? Ah no. She doesn't want those. She'd rather poke her eye out with a pin!'

"Well, perhaps it's not that bad," she answered it.

"Forgive me?"

"I said no, not that badly."

"You'll not miss being a mother?"

"No not really." To which her devil added. 'She'll miss it like a dose of the colic!' She did not add that.

"Like you, sir. I have little patience."

"That I cannot believe," he said, mirroring her own earlier statement.

Again there was a rather self conscious silence.

"Well...I must away. I came out to the castle barn - Grange barn, and thought to jog the short distance to see you and make sure you had recovered."

"I am quite returned to a normal state of health, mind, and strength, thank you. And it is most kind of you to think of me."

As he left the room, after bowing low and bidding her good day, she thought she heard him say,

"Every day, madam. Every day."

*****

It was a week for knights of the realm.

Once he had dismounted, the man took her hand.

"Mistress Jourdemayne. It is an utter pleasure to see you again."

"Sir Hugh. How pleasant. Do come in."

He kissed the back of her hand and lingered a little too long.

"I was passing on my way to the town and thought, 'now, why do I not go and pay a visit to the good Widow Jourdemayne.'

"Ah no, sir, surely you came slightly out of your way."

He tossed his hand as if he was flicking away an irritant fly.

"Madam, for you, I would brave Hell itself. I'd cross the River Styx."

She laughed at him.

"Well, sir...you almost had to. A few days ago and you would not have been able to reach us for water."

Bea thumped down a beaker of cider in front of the man. It slopped over the rim. He didn't glare or reprimand her as Rosalie thought he might, but he was not pleased, she could tell.

"Forgive my clumsy maidservant, sir knight, since our incarceration she has forgotten her manners."

Bea glared at her, stalked off and sat at the corner of the room to ply her needle. He ignored her.

Sir Hugh put his hand on his heart. "I am not a sensible man, madam. High water holds no terror for me."

"But surely the education of your knighthood has remedied those deficiencies, sir?"

"Ah alas. I am found out."

She looked down at his sword. It was the same size as Sir Maurice's blade.

"You are a fighting man, sir. "

"Sir Hugh preened himself."

"And so you must have been with the King to far flung places?"

"A few."

"In your role as a knight of the county…" Rosalie tittered. "Have you travelled much, Sir Hugh."

"A little. Though I am always happiest to return home here, to Wiltshire."

"Oh, I am anxious to hear about those places you found interesting. And those people you found most beguiling."

"France is boring. Ireland is…wet and Scotland is…rocky and cold."

"Oh. Did you learn nothing interesting when you were in these places, sir?"

"Very little."

"Oh," she said in a disappointed tone. "And did you meet no interesting people?"

"I must admit I developed quite an affection for the lassies of Ireland. They are good looking, have beautiful hair and an equable nature. Unless riled. Then they become as fiends incarnate!"

"I cannot imagine that you, a noble knight of the realm, could do anything heinous enough to turn these women into demons, Sir Hugh."

He smiled and preened his moustache.

"I think I can honestly say, Ireland is the only place I have been where I truly enjoyed myself."

"Pah!" said Bea from the corner. He turned to look at her but again, ignored her interruption.

"And yet, even the women of Ireland are not quite a match for our own English beauties."

"By English, I think you mean Norman?"

"English, Norman…now we are all one and the same, are we not."

Her little devil sat up straight on her shoulder and spoke into her ear. 'The cheek of the man. I am English and will remain English… even if I was married to a Norman.'

"Tell that to many of my farm workers, sir…and your own too, I suspect. But be careful should you do so. A knife in the ribs might be your reward. And you might end up buried in the forest in the dead of night. There are many who still take pride in their English name."

Even now, in place, a century later, was the process known as the 'presentment of Englishry.' This was the presentation of some kind of proof that a slain person was of English rather than Norman birth. It was a known excuse for not paying a fine levied by the Norman kings of England upon the tithings or groups of ten men, for the murder of a Norman.

He looked at her strangely then, with what she thought was a new kind of respect.

"Madam, you are wise beyond your years."

"No. I just keep my ear to the ground and my eyes open. I know that, even nowadays, after a hundred years or more, the resentment has not quite gone away. There are still some who are fighting the battle."

"But not you, madam," said a shocked Sir Hugo.

"No, not me. Although I come from Saxon stock, I have enough Norman blood in me."

"Oh do tell me the story. I am certain I would find your history fascinating." He settled in his chair more firmly.

"Creep..." said Bea under her breath, never raising her eyes.

"Sir Hugo, much as I would like to sit here and tell you the tale of my ancestors; that they were Woden born, that is descended from the Saxon Gods, and that the other half are directly related to the Angevins who have never denied they came from dark and uncertain origins..."

"Melusine...I believe," he said, his eyes large and enthralled.

"The very same... Much as I'd love to talk, I have a lot of work to do."

"And here I am, coming upon you unannounced. Forgive me, madam."

"Forgiven."

She stood and arranged her skirts.

"May I hope that you will give me leave to call upon you again."

Rosalie gave a huge and very audible sigh. "I cannot forbid you to visit, sir. You are a close neighbour when all is said and done. But please be aware that when I am able, I shall be making that vow of celibacy and Forceleap is not up for negotiation."

"Perish the thought, madam, that I visit you solely for the acquisition of your lands. Believe me when I say that I find you alone, utterly ravishing..."

Bea snuffled into her chest.

"Your humility can only grow amongst your other refinements. You surely cannot be blind to the fact that I am utterly captivated by you. I am being encouraged to marry, for I wish to comply with my dear deceased mother's wishes to marry someone, competent, able, who has a good standing in the community but is not on too high a pedestal as to be haughty and proud...or too lowly as to bring no benefit, or too far above my own station in life."

"Sir?"

"No madam. Give up this foolish idea of a vow..."

The word was spat out like a mouthful of mouldy food.

"No, sir. No, Sir Hugh. I must decline. I will not marry."

"But madam you could make me the happiest man in England."

"No. No. Thrice no. I would make you deeply unhappy."

"Oh I know that it is the custom of young ladies...to refuse..."

"I am not an untried young lady, Sir Hugh. I am a widow of thirty and I cannot be compelled to marry."

"What is age...?" He threw up his hands.

"If I were inclined to marry it would be to an older man. Not ...." 'Her little devil was saying, - a vacuous boy - "a man younger than myself."

Sir Hugh looked utterly deflated.

"Well...I will not give up. You must give me leave to try again... perhaps in a sennight."

"Nothing will have changed in seven days, sir."

She wrestled her hand from his and backed off.'

Bea came up to her side and opened the door.

"This way Sir Hugh..."

Sir Hugh bowed low. Rosalie looked carefully at his hair. 'Well at least he isn't bald like Master Pottinger.'

He left with Bea chasing him out to the yard.

She was shaking with laughter when Bea returned.

"What an absolute horror," she said, patting her headdress into place.

Bea tidied up the cider cup.

"I could tell you a few tales about our sweet faced Sir Hugh."

"You could?"

"Oh aye…"

"Oh! Do tell."

*****

Up in the privacy of their bedroom, sitting in her shift, Rosalie took up her mirror and looked at herself with a critical eye.

"Bea?"

"Yes madam…"

"Am I a beautiful woman? Tell me truthfully. I do not want you to tell me what you think I ought or want to hear. What do you think?"

Bea came up and sat by Rosalie in the light of a candle.

"You have really lovely hair - not that anyone ever sees it. And you have beautiful eyes but no…the whole of you is not beautiful. You are a handsome woman for your age as I have said before. You have no wrinkles. Your skin is very good. And you have all your teeth…you do have all your teeth, don't you?"

Rosalie grinned showing her teeth.

"Well then, yes, you are handsome."

"Then why are there suddenly so many men who are telling me they are in love with me, for myself alone and not for Forceleap Farm?"

"They lie. You know what men are like."

Rosalie felt deflated. "Tomorrow…we shall go to town and find the priest of St.Mary's and compel him to allow me to make a vow."

"Ah…tomorrow is Sunday. I doubt you'll be allowed to do that on a Sunday."

"Not on a Holy day? How foolish is that."

"Well, we can ask."

"Then I shall feel safe."

Bea started to brush her mistress' hair.

"Bea?"

"Yes ma'am."

"What is it you do know about Sir Hugh?"

Bea's voice took on the tone of one telling a salacious or spine chilling tale.

"Oh...he is the very devil."

"No...what does he do?" Rosalie felt a shiver cross her shoulders.

"What has he done? He's seduced half the locality that's what. From Beckhampton to Ramsbury his name is known to every virgin, high and low and yes, a few widows too."

"He is a seducer?"

"Oh yes. Promises the earth. He has practised the soft talk. I have heard the selfsame words from him; those which he spoke to you tonight..."

"Not you Bea? He hasn't tried to..."

"Ah no...not me. But he's tried my friend Alys. And my sister Fidela. She's the oldest of us."

"Did he succeed in...you know..."

Bea chuckled. "Not with our Fidela. She kneed him in the groin. Said it musta' hurt him being as how his p..."

"And this is how you know that the man uses exactly the same words with all the women he 'courts'?

"Aye. And the same words to Alys."

"What happened to Alys?"

Bea put her joined hands to the side of her face and effected a silly voice.

"Oh dear Alys. You must have known that our little bit of fun is now over. It can't go on. You must know that I don't love you. How can I? You are only a..."

"She didn't fall preg..."

"Oh no."

"It was just a fling, a bit of meaningless ribaldry. Now it's all over," was what he said.

Rosalie's fingers leapt to her lips. "Oh my! What happened?"

"She hit him with a log!"

"No!"

"No more than he deserved."

"And laid him out?"

"Aye…" giggled Bea."

"Why did he not report her? I am assuming he didn't?"

"And risk the whole neighbourhood knowing. And his dear, dear mother?"

"Ah yes… his mother, now deceased."

"I think there would have been a string of girls from here to Marlborough queuing up to tell his mother just what a despicable pillycock he was. How he's promised marriage to more than a dozen girls."

"I knew nothing. I never heard… a thing."

"You were a married lady then. He doesn't tackle married ladies."

"Oh Bea. If he turns up again. I am not at home. Ever!"

*****

"I have managed to remove the blockages to the leats and the tributaries of the river," said Master Hayward the next day.

"How?"

"A few lads and I went down under cover of darkness, last night and dragged them well away."

"Onto the meadow?"

"Aye."

"Then Master Dankworth will know that we are aware of what he's done," said Rosalie.

"It will do him no harm to know that we are conscious of his wrongdoing."

"I have no doubt that he'll deny all knowledge and blame someone else."

Ancelin gave a feral smile; such a smile as she had never seen on his face before. "Ah...but we know and he'll know it."

"Know that we know."

"And that might be useful."

*****

They had no chance to go to church in Marlborough that morning. Events overtook them.

"Mistress, have you seen Dyamant? I can't find her to put her away here whilst we go to church."

Rosalie was patting a little of her bryony rouge to her lips. 'Not too much now,' said the voice in her head. 'You want to make a good impression but not appear vain.'

She looked into her little mirror. 'Ah no. Off with you,' she said to herself as she wiped the stain off with a piece of sheep's wool.

"I am a widow. I am seeking to make a vow of celibacy. Whyever would I wish to make myself more attractive."

Bea came up and peered at her.

"You need to make yourself look more like that woman at Preshute church."

"What?"

"That ankleright."

"Ankleright? Oh, you mean the anchorite?"

"What's her name?" asked Bea.

"Alice, I think."

"Ah yes. That's her."

"But Bea, she looks like she hasn't washed for weeks, she has lice and her hair is..."

"She hasn't. Washed. And she rubs ashes into her hair."

"What did you say about Dyamant?"

"I can't find her."

During her marriage to Roger, the greatest consolation to Rosalie had been her dog. Dyamant had helped her over the worst of times. There had been many a day when she had cried into the rough fur of her aristocratic head and thrown her arms around her bony body for comfort. Dyamant was a small, arch backed, slender sighthound with short, pale grey, curly hair, long elegant legs and a pointed muzzle. Rosalie thought her eyes were as deep as a black ocean, if there could be such a thing. And she could, by gazing into them, lose herself completely. She would scoop up the small dog and push her face into the softness of her body, knowing that when she looked up, the adoration in her dog's expression would wash away all the wickedness of the world.

"She's probably under master steward's table. She likes to lie there when he's working."

"No...I've looked. And it's Sunday. He isn't at work."

"Ah no. In with Master Ancelin, in the barn?"

"No...not there."

"Then she'll be in the kitchen, by the fire."

"No madam. She isn't."

Rosalie's brow formed furrows of puzzlement, (even though Bea had said that it was a hideous expression which would cause her to look old before her time,) and scanned the room in which she sat.

"This time of the day, she's usually in here."

"I know. She has her routines but today..."

Dyamant was a dog of good habits and predictable moods. She could also be relied upon to come when called.

Rosalie raised her voice. "Dyamant, where are you?"

There was no scraping of claws upon the wooden floor; no sound of shaking which usually preceded a launch from some hiding place.

"We need to look for her."

"But we shall be late for church."

"I cannot go to church not knowing that she's safe," said Rosalie. "How would I concentrate?"

Bea quizzed her face…"Upon the liturgy…or upon the entreaty I shall make to the good Father Torold."

"Ah…yes."

They searched all the outhouses, the barns and the close cottages. No one had accidentally closed a door upon the little dog. Dyamant was well known around the place and soon, Rosalie had everyone looking for her.

Master William Newbold, who was as fond of the dog as anyone, suggested a search of the nearer parts of the farm fields. "You know how she enjoys chasing rabbits. I expect she's just been carried away…"

Rosalie looked worried. "Carried away?"

"I mean that she has a great deal of excitement when she is out in the field, chasing the rabbits and digging for…"

"She always comes when called."

"It's true, master steward, she is a well trained dog," said Bea. "She always returns. It might take her a while but she comes back."

Master Hayward and the Forceleap Farm steward exchanged looks.

"Then we must go further afield to search."

They began at the meadows behind the barns. Rosalie knew that Dyamant wouldn't go too far in the field as she was a little afraid of the cows.

There were a few folk out taking advantage of the good Sunday weather, sitting upon the grass and under the trees. None of them had seen the dog.

"Well if she hasn't been seen coming this way then she cannot be any further along there," said William thrusting his arm out over the down.

Rosalie surveyed the land, over the dips and dry valleys.

"She has never come this far out before on her own."

Their eye was taken by a small black speck moving at speed over the undulations of the turf.

As it got closer, they recognised it for a horse and rider.

"Is that Master Dankworth?" said Rosalie

"No, it's coming from the south. He would travel due east, if he came across the downs," answered William.

Bea shaded her eyes with a flattened hand. "It's Master Godechepe. You remember you met him at the betrothal festivities."

"The gentleman from Boreham, out near Pewsey?" said William Newbold.

"What can he be doing out this way?" asked Rosalie, utterly perplexed.

The man rode nearer and then after a while saw them and hailed them.

"Ho! Mistress Jourdemayne!"

The man was sitting his horse a little stiffly and had his dark cloak wrapped around him. Odd as it was a mild day. They noticed, then, that he rode one hand only on the reins.

"Master Godechepe. God's blessings on you. What brings you five miles across the downs?"

The man laboured up the slope on his bay horse and clicked his tongue when he held it back on the last leap.

"Whoa there, Augustus!" He seemed to have difficulty staying in the saddle.

Bea ran to grab his stirrup.

"Oh, sir, are you alright?"

"Well, that was quite a run...but yes, I am alright. Thank you."

"Madam." He bowed from horseback breathlessly. "I am glad to have met you here."

He fiddled with his cloak as he addressed Rosalie.

"I have come by the most direct route I could. I was on my way to a cottage just north of Alton Priors to meet with a friend of mine, for we were to take dinner together and, since I had a little time, I thought I would just sit awhile and stare out over the view."

"It is a particularly fine view, sir," said Rosalie. "From the hills about."

"Over Cutforth down and over towards the farmland of our neighbour Master Dankworth."

"Yes indeed."

"When I spotted a sight which I had not seen, well, since the winter, when these things are scattered over all our grounds."

"Things?" said Ancelin Hayward, speaking for the first time since they had left home.

"Sheep folds, my good man."

Ancelin nodded. "Not since lambing have we had them out so far from habitation."

"And my interest was piqued, for coming from this solitary fold was a pitiful yapping and barking."

The man took out a grey bundle from his cloak and handed it down to Ancelin.

"Upon our conversation at the betrothal feast of my Goddaughter, I remember you describing to me, the outward form of your canine companion, Mistress Jourdemayne."

"Dyamant!"

The dog struggled in the arms of Rosalie's farm manager and yelped to be let go. She leapt into the arms of her mistress and began licking her fiercely.

"Oh Dyamant!"

"She was penned in. In the sheepfold where, of course, there were no longer any sheep."

"We use these for our milking ewes, Master Godechepe but closer to home," said Hayward. We have none at present out in the fields."

"I cannot imagine how your poor beast got in there, so far from home and all alone."

Rosalie was holding her dog as close as she could to her body and the dog submitted, going limp with happiness.

"She never strays too far from the farm, sir. Never. She is too afraid of the cattle in the fields around."

"I knew at once that she must be the little creature you described to me, for I think there is not the like in the whole of Wiltshire," said a rather pink in the face, Master Godechepe.

"Please sir, come up to Forceleap Farm and take some refreshment. It's the least we can do," said Rosalie sweetly. "You may take your ease and rest there a while."

"Alas, I am late for my dinner appointment…"

"Might we send a boy to your friend to inform him that you are detained and will be along shortly?"

"That would be most acceptable. Thank you."

As they walked back, up and down the slopes, Dyamant now completely recovered having been given water from Master Godechepe's flask, they discussed the past good and bad weather, in spite of the prediction of St. Swithun.

Gradually they strung out, Master Godechepe speaking to William Newbold with Bea trailing them, then Master Hayward and Rosalie with Dyamant leaping and circling around them.

"How can Dyamant have gone so far Master Hayward?"

"When did you last see her?"

"Last night. She had decided to stay downstairs, I thought. As you know, she is particularly fond of William and I wondered if she had decided to sleep in his room last night."

Ancelin chuckled. "It's not unknown."

"I know…it's because he feeds her tidbits kept back from his own supper," said Rosalie with a knowing smile. "He thinks I don't know."

"And so you did not miss her for quite a few hours."

"All night and part of this morning."

Ancelin Hayward looked sidelong at his mistress. "Well…it's all turned out well, though if we hadn't found her…or Master Godechepe hadn't found her…"

"It does not bear contemplating, Hayward."

A strange look came over him and he jogged the few feet to catch up with the forward party.

"Master Godechepe, might I ask you…how was the fold fixed?"

Henry turned and mulled over Ancelin's words.

"Fixed….fixed? Well, the hurdles are all…"

"Yes but the gate, how was it fixed?"

"I had to undo it, if that is what you mean? To get the little dog out. She could never have jumped out. Or in."

"Thank you."

"It was fixed in the usual way; a stiff rope around the upright of the gate, tied twice."

Ancelin nodded.

"And no sign of anyone around? No other animals?"

"None whatsoever. The down was bare."

"Thank you for your help."

Once home and after a good jar of cider, Master Godechepe was invited to dinner but alas, he would return to his friend to the north of Alton Priors. He had promised. And he kept his promises. But he did agree to return another day to take dinner with them all at Forceleap by way of a thanks.

When the man had departed, Ancelin took his mistress aside and spoke quietly.

"The good master described the sheepfold to me. It is highly unlikely that that fold has been left on the ground from the winter and if it has, then why was a new rope attached to the gate?"

Rosalie took in a sharp breath. "The gate was closed deliberately?"

"Dyamant could not have lost herself in that fold. She could not have shut the gate and fastened it."

"It's the work of man, then?"

"Madam. You have enemies," he said.

This information felt like she was coming from noon into night.

❧

CHAPTER FIVE ~ THE ARGUMENT

What none of them could understand was how Dyamant had been lured out of the farm in the first place and how no one had been seen taking her.

"I want to go out to that sheepfold. Explore the ground. It might tell me something," said Hayward.

"I will come with you," Rosalie reached for her surcote and gave it to Bea. "I'll wear this, rather than a cloak, Bea."

"Madam, you have no need to come," said her farm manager as Bea passed the yellow wool over her mistress' head, taking care to avoid catching her veil in its folds.

"Two sets of eyes are better than one, Ancelin," said Rosalie. "What you miss, I might find."

Ancelin tutted. "Mistress Jourdemayne...it will be trespassing."

"Nonsense. The downs' tracks and ways belong to us all."

"Let us hope we do not meet Master Dankworth and his cronies. He may have another view."

"If we do, rest assured, Master Hayward, I will send them packing."

She heard her manager tut again and a sudden swift irritation crossed her breast but she did not give voice to it. Although her position of absolute mistress of farm and house was new to her, and the novelty of it had not yet worn off, she did not yet wish to give in to any disquiet.

They jogged down the slope and onto the flat, making good pace on the flinty turf.

Riding hard up the following slope where they had first seen Master Godechepe, they stopped on the brow.

"So he came from that direction," said her manager.

"And Alton Priors is over that brow."

"Quite a way over that brow."

"Oh is it?"

"Four miles with quite a few hills."

"I have never been this way before," said Rosalie.

"I know."

"How far does Forceleap Farm land stretch here, Master Hayward."

"The boundary stone is just over by that large ash tree to the west and our southern boundary is just over those old ridge and furrow at the next slope"

"We are still on our own land here?"

"Yes."

"I cannot recall Roger ever complaining that people trespassed anywhere," she said.

"No. When he was alive, people were aware of the boundaries and kept to the common paths."

"Are you implying that now I am in charge, things are more lax, Master Hayward?"

"No, not at all. It's just they might take the opportunity to move the boundary stones or grub up a hedge. Filch a few feet. Master Roger told me that was

what happened when his father died and they had to beat the bounds once more, to make sure of the boundaries."

"Who was at fault?"

"He didn't actually say."

They looked at each other and a meaningful look passed between them. They both knew who they *thought* might be at fault.

"But Master Godechepe passed without incident over Master Dankworth's land?"

"It's Sunday. And there are no sheep here. So no shepherds."

"Talking of shepherds and passing onto cattlemen," said Rosalie swivelling in the saddle.

"Tell me and tell me truthfully, what do the men think about having a mistress instead of a master now?"

Hayward set his face.

"Any discontent will be dealt with. By me."

"I heard that one man wanted to leave Forceleap because it is now ruled by a woman."

"That man is a fool. His wife soon sorted him out."

"He is still with us?"

"At present."

"There is no wholesale discontent?"

Master Hayward looked out over the downs.

Rosalie recalled the speech she had made shortly after her husband's death, to many of her workers and tenants, as many of them as she could gather together at the farm.

"I know that you are all a little nervous now that you have a mistress instead of a master."

Some of them had shuffled their feet.

"And I do not know, as yet, how I will get on, save that I know I have a good manager, excellent stockmen and shepherds. I will do my best to serve you all and I hope that you will do your best to assist me."

Some smiled, some scowled.

"But should any of you feel unfairly done by me...and I hope that will not be the case... it will be remedied. Please do not think that because I am a woman, I am unable to learn the business of the farm; of the cattle, of the sheep."

One or two shook their heads.

"And that I cannot comprehend the difference between good work... and false."

"Your speech won most of them over ma'am," said Hayward at last, not looking at her.

"And you Hayward? What is your view?"

Master Hayward shifted in the saddle as if it had become uncomfortable to him.

"It's neither here nor there to me."

"Would you sooner I married and brought a man to the top table?"

"I know how you'd feel about that."

"That I am not about to join my name to anyone else's…?"

"No."

"What *has* been said, Master Hayward?"

He sighed and rubbed his forehead. "That before the year is out, you will have married. Brought Forceleap to Master Dankworth or Master Pottinger or Sir Hugh…or someone else."

"I suppose they have seen these men visiting."

"Word has reached the furthest corners of Forceleap."

"Then I wish for you to deny this rumour. I will never marry any of these men. Rest assured."

Master Hayward regarded her with round eyed puzzlement.

"Do you not see, madam, people will think what they think. They cannot imagine a woman of your beauty and sensibilities not wishing to marry. It is beyond their understanding. These are simple folk. To them women such as you are always attached to a man…."

"This one is no longer attached."

"Even if you make this vow, they say that you will not keep to it. That it will be broken."

"Do they have such little regard for me then?"

"Imagine it, madam. The women they know…marry as soon as they are able. Then if they are widowed, they marry again. It's prudent."

"But they are not in my position. Many of them *must* marry, for they cannot keep themselves and their children. They will marry to keep them from beggary and parish charity. I do not, with God's grace, fall into that pit."

They had not moved from the top of the slope and a siffling wind came up from the south west.

"You are fortunate madam. You may do as you wish. You may make your vow…"

"Aw…don't tell me that *you* think, as does the noble Sir Hugh, that I will make my vow and then immediately regret it."

"I know you, madam. I know what you believe, how you think…"

"You most certainly do not, sir. For the last ten years you have dealt with my husband Roger. You and I hardly know each other. We have been thrown together in the past few weeks and have rubbed along well. How much do you think you know of me in those few short weeks?"

"I know you are stubborn and headstrong," he said jutting his chin.

Rosalie's mouth fell open.

Her little devil shrieked and fell from her shoulder. 'Oh, I wouldn't stand for that. Oh no. Not at all!" it said as it clawed its way back up.

"And will not listen to advice."

"And I thought…all this time, that you were helping me to understand the business of Forceleap Farm when you were merely tolerating my feminine blunders and lack of understanding!"

"I have tried to…"

"And this is your opinion of my conduct?"

"I am a bold man. I speak my mind."

"Rude, you mean?"

Ancelin Hayward almost blushed.

"If you think it is rudeness then it is rudeness but only for your own good."

That utterance was a big mistake.

Rosalie turned her horse. "Oh how many times have I heard that? I cannot count them. That something is for my *own good*. For my own good, Master Hayward, and for yours, I now remove myself from your sight. Obviously, I do not meet with your approval at all."

And she galloped off down the slope.

*****

She set a furious pace over the downs; she was so angry. If she could do without him, she'd send him packing immediately. Then she came to her senses. There were no hiring fairs in the vicinity until the following August and she did not know where she would be able to acquire another farm manager. She was certain she could deal with most of the matters arising from farm business herself, but knowledge of cattle and sheep she didn't have. That is what she had been attempting to learn. Perhaps he felt that it was no business of hers to learn these things. She was a woman. She really had thought that he had not penalised her for her sex but perhaps he had and just kept quiet. None of her other men had Ancelin's experience. None of them knew Forceleap Farm like he did.

The further away from him she rode, the more she regretted her bitter words. But she would not apologise. Oh no! She had meant it. He was rude. He was blunt. She was the mistress and she made the decisions...be they good or bad ones.

'No!' said her little demon. 'You have made no bad ones.'

"None yet," she said out loud. "And that, I suppose, is mostly because of Ancelin Hayward."

She slowed her pace and thought back over the last few weeks.

What had he advised that she had ignored or not implemented on the farm? She could think of nothing. Why did he call her headstrong? His opinions of her could only be as indistinct as vapour or mist.

'Oh he's just being a typical pig headed man,' her voice said to her. 'He must always be right. He cannot be seen to be bested by a woman.'

"What have I done to warrant such treatment?" she muttered as she rode up an unfamiliar slope of clover. And down a thorny bank of thistles.

"How can he make such a judgement of her on this short acquaintance?" she said aloud.

Her breath came now in short puffs for she had difficulty controlling the large stallion, Goliath which she'd chosen to ride, at this punishing pace. He had picked up her mood and raged onward as if he was riding to battle. "Whoa...Goliath...whoa horse," she said with one part of her brain and with the other said, "I have agreed to marry no man. How dare he think that as soon as a rich or handsome man comes before my eyes, I will fall down at their feet and...."

"Oooh!"

Goliath came to an abrupt stop, for he had reached a body of water and was not inclined to cross it. In order to stay on his back she had to make a grab for his mane. Once she had recovered herself, she patted Goliath's shoulder. "Right...good boy...I don't remember this." She had not been paying attention to her surroundings.

She realised that in her musings, she had allowed the horse to travel wherever he wished and that somehow, they had strayed from Forceleap Farm land.

'That's what happens when you aren't paying attention, you silly woman,' said her demon.

She looked around carefully.

Where on earth was she? She was sure they had no large bodies of water like this on their land. She had scoured the maps that Roger had had made. This was a large pool with rushes and reeds to the edge. Forceleap had small dew ponds up on the chalk but they were never as deep nor as intimidating as this one.

All was silent save for the call of a moorhen and the soughing of the light breeze through the reeds.

She backed Goliath away and stood in the stirrups to see if she might discover a landmark. A copse, a sarsen stone, a building?

There was nothing in sight. Merely miles of down. And a few sheep.

She began to canter along the edge of the pool hoping to find the end of it so that she might travel round it and find higher ground.

Suddenly and with a hissing noise, a hideous thin, white creature rose up from the bank and the concealing reeds. It unfolded itself as if it had been reclining in the mud of the pool's edge and stretched long bony arms up to the sky.

She gave a shriek.

Unnerved, Goliath reared on his hind legs and, like the tournament destriers she had heard described in the stories told around the fire at Christmas, leapt up and pawed the air dramatically. Rosalie let go of the reins.

She leant forward in a vain effort to stay on the horse's back but was unable to keep her seat. She slid from Goliath's saddle and landed on the hard ground, striking her head as she came down.

Mind you, not before she had taken as good a look at the creature as she could.

She had tried, in those few moments...not even long enough to call heartbeats... perhaps an eye blink...to keep her gaze upon the thing's dripping head, but her eye did, nevertheless, travel downwards to the patch of dark with its pink centre, above its thighs, to realise that this was a naked man.

*****

She hit the ground and knew no more. And so she did not see the man scurry up the bank, reach for a concealed shirt and pull it up over his nakedness.

He rubbed himself dry, as well as he could whilst he leaned over the insensate woman.

"Oh my Lord."

He lifted her hand and felt for the pulse which he thought indicated that life was present. He'd heard that somewhere.

There it was, thrumming under her skin.

He gazed on the angles of her relaxed face. "Oh how beautiful she is," he said to himself.

His eyes raked the ground about to discover where her large horse had come to rest.

"Oh yes, I recognise this one." He set off to recapture the beast. "This is Roger Jourdemayne's stallion."

The man brought the now docile horse back to the edge of the pool and tried to lift the unconscious woman to its saddle. Impossible on his own.

Rosalie was laid back down on the turf and murmured in her hurt. The man searched out the rest of his clothes and determined that he would have to carry the poor woman to her home or to his.

Now which house was nearer?

He was just thinking that his own house was closer but that he supposed she would be most upset to find herself awakening there, when he heard in the distance, the pounding of hooves on chalk turf.

He ran his hands through his wet hair and tried to bring some order to its appearance.

Over the brow of the hill came a man on a brown horse. When he espied the pair of them, he dug in his heels and the horse doubled its pace.

The first man drew himself up.

"Hayward"

"Master Dankworth!"

Ancelin Hayward threw himself from the saddle. "What in the name of God has happened?"

Ancelin began to search his mistress' body for broken bones or evidence of other hurts.

"I came upon her on that great brute and he was frightened. He threw her from the saddle." He didn't tell Hayward that it was he who had caused the horse to rear.

"I told her not to ride him. He is too strong for her."

Rosalie gave a moan and took a deep breath and, even though they waited she did not regain her wits.

"As far as I can tell she has no broken bones," said Dankworth.

"She hit her head, here," he said, trying to show Ancelin the site of the damage.

Ancelin pulled Rosalie's disordered headdress closer to her hair and wrapped it around her neck. The action did not allow Master Dankworth to see anything at all of Mistress Jourdamayne's permanent injuries.

"I will carry her before me on Filbert, (this was the horse which Master Hayward was often to be seen riding.)

"We must get her home."

Ancelin picked up Rosalie as if she were a doll made of twigs and rags. Then suddenly, he said "What are *you* doing here, sir?"

Master Dankworth bristled. "What am I doing here? Why, this is my land. What should I be doing here?"

"Your horse, Master Dankworth? Where is your beast?"

"I have no beast today. I often walk."

"Walk...to this pool?"

"Especially to this pool."

Hayward looked the man up and down and realised that he had recently been wet.

"Did Goliath toss you into the water?"

"No. Of course not."

"Then...?"

"I come here to swim in the water. I find it invigorating. A swift walk home and I am warm and dry again." He looked a little awkward. "It's one of my little pleasures. Some men have their drink...I...swim."

Suddenly Master Dankworth's eye grew hot. "What are you doing here? On my land?"

"We were not originally on your land but Mistress Jourdemayne mistook the path and ended up here by mistake."

"You left her, sir?"

"No, Master Dankworth, she left me."

"Ah," he said, as if he understood perfectly. "Then off we go. I shall bring the great brute behind."

"That is most kind, sir. We have a two mile walk."

"Nothing to me, young man. Nothing."

CHAPTER SIX ~ RECONCILIATION

Of course, Rosalie heard naught of this conversation slouched against Ancelin Hayward's breast even after they'd reached Forceleap Farm. He gently took her up again, passed without a word through the house and laid her down on her bed.

Bea came running,

"What on earth has happened?"

"Master Dankworth found her. Goliath threw her and she's hit her head."

"Should we send for the doctor?"

Ancelin chewed the side of his mouth. "No, let's wait and see if she comes to. If she isn't right by this evening, I will go myself to Marlborough."

"What's this?"

Master Newbold now came into the room but no further than a few steps beyond the door.

"The mistress has been thrown and has hit her head, master steward," said Bea worriedly. "Master Hayward thinks we should wait a while before we send for the doctor from the town."

Newbold shook his head. "What was she doing?"

"She came out with me to...oh...come and I'll tell you." He caught his fellow worker by the elbow and they moved out of the room. Ancelin shouted back. "Take care of her Bea and let me know the moment she wakes."

"Aye sir."

Master Newbold came down the stairs and into the hall.

"Oh...Farmer Dankworth... I didn't realise you were here."

Dankworth's blue eyes scanned the long figure of the Forceleap Farm steward.

"Ah, William. I had the misfortune or might I say fortune to find the lady fallen from her beast."

"You did?"

Hayward came up behind the steward. "For which we thank you greatly, sir. I am sure that Mistress Jourdemayne will wish to thank you in person, when she is fully recovered."

Ralph Dankworth shook his locks, now dried to clumpy, weedy waves. "That I doubt, sir. We parted on poor terms upon the last occasion we met."

"Oh?"

"It was at the celebration given by my merchant friend in Marlborough. I was too...hasty and insistent, I grant it. I do not have much experience in the wooing of the ladies."

The two Forceleap men gave each other a surreptitious grin.

"I overstated my own capacity for love and underestimated her desire to...I had thought it was merely womanly dignity which made her..." The man tailed off. He looked up and saw that both men were smiling.

"Master Dankworth, you have obtained the same answer many other men in the locality have received."

"Sir?"

"The mistress is not inclined to become...attached... to any gentleman," said William.

"It is not for you alone...merely that being a widow, she is exercising her right to remain...single."

"But I am certain that my behaviour has led her to think very badly of me."

Ancelin approached the distraught man. "Think nothing of it. We shall explain that your tender feelings for Mistress Jourdemayne escaped the control of your normally excellent masculine reserve."

"You would explain…?"

"Yes of course we will."

"Ah…well then." Now the man positively glowed with good humour where a moment before he had been inconsolable.

"That would be most kind of you. And please, give her my best regards when she recovers her wits. Tell her that from the bottom of my heart, I adore and…"

William coughed "Sir, I think that a simple wish for her well being will suffice."

'Best not appear too…keen, eh, Master Dankworth?" said Ancelin gleefully.

"Ah…no…you are right, I suppose."

Ancelin's fingers pressed into the wool of Master Dankworth's cote in order to lead him away when he said,

"Would you allow…would she allow…do you think that I come to ask after her welfare tomorrow?"

"I am certain that would be fine," said William, eyebrows raised.

"She won't look at him," said Ancelin Hayward when he had gone. "I know what I said to him, but she'll not entertain it."

William sat down at the table. "What was he doing there, wherever the mistress was found? I thought that you had gone out with her."

"I did. But she rode away from me in a high dudgeon. I carried on to the place where Dyamant had been confined to discover…"

"Yes?"

"That there was nothing there."

"Nothing…there?"

"Not a hurdle fold…not a scrap, neither straw nor string… I searched for a while to see if I could find where one might have been positioned but there was nothing, William. No sign of Dyamant's incarceration."

Hayward had ridden around the field his eyes to the ground. He would be certain to miss no sign of the fold's hurdle pegs being driven into the ground. He would see evidence of feet passing and the gate opening and closing, if nothing else. He could not even detect any new sheep droppings indicating a fold had been used recently for the purpose for which it had been created.

Newbold rubbed his small beard. "That is a puzzle."

"Then I thought that I had better go after the mistress and when I couldn't see her ahead of me, up on the down, I scouted around for a route she might have taken and…"

"Came upon Master Dankworth with Mistress Jourdemayne?"

"A few moments after the incident. The man had been swimming in his pond and was wet through."

William looked up quickly. "Swimming?"

Ancelin, with a chuckle to his voice said, "Aye, swimming like an otter."

"For the pleasure of it?"

"It seems so."

"How strange."

"I haven't been swimming since I was a lowly shepherd of about thirteen summers, said Hayward wistfully."

"Yes indeed. It isn't something one imagines a gentleman of two score years might…"

"But he does it often, he tells me."

"Deary me."

Ancelin sat down wearily at the long table and rubbed his face.

"So what do you think this means, William?"

"I cannot fathom, Ancelin. Unless…"

"Yes?"

"You are mistaken in your observations."

Hayward chuckled. "You think I can't find a sheepfold in a furlong or two of deserted down?"

"Well then…we must think, must we not, that Farmer Godechepe is mistaken in his directions?" The look on his face said that he was giving the man the benefit of the doubt.

Ancelin leaned over the table. "Frankly, William, his story; it leaks like a toad."

*****

Rosalie returned to the world just before the light went from the sky over Avebury.

Bea fussed over her until her mistress told her to go away and sit elsewhere quietly, for she had the devil of a headache and could not abide her chatter.

Rosalie sat upright and felt instantly dizzy. She prodded her rump. Oh no, another bruise. And her elbows hurt too.

"Bea!"

'Where is the damned girl?' said her little voice.

"Bea...I need you."

'Never there when you need...' said the devil on her shoulder.

"And you can shut up!" Rosalie was in a bad mood. "And go away!"

Bea poked her head around the door.

"Can you fetch me some tumbler's cure all? I am a mass of bruises."

Bea just stared.

"Please."

Bea disappeared.

Her bruises salved, she began to piece together the story of her accident, in her head.

"And then Master Ancelin and I...oh..."

"Oh what ma'am?"

"Nothing...just..."

"What?"

Rosalie sighed. "We had an argument."

"Oh."

"And things were said which..."

"Who said them?"

"We both did."

Rosalie caught her maid by the hand, "He is still here isn't he? He hasn't gone off to find himself other employment?"

"He is still here and sitting on a bench in the hall with a jug of cider."

"He hasn't gone home?"

"He won't go home, he says, until he knows that you are alright. If you aren't, he will ride to Marlborough for the doctor."

"Well then go down and tell him that I am...alright."

"No other word?"

"No. I...I think not."

Bea departed and Rosalie lay back on her bed.

She went over her memory of the day. Kind Farmer Godechepe bringing dear Dyamant back home. She patted the soft head of her bedfellow who was, at that moment, warming her knees. The quarrel at the brow of the hill. Her flight on Goliath and then..."

"Oh..Heaven forfend!" She sat bolt upright and regretted the action.

She became suddenly hot and threw off her coverlet. It landed on Dyamant and she shook and jumped off the bed in disgust, slinking away with a disgruntled, white edged eye.

Rosalie Jourdemayne swallowed. "He was completely naked!" Master Dankworth had been as unclothed as Adam in the Garden of Eden. He had not even the benefit of the fig leaf she had seen over the vital parts of that first man, on the wall of the church at Marlborough!

"Oh..oh..goodness."

"Ma'am?"

Bea had come back into the room. "Are you alright? Might it be a good time to let Master Hayward come up to see you?"

Rosalie shivered despite her heat. "I suppose if he must, he must."

They then spent a few moments putting her into a shift and a large blanket and carefully winding her hair in an oblong of cloth, taking care of the duck sized egg on the back of her skull.

Quickly she took up her mirror. Well, there was no need for a helpful rouge for her cheeks now. They were as incandescent as the burning bush in the Bible!

She sat in her chair and took in a few deep breaths.

"Ma'am."

"Oh Master Hayward. I..."

"Let me say..."

"I thought perhaps that..."

"I should not..."

"No you first.."

"Say what you..."

There was a little uncomfortable silence.

"How are you feeling?"

"Like I have been tossed from a great height upon a hard surface."

An infinitesimally small smile crossed Ancelin's lips.

"You have no lasting damage to the head?"

"I don't think so...no. Just a lump as large as a loaf."

"Good."

"Though my eyes will never be the same again."

He peered into her eyes. He swallowed. "They look...perfect...I mean...alright to me."

"Ah no..it is the inner eye."

"Forgive me?"

"What I saw, Master Hayward."

"Saw?"

"Saw. Master Dankworth crawling from a muddy pond, his hair covered in weed, his dark haired...body glistening in the sunlight and his...privy parts dangling open to the fresh air as bold as a bawd!"

"Yes. Apparently he enjoys swimming in that pond," said Ancelin with an unconcern that riled her a little. "Naked."

"And coming out like a monster of fable, and the devil he is, to frighten ladies from their horses."

"To be fair, it is his land and you were not meant to be there."

"He was totally naked!"

"He does it often, he tells me."

"You have spoken to him?"

"I have and we have him to thank for staying with you whilst you were insensate and then accompanying me back to Forceleap and leading Goliath by the rein, for I could not manage you up before me and Goliath too."

Rosalie's mouth was a perfect 'o'.

Her mind could not contain the facts that Ancelin had had her clasped to his breast and that the enemy, Master Dankworth had been left alone with her unconscious self.

"He has been here?"

"Indeed. He was most upset by the incident."

"I should think he was. If he hadn't sprung up from that pool…"

"Well he gives you his best wishes for a speedy recovery and he will visit tomorrow, just to make sure you are alright."

"NO!" Rosalie's voice rose to a high pitch "I will never be able to look him in the face again."

Once more there was that strange look on his visage.

"I will only ever see…" She closed her eyes, but the vision was still there.

"Madam, you are not a green girl. No blushing virgin…"

"Ancelin Hayward!"

"You will forget…that…in time."

"I have no wish to see him."

"Ma'am, he is really worried that he has pressed his suit too violently and wishes to apologise for his previous behaviour. He has asked me to explain that…"

"No. I will not listen."

Ancelin folded his arms across his chest.

"Speaking with him in a civilised manner will cost you nothing."

"Oh here you go again. Advice!"

"He is genuinely worried for you ma'am and feels strongly for you."

Rosalie narrowed her eyes.

"And not too long ago, you thought the man was responsible for the damage done to Forceleap Farm. You were not so fond of him then."

"I told you I cannot prove it. And there is more news."

"Oh no...not more awfulness." She turned her face away .

Hayward hooked a stool with his foot and sat before her looking up.

"The fold where Master Godechepe said he had found Dyamant?"

"The one we were going to try to find?"

"The same one. I could not find it."

"You...could not find it?"

"No, neither could I find any trace of it or of a dog. Not a wisp of straw, nor a pawmark."

Rosalie blinked. "Then it is not where he said it was."

Ancelin shook his head. "It has never been on that down. Not this year."

"Then where did Dyamant go?"

Hearing her name the dog crept back to her mistress and sat on her feet.

Hayward reached out and tousled the curly hair of her head.

"Master William and I cannot fathom it."

"Well, if you two men cannot fathom it, how am I supposed to do so, a mere woman with a sore head."

Ancelin looked up at her. Two cheeks burning in round patches, her eyes bleary and tired, her brow a little moistened with perspiration.

"Madam, please."

Rosalie sighed. "I am sorry Master Hayward. Thirteen years of submission. Thirteen years of subjugation; feeling like a slave in my own home, has made me suddenly want to break out and become... outspoken."

"I know that...you..."

"Please listen. I realise that I have not been easy these past few months. This is all very new to me, not least the freedom I now experience. It may have lodged in my head a little. I may have thought that...I needed to..."

"Become as blunt and as rude as me, madam? A mere hired man?"

Rosalie laughed. Was this an apology?

"In chess, Master Hayward, I would now be saying that you have made a move which compels me to capitulate."

"Oh yes, I forget. You play chess don't you?"

"Oh it was something else that I had to learn 'for my own good'," she said.

Ancelin smiled but looked away.

"And I was too good at it, in the end."

"So you had to contrive always to give in?"

"Always."

There was a silence punctuated by the snores of the small scent hound at their feet.

"I do understand what your life has been like."

"I doubt you really do. But thank you for trying."

"And I apologise for calling you headstrong and stubborn."

She wanted to laugh out loud but thought it not a very feminine thing to do and just tittered. "Oh but Master Hayward...lately, I have been."

"I like it better when you call me Ancelin."

Rosalie gave a quick look to the corner where Bea was sitting but it was alright, the girl was nodding.

"I must sleep, I am exceedingly tired. And I ache like the very devil."

She rose and staggered a little against him, for she had not really recovered and was dizzy. He leapt up. The dog jumped and squealed.

Bea snorted and woke. "What..?"

Of course, what she awoke to, was the sight of her mistress and her manager embracing.

"Oh!" she said, her mind processing something she did not fully understand. She saw two...and made twenty.

"Goodnight. And thank you."

He bowed.

"Ancelin."

CHAPTER SEVEN ~ THE GIFTS

Farmer Dankworth was not the first to arrive the following day. Master Godechepe came riding up cheerfully on his lively roan mare half way through the morning.

"Good morning to you." And indeed it was a good morning, for the sun shone and the autumn air was still and calm.

Master Newbold greeted the man on the step of the hall.

"I will tell madam that you are here."

"Oh Master Newbold, I am sorry to come unannounced but being in town earlier today, I thought I might call on my way home. I hear some distressing news. Mistress Rosalie is unwell...is this true?"

"Mistress Jourdemayne took a tumble from her horse and whilst she is a little indisposed by her... 'adventure', I am sure she will be pleased to see you."

Rosalie, listening from the doorway of her solar growled to herself. "Oh why must everyone know my business. Why can I not fall from my horse without everyone in the area knowing about it a day later!"

Bea tidied her mistress' appearance quickly and Rosalie, composing herself, walked as gracefully as she could down the steps, followed by her maid servant.

Much as the operation pained her, she was not about to let any indication of that pain show on her face.

"Master Godechepe, how kind of you to call." She sat down gingerly upon a cushioned bench.

The man took her hand and bowed.

"Now ma'am, what is this I hear? That you are being careless with your good self? Your friends are most worried about you."

Rosalie bridled and took away her hand.

"I have no friends," she said flippantly. "Sir."

"Madam. That is simply not true. I count myself a friend, even though it is a friendship of such a short acquaintance."

Rosalie's patience was in short supply that morning.

"I thank you again very much, sir, for returning my dog to me. I should be lost without her. *She* is my one and only true friend."

Master Godechepe took a step back.

"She is loyal, does not require favours in kind, is unchallenging and does not give out advice where it is not required. She loves me for myself alone and gives that love unconditionally, no matter what I do."

"I…"

"Do you know of any other creature who is so perfect a friend, sir?"

"But madam, she is *just* a dog."

"Anyone who calls themself a friend of Rosalie Jourdemayne will know, sir, that the words 'just' and 'dog' cannot be uttered in the same sentence."

Bea tried hard not to laugh and it came out as a strangled sneeze.

"This is why, of course, I returned Dyamant to you so promptly after I found her. I know how much you value her. How much you must have been worrying about her."

Rosalie watched him under her eyelashes.

He was not in the slightest bit put out by her words.

"Well, I am glad that you are recovered and no real harm has come to you."

Bea came up and offered the man a beaker of cider.

"You have been in town I hear. From whom did you hear the awful news of my… accident? It was quick upon the air was it not?"

"Well, madam, I think that my sister, who was the bearer of the news, got it from one of the dairymaids who serves her house."

Rosalie gave Bea a look across her shoulder.

"I see."

"But I am sure it will not be well known."

"Oh what a foolish woman I am to be riding alone on a great brute of a horse..." she said sarcastically.

"Mistress Jourdemayne, I do not think the particulars were spoken of. I for one do not need to know and am just happy that you are unhurt."

"I am hurt, Master Godechepe. But I can bear the consequences. I have had worse."

'Now that will set him thinking,' said the little devil in her ear. 'What will he make of *that?*'

Rosalie smiled at him properly for the first time.

"What have you there in your hand?"

"Ah...yes..."

"Please do sit."

The man sat upon a stool, spreading the brown woollen split cotte which he had worn to ride across the downs and into town and laid a felt wrapped bundle on the table before him.

"I have it from the town this morning."

"Oh?"

"I bought it on a whim, you understand. I am not usually so extravagant with my funds but when I saw it, I had to have it."

"Oh it is a costly item then?"

"Oh yes indeed. I can scarcely believe how much I paid for it. All upon a whim of a moment. But then...it is beautiful."

Rosalie did not wish to appear too keen and so she simply stared at the wrapped bundle.

"And it had travelled a great distance over the sea even before I saw it, and quite apart from it being a thing of great beauty and worth, I am told it is a thing of rarity."

"Where did you get such a ...a ... without seeing it, I know not what to call it...Quintessence?"

"There is a merchant lately come to Marlborough. His daughter has married in the town and he, having no other family, has travelled to be with her. I think he has plans to retire from his business soon."

"Oh...a merchant in what?" said Rosalie, leaning forward to see if she could catch a glimpse of this item.

"Precious goods from the lands of the heathen."

"Ooooh," said Bea.

"For sale in such a place as Marlborough? Surely there is little demand for them?"

"Master Godechepe shrugged his shoulders. "Well...I knew this man in Dover in the county of Kent from whence he hails..."

"When you were a wine merchant, sir?"

"Yes...it was my birthplace and my home for many years. I knew him and reacquainted with him when he arrived here in Wiltshire."

Now, Rosalie understood the slightly different accent with which the man spoke.

"And you took a look at his wares?"

"Oh...mistress...you have no idea what treasures the man has."

"Well, you have acquired one treasure, sir. Do not keep us in suspense."

The man almost giggled like a child keeping a secret and began carefully to unwrap the felt package.

"I don't know if I have managed to get it here in one piece. I do hope so. Oh I do. It is so delicate you see," he said.

His hands shook as he took the thing out and something between his fingers sparkled as the light hit it.

"It is made of glass."

"Glass? That is costly indeed."

"Oh not the crude window stuff you see in the houses of God but...er."

He brought it out to view.

It was a small beaker of translucent, pale green glass, so fine that his fingers could be seen through it, grasping it tightly on the furthest side.

Around the body of the cup were several rows of blue, raised from the surface in rising lines and at the base was a wavy line of dark blue, deep and as dusky as a winter sea. The whole was like the trumpet of a flower but transparent.

"Oh that is beautiful indeed," said Rosalie. "See how it shines."

"It has a particular lustre. They tell me this is achieved by adding gold to the glass."

"Gold!"

"Things like this are made by master craftsmen in faraway places and transported across the sea to…"

"How is it that it has not broken on its long journey?"

"That is a miracle."

"It is indeed."

Master Godechepe turned it around in his hands. "Might you like to hold it, Mistress Jourdemayne?"

Rosalie took in a little breath. "Touch it?"

"Why, yes indeed."

"If I may…" she held out her hands. "I will be very steady."

"Of that I have no doubt."

Rosalie closed her fingers around the little thing. It was no bigger than could be encompassed by her few small fingers. It weighed not even as much as a little bird.

"What would be served in this small amount, sir?"

"Ah now, I made inquiries of Master Hoare…the man who fetched the thing from Persia, I believe. He says there is a beverage which is quite unlike anything else; nothing of which *we* are aware, which the people of those hot lands drink."

"Oh what is that Master Godechepe?" said Bea her eyes as round as the moon.

"Sharbat, is what they call it. It's drunk in small amounts and is very refreshing."

Rosalie handed the little thing back to him and he gently laid it down on the table top.

"He tells me that the oldest mention of sharbat is found in a Persian book of the last century. But its recipe goes back a very long way. I of course have never tasted it."

"Will you learn how to make this - sharbat?" said Rosalie pronouncing the unfamiliar word carefully.

"Ho no! That sort of thing is not for me. I am though, I must say, partial to a little honey wine."

"Mead?" said Bea.

"Shall I take a little every day, in this exquisite vessel?"

Rosalie mused, "Oh how I would love to own such a beautiful item. But it is far too pretty to use, sir."

"You think, I should just put it on my pot board and look at it?"

"I would be terrified of breaking it, if I had to wash it," said Bea.

"Well then young lady," said Henry affably, you had better practice carefully."

"I beg your pardon, sir?"

"For you will have the care of it."

"No...I..." Bea looked completely flummoxed.

Henry Godechepe picked up the little beaker again and presented it, with a nodding bow, to Rosalie.

"As a token of my esteem and friendship...madam. Please accept this as a gift. I knew that you would simply love it! A beautiful glass for a beautiful lady."

Rosalie didn't reach out to take it but rose slowly from the table, the shock of his utterance sinking in.

"A gift?"

"Indeed. I have bought it for you."

"No...I cannot accept it."

"Aw come, mistress, you know that you love the thing. You said yourself you should like to own something like it. Well it is *yours*."

"And what do you want in return, Master Godechepe?"

"Want? Why nothing. This is a gift, Rosalie."

Rosalie backed off a few paces. "Sir, I hardly know you. Our acquaintance is short, these were your own words not a heartbeat ago. We have met but three times, I think, why should you want to present me with so valuable a gift?"

Henry wrinkled up his nose. "Well, maybe I exaggerated a little about the cost of it. I *did* drive a hard bargain but, yes it's still a valuable item."

"Then why give it to someone whom you have not known for very long?"

Henry was now beginning to be a little put out.

"Rosalie. I'd like to make you happy. You have lost a husband, your rock and master. I know that you have had a hard time this past few weeks with the flood and your injuries. I simply seek to make you happy." He grinned from ear to ear.

"And I say again, sir. I cannot accept it."

"Whyever not?"

"If it had been a flagon or even a cask of your excellent wine, or a basket of apples from your orchard, I might have said thank you and taken it with gratitude, but such a gift. It is truly too much."

"You think that I will use this to influence you to...do something?"

"No sir. I have no doubt that you are in earnest. But it is too valuable."

"Mistress Jourdemayne." He smiled widely. "I have no intention of taking the thing back and I am not about to travel across the downs to my home with the thing in my saddle bag."

Rosalie bit her lip. And her tongue.

Her little demon however said, "Aw go on. What can possibly be the harm?"

"No sir, it must go away with you." She carefully wrapped it in its woolly cover once more.

"I will leave it here today. If you are still persuaded to part with it on another day. Then so be it."

"Please do not be angry that I have refused it."

"Not at all!"

"And to make up, perhaps you would like to take dinner with us here at Forceleap, next week?"

The man stood and bowed low. "I would be delighted."

*****

No sooner had Master Godechepe put his backside to his saddle and ridden away, than another horse trotted into the farmyard.

Rosalie looked up from her business parchments. 'Oh what now?' said her little voice. 'Are you ever to get these tasks finished?'

She heard a man's voice say,

"Was that Henry Godechepe I just saw, Newbold?"

"Aye Master Dankworth, he was here for a little while."

"Hmm." The man seemed irritable but as soon as he saw Mistress Jourdamayne, his face creased into a smile. Rosalie could not, without complete rudeness, avoid him, for his demeanour was one of solicitous kindness. Even the evil blue eyes seemed more friendly.

"Oh...you are up and about; that is good. Yesterday I was so perturbed that..."

Rosalie's face grew sunset red as she remembered the state in which she had last seen Master Ralph Dankworth's body. He seemed not to remember at all.

"My injuries would not keep me confined, Master Dankworth and I have so much to do."

'*You* cannot go gadding about the countryside visiting all and sundry!' said her little devil. 'You have a farm to run.'

"Have you no tasks which keep you at Falkner's Farm, today?" She regretted the tone as soon as she uttered the words and she heard her devil tut in her ear.

Bea was clearing away the cider beaker used by Master Godechepe and swivelling her eyes to Heaven, gave it a cursory wipe and filled it for Master Ralph Dankworth.

"Oh I have tasks; we are coming up to reaping and to fruit picking. I have a good orchard at Falkner's and make excellent cider but my man can take care of all that."

"I like to keep my finger on the spot, sir. It's all too new to me yet."

"Ah yes, you haven't had a full year of the farm yet, have you?"

Rosalie settled herself on her favourite chair.

"I am still learning."

"Are you certain that it is necessary for you to ride about the furthest corners of your land in the pursuit of this learning, dear lady?"

The man's eye strayed to the mysterious felted package still lying on the table top.

"I must know all the boundaries, must I not, Master Dankworth, if I am to be able to stay within my own land?"

"Well, yes but…"

"And I cannot do so well sitting in a chair here, staring at a map."

"Well, no."

"And I am told that unscrupulous people have often taken the opportunity to extend their own boundaries at our expense when there is a change of ownership."

"Oh dear…have they?"

His fingers longed to touch the soft felt of the parcel. And the soft skin of her hand.

"And so, there are, I believe no dictates about where and when I cannot ride my own land."

"Certainly not." He pursed his lips as if he was tasting something and made a strange almost silent noise like a cat lapping some milk. Suddenly, in Rosalie's mind's eye, Master Dankworth became a feline creature with black hair and pointy ears. Oh - and narrow, blue eyes.

"However, I think there must be a rule, for your own good of course, about travelling alone about the countryside, mustn't there? A lady of your quality."

Bea clattered a jug on the pot board and then….silence.

'Those words again,' Rosalie's inner voice said.

She took in a long and audible breath through her nose.

"Sir, I must say that I do love the sound which the word 'rule' makes, when I break it."

Master Dankworth cocked his head like a little bird when it spies a worm. He had no idea what she had just said.

'Oh another one who doesn't understand you,' said her voice 'and has no humour.'

"Please, good lady, take more care of yourself. Your friends…"

"Please, spare me the advice, sir. I have had a deal of that already today."

Ralph looked up quickly. "Ah…Master Godechepe?"

"Yes. He brought me advice and a gift." Rosalie touched the felt parcel.

The man's face fell. "Oh…well…I too have brought a gift. Though I am sure that mine will no way…erm…"

He lifted a basket from the floor at his side and peeled back a white linen cloth.

"From my own orchard. The very best that Falkner's Farm can produce." The man fairly puffed out his chest.

All Rosalie could see was Master Ralph stark naked crawling up the bank of the pool.

"Oh…how…lovely… plums."

Her little devil chuckled with such fervour she was sure he would hear it.

"And we have cherries in season…we have the best cherries at Falkner's. I must get you some one day."

"That is a very kind gift. Thank you." She handed the basket to Bea whose creased face was as purple with amusement as were the plums .

"I do not need the basket returned."

"Thank you."

Now they had nothing about which to talk.

Eventually, "Did Master Godechepe stay long?" asked Ralph.

Rosalie was aware the man was fishing to find out what stage the 'relationship' between them had reached.

"Not long. He was on his way from the town and called in."

"Ah…"

"To bring me this…"

She unwrapped the glass cup and stood it gently upon the board.

"Oh my! That is…Oh Heavens. Beautiful."

'Go on…' urged Rosalie's little demon voice with a brisk and cheerful alacrity. 'Go on tell him how expensive it is.'

"Yes. It is, I believe it's Persian glass and fearfully expensive."

Master Dankworth's face dropped and he sucked in his cheeks.

"He is a very wealthy man."

Rosalie sighed. "Yeees. He is. But…I am not really inclined to accept such an…immoderate gift."

She folded it once more in the felted outer.

Ralph perked up once more.

Their conversation then fell to the yields which might be expected of their ground owing to the inclement weather earlier in the year.

"I believe those who are in the know say that we shall have yet more of the kind of rain we have already experienced."

"Oh? How can they tell?"

"They can certainly tell when we are about to have a storm. I have had it with my own eyes and ears."

"I suppose they look at the clouds massing and the winds gathering?"

"Oh this might be days before the bad weather arrives."

"Then it is witchcraft, Master Dankworth," giggled Rosalie.

"Ah…well…just people in touch with the signs of the earth, I suppose."

"Do you have any such people on your land?"

"Yes, yes, I do."

"And do they…"

"He."

"Ah, yes. Is *he* able to predict when the rain might cause the rivers to flood and springs to break out where previously there were none?"

She watched him very carefully.

Again he tipped his head sideways.

"Yes, I suspect the man might be able to do that."

"You know, of course, that we have been cut off here at Forceleap

Farm?"

The man looked sorrowfully at her. His evil blue eyes, no longer quite so evil, betrayed not a jot of the culpability she had expected.

"I do indeed. In my lifetime, that has happened only twice. If we all keep our parts of the river flowing and our leats clear we should have little problem. But..."

"This year, despite good management of the river and the leats, our land was flooded and our cattle put at risk."

"Oh dear me...no."

"It was only through the good auspices of my manager Master Hayward, that we managed to lose no animals."

"He is a very competent man. You are lucky to have him."

"He is. So skilful is he, Master Dankworth, that he found that our leats had been purposefully dammed. Can you imagine it?"

Ralph Dankworth didn't shift. He didn't show any guilt or knowledge.

"Nooooo."

"Oh yes. And so Master Hayward and a few of his lads went and shifted the blockage and well, you must know that the water receded and there we are."

"Noooo."

"We were lucky indeed."

"That is awful. Who about these lands here could do such a thing? Oh Mistress Rosalie, who could be so...evil?"

"Evil indeed, sir."

"There is no smidgeon of doubt but that it was ...deliberate...?"

"Oh no Master Dankworth. It was deliberate."

"Heaven forfend."

"Well, I can assure you that now, I have my eye all over my land. That, sir, is why I ride out to travel Forceleap Farm from corner to corner. I'll not have something like this happen again."

"No indeed. But madam," he stretched his neck and tried to take her hand. "Please do be very careful. It seems there is someone who wishes to injure you and yours. Promise me you will not ride out alone."

"I cannot promise it, sir."

He sighed and once he had realised she would not allow him to touch her, he withdrew his hand. "And no more falling from horses."

Rosalie flexed the corners of her mouth by way of a smile, soon stilled, "I am persuaded that I must buy a smaller horse. I have been riding my husband's great beast and frankly it is too large for me."

"I'm glad to hear that you are thinking of your safety."

"I will go with my steward and manager to the fair at Maugersbury in October. There I will buy myself a good horse."

"Capital," said Ralph.

"One I shall not fall from." She looked him straight in the eye. "Mind you. I hope never again to see anything which makes me do so."

He cocked his head again as if weighing up her words.

"Madam?"

"You know sir?" She leaned forward conspiratorially and he could do nothing but follow her lead. His face was close to her's.

"I saw a monster just before I fell from Goliath's back? This is why I fell. I was shocked into it."

"Nooo! A monster...where?

"Rising from the pool on your land. Oh it was awful. Hairy and black and moaning as if Hell was refusing to contain it."

"Nooo."

She saw his eyes change.

"I never wish to see the like again."

He pulled back.

"Did you know, Master Dankworth, that such a creature lived in your pool. Such an *ugly, hairy, naked,* denizen of Hell?"

"Oh no!"

"Oh yes. I saw it...all of it, in all its...glory."

"No! Oh my! How awful."

The man rose from his chair."

"I had no idea." He started off and then came back. He rubbed his face and then forced his fingers through his dark hair.

Rosalie followed him to the door as he muttered and chunnered to himself.

"AH yes...I must be going home. I have so much to do."

"Master Dankworth," she said with grin. "You must rid the pool of that monster. I am sure the priest will help you."

"Yes...yes...Oh my dear Lord. I had no idea."

"Oh and thank you for the...plums."

*****

The crops were gathered in. The sheep had their autumn shearing, for the Wiltshire breed had two shearings a year, which brought great prosperity to the farmers.

Rosalie watched as the sheep were brought into the pens and the men turned them this way and that, snipping so quickly, the sheep hardly had time to protest before they were slapped upon the rump and sent along the tunnel of hazel-made hurdles to feed once more on the pasture.

Master Hayward was there supervising and checking the workforce, sometimes doing the job himself.

"Hoi... Baxter! We need the tar pot here." One ewe had been nicked by the shears.

"Do they often get damaged, Hayward?" asked Rosalie, leaning over the hurdle wall.

"No not often, ma'am. When a man is new to the shearing then sometimes they get cropped but there is a tendency for a new shearer to go slowly...until he gets the measure of it."

"How quick some of the men are!"

"Ah, that is years of practice."

She nodded and smiled.

"I will go and supervise the bringing out of dinner for you all," and she turned and walked up the hill, her blue cotte swaying as she strode boldly away, two hands holding up the hem a little.

He stood up and watched her back. He wiped his hand over his brow. It was a warm day again and he'd pulled down his cotte to his waist and tied the sleeves of it, so that it looked as if he wore some kind of shirt and skirt. His linen sleeves had been rolled almost to his armpits.

Rosalie disappeared up the hillside until she was a speck and was gone, her white head cloth visible to the last in the bright sun.

He turned back to his work.

"Go to it, Adam...no slacking now."

Dinner in the field was a short lived thing for they were keen to get the sheep finished and back out on the pasture as soon as they could. The animals skipped and tripped away and then finding the shade, they lowered their heads again and began to crop the turf.

Ancelin Hayward looked up to the horizon. Up from the south west the clouds were banking and the sun would soon be blotted by them.

"I think we need to be indoors soon, for there is a devil of a storm coming."

"Aye," said one of the old farmhands, "me missus said as such this mornin'"

"I am only glad that it's held off long enough for us to count, shear and mark the ewes."

"First of the autumn storms, I've no doubt," said another hoary headed Wiltshireman. "T'is the season for it now."

They loaded the hurdles onto a wagon and trundled across the down at a slow pace, keeping alongside the cart which held the fleeces.

They were close to the barn where these were stored, when they heard the first rumble of thunder.

"Thunder in the day without rain or lightning?" said one of the shepherds, shaking his head. "That don't bode well."

Ancelin thanking his men, wearily trod his way into the yard. He plunged himself to the shoulders into a horse trough and came up, shaking his head like a dog. The droplets flew all around and stained the warm beaten earth and cobbles of the farmyard. The light had changed dramatically. From a pleasant autumn brightness, the day had become one of a strange light, where everything which one viewed was tinged with a brown, yellow hue. And then the sunlight went altogether and the day became an early grey dusk.

There was another far off rumble .

Ancelin looked up at the sky to the south west. Was he mistaken? Did he see the flash of lightning?

He dried his hair on his cotte and then dressed again, taking off his belt and repositioning it over his shirt and damp clothes.

He smelled himself. Stale sweat, sheep fleece, and now rank water but there was nothing for it. He would go in and see his mistress before he retired for the day.

One more look at the sky told him he would not be sleeping in his own bed tonight, for he would not make a journey out in the unprotected down in a storm such as was coming *this* night.

He jogged tiredly to the hall and called into the door. "Master Newbold...is the mistress about?"

"Aye, she is," came a hollow voice from the pantry. "She is in the office."

Hayward picked up his tired feet and poked his head around the door.

Rosalie heard him coming and turned from her work.

"Aw, Ancelin. It's so dark suddenly. Have I misjudged the time? Is it dusk already?"

"No ma'am. The sky is full of rain. We shall have a storm 'ere long. Unless it skirts us and goes up to Baydon and Lammy Down."

"Do you think it will?"

Ancelin thought for a moment. "No. It will come here. I think we shall need to secure everything for there will not only be rain but wind too."

Rosalie jumped up from her stool.

"Then let us do what we have to do."

This time Ancelin Hayward was having none of her forwardness.

He took both her arms in his capable but rather dirty hands and squeezed.

"Madam. Rosalie. Please, stay inside. There is nothing you can do. The men and I will have it all under control. There is the great danger of lightning."

Rosalie thought back to a day in her youth when a young man had been caught out on the treeless Berkshire downs in a storm such as they said was coming now. His charred body had been found a day later, black as pitch and contorted into terrible shapes. The superstitious amongst them complained of the evil one - demons disgorged from Hell. Others tutted and said that, poor foolish man, he might have known to stay put and wait out the storm, not walk across the bare turf and invite the furious gods to strike him down.

Rosalie nodded. "Take care, Ancelin."

He did not let go of her arms. He looked earnestly at her for a matter of a few heartbeats for, surely it was impossible that she would not defy him or at the very least dispute with him.

"Good."

Ancelin and a few of the sturdier men then secured carts in barns, dragging them into any spare space. They closed all the doors and bolted them with large lengths of wood through iron loops.

Anything which might blow away was secured with rope. Tarpaulins of oiled cloth were laid over any unstored crops or roots and secured by large stones ready for just such an emergency.

The cattle, many of whom had been driven into the nearer fields now, ready for the autumn killing, were herded into the barns where those lucky enough to be kept overwinter, would be housed until the lush grasses grew again in the early spring. They lowed and tussled in this unfamiliar confined space but were made confident by the presence of the older cows who knew this place from last year and remembered it meant safety and food.

The barn door lit up with a ghostly light as the lightning flickered and showed Ancelin's shadow huge on the wood. Finally it was closed leaving a couple of the young lads inside amongst the straw to look for any dangers.

They had done this with every building. There would be many men this night who would not go to their own beds.

Suddenly there was more light, showing the large lime tree which grew just outside the main gate reflected as a black shape on the wall of the barn. Even Ancelin thought for a short breath that it looked like a demon stretching out its arms.

And still there was no rain.

Hollering for everyone to go home if it was close, or find shelter if it was not, Ancelin ran across the yard towards the hall door. He would find a blanket and his cotte would make a pillow for his head and he would sleep on the floor. It wouldn't be the first time.

With the shout of a fiend the lightning struck, emerald green in its light...somewhere very close and the thunder rolled immediately after it with a stunning reverberation so loud that the farm manager had to put his hands over his ears. After a while he took them away.

Then he heard his name being called. "Ancelin...are you there, Master Hayward?"

"Here Master Steward...coming."

He carried on his run. Still there was not a drop of rain but the wind was rising.

Another lustre of lightning struck, followed by an immediate peal of deafening thunder. Ancelin staggered in the door as the biggest sheet of lightning yet, scoured the ground and lit up the surrounding countryside. There was a stupefying crack which made the ears ring and hurt and rendered them deaf for a moment.

Master steward came forward in the dark, for the light had blinded them both and he waved a candle in front of him.

"There are victuals in the hall, Ancelin, go in and take your ease. You have worked hard this day. Wash in the pantry. There is soap and water."

The farm manager pulled off his shirt ready to wash and then looked back out of the door. Another horizontal flash showed him that the major blast had struck the old lime tree outside the gate. There was a terrible sulphurous smell, like the stench of Hell and Ancelin saw that the tree had been struck down the middle and was cleft almost in two.

Now it was burning.

And still there was no rain.

CHAPTER EIGHT ~ THE STORM

Ancelin threw away the towel which William had given him. There was no time to wash himself; he had to douse those flames, for if a spark was to fly up and land upon the barn roof, any of the barn roofs, there would be disaster.

Yelling to Master Newbold that the tree was on fire, he dashed out of the door, pulling on his dirtied shirt and doing his best to tuck it into his braies.

He yelled for help as he ran but, of course, most folk had gone home already or were making their way there. One or two heads peeked from the unsecured and smaller barns.

"Adam, get out here and help. Get water, water in anything and blankets to smother the sparks."

"Aye sir."

Ancelin Hayward ran to the horse trough where he had so recently dunked his head. He plunged a bucket, lying close, into the water and looked up, out of the gateway to the old tree. The leaves were turning and beginning to fall; they were dry and as flammable as kindling. The forms of the branches showed against the dark sky like skeletons with licking flames for bones, leaping and dancing.

Adam came up with a bucket and he too filled it.

Next came Master Newbold in his long cotte of cabbage green, running with armfuls of blankets from the house.

"William, the sparks must not be allowed to catch the thatch. Wet the blankets and throw them onto the roofs. Adam will go up a ladder for you."

Young Warin Logge, who lived close by, came running into the yard, his blond hair caught and turned blue by the next flicker of lightning.

"The tree, sir the tree, it's on fire."

"I know. Here take this." Ancelin thrust the bucket at him, get as close as you can and throw the water at any of the burning parts. I'm off for the orchard ladder."

He ran out of the gate, past the burning tree and into the orchard of pear, apple, nut and medlar trees.

Rosalie had heard all the noise and shouting and now came out of the hall door with Bea trailing her.

"Woe Sakes!" shouted her maid servant, "It's the old tree!"

"William looked over his shoulder. "Ma'am, Hayward has gone for the orchard ladder."

"He can't use that surely, against a burning tree."

William shrugged. "He knows what he's doing." They all understood Ancelin's innate practicality.

The two women rushed through the gate and stared at the venerable lime, dancing with flame. They were almost blinded by the next fork of lightning which snaked down some way away from them.

Rosalie shielded her face with her arm, from the fierce flames which licked around the poor tree.

"He's mad. What does he think he can do?"

"Can we not wait for the rain to come?" asked Bea, "It will. And then the flames will be put out."

William was now at their elbow with the dripping blankets.

"Master Hayward is concerned that the thatches will ignite before the rain can douse the flames. There are some storms which never turn to rain, you see."

Adam and Warin now came up and threw the water onto the

flaming tree. Their aim wasn't good for it was difficult to get close but there was some sizzling and smoke.

"Quick, the kitchen, anything which will hold water," cried Rosalie. The women ran back into the building to gather up what vessels of water they could carry.

A few more men had now arrived from the nearer dwellings.

One older man came armed with a besom and began to beat out the tinder sparks at the base of the tree.

Another stupefying blast hit their ears and they all recoiled in their tasks to hold them, so painful was the noise.

There was another loud crack and William saw that one of the trees in the orchard had been struck.

"Ancelin!" he cried, worried that his friend might have been close and struck too.

But a black shadow in a black landscape came staggering through the orchard gate, a strange shape; bowed with a long horn protruding from its head."

"Ah, Ancelin," said the steward as he recognised the shape for the farm manager with a ladder on his back.

Hayward approached the outer wall of the main cow barn and put up his ladder. "Up you go Adam me lad. Master William will hand you the blankets, though we'll not have enough to deal with the whole roof. Do your best. If sparks land, we'll beat them out with our bare hands if we must. Now you Warin, you get your buckets and up that ladder and wet the rest of that thatch as if your life depends on it."

He then turned his attention to the tree.

"Here, William, throw it here!"

More water was thrown on the tree.

The sky was now filled with ceaseless light, as bright as day, frequent strikes liquefying into a completeness, as waves on a pond run outward from one small pebble.

Ancelin took a bucket and, shielding his head with his arm, he threw it one handed as high as he was able onto the branches.

"We need to get higher."

"We cannot, safely," said Rosalie, coming up to his shoulder with a kitchen jug. "You cannot go up a ladder. You will be incinerated. And there are several boughs which are close to the thatch of the cow barn."

"I cannot take off the boughs, there is nowhere that is safe from flame, to saw them."

"What shall we do?"

"We have no choice."

Ancelin ran to the shed at the side of the hall building and came out with an axe.

He pulled Rosalie back from her flame dousing and told her to stand well away.

Black smuts were now flying through the air, one or two of them reaching the cow barn. The black smoke was fearful.

"Are you abreast of it, Adam, Warin?"

"We are, sir," came their shouts.

"Then prepare for a barrage of sparks."

William came up behind him. "Ancelin, can I help you?"

"Take the women folk away. And prepare for sparks everywhere. I am going to fell the tree."

Before anyone could argue with him or even take in a breath to do so, he had poured a bucket of water over himself, bent his back and dashed to the half trunk of the lime.

"Keep throwing the water. It doesn't matter if you douse me. It'll be all the better. But keep your distance. Branches may fall."

Rosalie threw her cauldron of water at the slightly drunken side of the tree, where ribbons of fire licked up and down the hollow.

The light of the storm caught her face and turned her to white marble.

The lime was a tree which bore a very light wood which was easy to cut, but alone, Ancelin would need all his strength to achieve a fall of the tree as quickly as he hoped and in the right place. He had after all, been in the field since dawn and was weary.

"Mistress."

"Yes Ancelin…"

He took a deep breath and struck the trunk with a mighty thwack,

"If I should die today."

"No…!"

"And I might. You never know."

"No, Ancelin, don't speak so."

"Then I…" One more huge strike and flakes of bark flew off the wounded tree.

"…Want to say something which I need…" Another swingeing blow struck the tree.

Another peal of thunder, but further away, interrupted his speech, but not his Herculean efforts with the tree.

"…to say."

Bea arrived with a bucket and threw her water, turning immediately on her heel to run off to replenish it.

Master Newbold came up after her and threw another, higher for he was a tall man and could reach. Off he went for further supplies.

The fire above Ancelin Hayward crackled and spat and now and again embers of ash or burning leaves struck him. He could feel the heat of the burning tree above him and smell his hair singeing. The smoke made him cough.

He cursed as his hands, gripping the axe tightly, were scorched with falling embers.

"Rosalie, mistress." It spurred him onto faster speech.

"I am listening."

One more thwack.

"I am not asking for anything…"

"Thwack!"

"I am saying…"

The chopping sounded a different note.

The tree shuddered.

Ancelin redoubled his action.

"That should I die today...or any day...soon..."

The tree began to give in.

"In the service of Forceleap Farm..."

There was a deafening, splintering, shiver in the tree.

"Remember this. That I love you..."

The rest was taken up by the noise of the poor tree's death as it keeled over and came to rest in exactly the place Ancelin had wished it to land. Away from the barn. Away from the buildings, away from them.

*****

"Now douse the tree...wherever there is flame. Do not let any live cinder remain," he said, matter of factly, turning, as if his soft words had not been uttered and they were the sort of thing a girl heard every day of her life.

Rosalie was rooted to the spot. No one had ever said that to her. That they loved her. Not even her parents. Certainly not Roger.

'No. That isn't what he said. It cannot be what he said,' said her little voice.

'You are mistaken.'

"Yes, Ancelin," she said as if she had heard him say *something* but that she had not caught the meaning of it and did not wish to offend by asking him to repeat it.

He backed off from the tree and panting hard he took up a besom and began to beat out the flames of the tree's canopy with it. He didn't look at her at all.

Rosalie watched him carefully. He showed no sense of what he had just said but carried on with his task, battling with the flames wherever he saw them arising, coughing with the smoke and narrowing his eyes against the floating debris.

Henry Armstrong now arrived with a sweating face.

"Sir, Master Hayward, the orchard is on fire!"

Ancelin Hayward swore and, wiping his arm across his sweaty forehead he threw down his besom.

"Carry on here, Henry. Who is in the orchard?"

"Humfrey, Harris and Cowman, sir."

He nodded and ran off towards the smaller trees of the orchard.

Halfway there, he turned and bellowed up at the barn roof.

"You doing alright there lads?"

"Aye, sir. We have it under control, we think," came the bass voice of Adam Hartnoll.

"Well done!"

And he ran on.

Rosalie, still rooted to the spot, shook herself and ran after him.

"Wait, wait for me."

The two of them reached the orchard and swept their eyes over the trees, as well as they could.

The fruit and nut trees were not planted close together and as luck would have it, the only damage had been to a notably ancient apple tree to the middle of the field. But there was still some damage likely to other trees from sparks flying in the breeze which had arisen. It was now getting dark and everyone could see them as they spun across the air like little fireflies. The pond in the middle of the orchard now became the focus of their activity.

Luckily the thunder was moving off and no more lightning pierced the sky, though they could have done with it shining, to be able to see what they were doing.

"What do we do here?" asked Rosalie

"Douse the flames of this tree. Like the lime, we cannot have the sparks ignite the rest. This is our cider crop and our drink for the rest of the year."

In the end it took just four of them to extinguish the flames of the small spreading apple tree. As certain darkness fell, it sat, a forlorn and mangled shape and daylight would show them the extent of the damage. The rest of the trees of the orchard were saved.

They laughed joyfully as the last of the flames fluttered out and they both fell to the soggy ground, exhausted, amongst the fallen apples, dislodged by their antics.

Some of them were split with the heat.

Rosalie picked one up and looked at it as if she had never before seen an apple.

"Look! Anyone for a baked apple?"

Hayward had fallen on his back, his knees raised, his exhausted arms resting out like a cross beside him, his eyes closed.

It was then the rain started.

Huge droplets now began to fall on them. Great, fat, heavy droplets which spat as they hit the earth.

Rosalie struggled to her knees, stretched out her arms and lifted her face to the rain, still laughing.

"Now there will be no more thunder...just rain," she said quietly. "A bit late."

The rain increased and began to hiss around her. She shivered.

"Up Ancelin. We need to be under cover now or we shall take cold after our exertions. Especially you."

The man lay there unresponsive.

Rosalie fell forward towards him, resting on her knees and wrists. "Ancelin. Get up!"

He did not move. The rain hissed around them like angry snakes.

Ancelin's linen shirt and braies became almost transparent with the wet. She tried not to look. She shook him but he did not respond.

"Oh!" A huge blockage now arose in Rosalie's throat and though she tried to call for help, nothing came out. The back of her throat constricted and she knew she was about to cry.

The little voice in her head said, 'He knew...he knew he would die. He told you. He *told* you and now he IS dead.'

*****

"Ancelin...oh Ancelin. Do not leave me," she wailed and she threw herself bodily over him."

Henry Cowman now came up and took in the strange scene before him.

"Master Hayward, sir. Don't you fright us. Wake up!" He grabbed the farm manager by the shoulder and gave him a hearty shake.

Master Hayward groaned. "Nah...let me sleep a moment longer."

Now Adam ran up. "Sir...wake up!"

Ancelin Hayward, fatigued beyond movement, opened an eye.

"It's dark now, sir. Are we finished? Can we go home? Those of us who can, that is?"

With some reserve of superhuman strength, the farm manager pulled himself to his elbow and Rosalie fell from him like the apples which had fallen from her trees.

"You live?" was all she could say.

"Aye, you can all go home. We are past danger."

He rolled onto his knees and stretched out a hand to the now charred and soaked form of the apple tree's trunk and pulled himself to a standing position.

He wavered for a moment.

"Aye off you go home. All of you."

Rosalie also crawled her way up and retied her headcloth, now absolutely soaked.

The men trudged away, leaving the both of them alone by the tree.

'This is not the time for you to take him to task for his words,' said her devil. 'Give the poor man time. He's exhausted.'

"Come, I'll give you an arm. We shall walk back together," she said to her manager.

Ancelin levered himself up from the tree where he'd been leaning.

"Master Hayward...Ancelin?"

There was no response.

"The words you spoke..."

"Hmmm?"

"When you were taking down the lime…"

Hayward was inattentive and seemed perplexed by something and suddenly he filled his lungs to shout after the departing men.

"Adam!"

"Aye sir?"

"Have we tethered a goat here…or has one of you had one of your dogs here?"

"Ah no sir." Adam came jogging back on his young man's legs not yet exhausted.

"You'll remember we've had the sheep cropping the orchard till lately. No goat, no dogs."

"Then why do we have a chain here? A chain hung on the branch?"

Adam came forward and peered with his twenty year old eyes at the metal which shone in the rain and dark.

"Chain…sir…?"

Hayward's hands moved up the chain, which incidentally had not touched the ground.

"It's driven into the tree with a groom."

"Aye sir. A pointed groom."

A groom was a thatching tool; sharp and long and used to hold the thatch in place before fixing.

"It's metal, Adam."

"Why would it not be sir?"

"It is known that lightning is attracted to metal."

"Is it, sir?"

"It is something I have heard."

Adam and Rosalie stood transfixed as they watched Ancelin pull the metal spike from the tree trunk.

There was no doubt that it had been struck by the lightning, for it was blackened and slightly bent.

"Lightning, metal and trees, do not go together."

"You mean…?"

"Has someone deliberately…?" said Rosalie at a whisper.

"Ah sir, it's just someone forgetting to take their groom back with them when they've tethered their goat…or their dog."

"Would you?"

"I don't thatch, sir."

Ancelin looked up with tired eyes to the, now black, and pouring Heavens.

"Hmmm," he said, meaningfully. "Forgetful?"

CHAPTER NINE ~ THE CHURCH

They slept well beyond dawn, that day. All of them, for they were thoroughly spent. It took Bea several moments to rouse her mistress and it was Dyamant who, desiring her breakfast, jumped on Rosalie and, licking her all over, eventually made the woman sit up in bed.

"Did I dream it, Bea, or did we have a terrible storm yesterday?"

"We did." Bea brought her mistress some warm water in which to wash.

The soap was contained in a little bag and was made almost entirely of oatmeal flakes.

Rosalie patted herself dry and the linen towel was grey with smuts.

"Oh...I stink of smoke!"

"It's your hair. I'll help you wash it."

"I must go around and have a look at everything this morning. It was hard to assess the damage in the dark. I hope it's no longer raining?"

"No ma'am. That ceased about midnight, I'm told."

"Then flooding is not something with which we need to concern ourselves...again."

"No ma'am."

They slopped around for a while in a basin of water whilst they washed Rosalie's fire smoked hair.

"Oh...I have a few little burns. I hardly noticed them at the time."
Well, such little fire burns were as nothing compared to those she had
endured whilst Roger was alive.

"They are from the smuts, madam. I have some too."

"And I suppose my blue cotte is completely ruined?"

"Completely, as is my grey one."

"Then we shall need more cloth."

Bea's eyes lit up.

"Another visit to Master Mercer?"

"Aye. And our long awaited visit to the church in town...and my
vow."

It was then that Rosalie remembered the words which Ancelin
Hayward had spoken to her.

No, he could not possibly have spoken such words. They were
figments of her imagination. Whyever would he say such a thing? They
were words conjured up by her fevered brain; her overwrought brain
full of the anxious hazard of the moment."

'Well..there's one way to find out,' said her devil, 'ask him.'

"Oh no...don't be foolish!"

"I beg your pardon ma'am," said Bea.

"I said, it would be foolish... not to take the opportunity to go to the
town and speak to the priest of St. Mary's... at the same time as going
to Master Mercer's."

"Yes, madam."

"But now…" said Roslaie, tousling her hair with a linen towel. "I will
make a perambulation of the farm."

"Not like that you won't," said Bea giggling and reaching for
Rosalie's mirror.

"Oh Heavens! No." Her hair stood on end, like a cockerel's crest.

Bea moved a comb through it carefully.

"Bea, do you know how Master Hayward is this morning?"

"I do know that he was sleeping in the hall last night. I passed him
late on my way back to bed and he was gently snoring. I passed him

again this morning and he hadn't moved an inch."

"Are you absolutely certain, when you passed him this morning that he...he...was still...alive?"

"Alive, madam?" Bea laughed out loud. "Why should he not be alive?"

"No reason," she answered sulkily. "Just something I think he said."

"Oh? What did he say?"

"I cannot divulge."

"Oh ma'am." Bea pulled at a knot and tugged a little too hard. "Ouch!"

"Aw sorry."

"Well if you must know, he said that he might...might...die...soon."

"Die?"

"Yes. That is what he said. That if he was to die..."

"Yes?"

"Then I must...think...favourably of him."

"Why should you not? He is a nice man as I've said before and such a clever soul."

"It's true that we might all have burned to the ground last night, if Master Hayward had not been so quick thinking."

"That is true. Oh, he isn't the most handsome man in the world..."

"Not like your Master Sommar eh?"

"He's not *mine*."

"I know. You just like him."

Bea cleared her throat. "He isn't the richest. He doesn't have perfect manners."

"You mean like Sir Hugh?" laughed Rosalie.

"Or your Master Godechepe."

"He is not *my* Master Godechepe."

"But Master Hayward is loyal and kind and he loves..."

"Yes...?"

"Forceleap Farm with all his heart."

Rosalie almost felt sad that Bea had not said something else entirely.

*****

"Master Newbold, might you put this in the cart for me please?" said Rosalie as she struggled with two parcels of wool fabric bought from Master Mercer in Marlborough High Street.

"Where are you off to mistress?"

"To the church at the top of town."

"To pray, ma'am?"

"To debate, I suspect, if my previous experience is anything to go by." Rosalie did not expect to come away with a promise that she'd be able to make her vow at St. Mary's at any time soon. But she had to try.

As she walked the market on the street, Rosalie purchased a few other items from other shopkeepers and these were all stowed away in the body of the cart slowly driven by Fulk, from venue to venue.

Master Newbold walked beside his mistress and Bea as usual brought up the rear, lagging behind as she feasted her eyes upon the different wares to be had.

"Geese, geese good laying geese. Larders, larders buy my larders!" The hubbub was deafening, the traders all crying their wares with the full force of their lungs against the background din of some of street musicians who had set up by the market cross.

"Mend the old bellows," cried one old man bent beneath a huge basket full of leather pieces and old bellows, his white hair disordered and dirty.

They were about to pass the Green Man ale house. Rosalie looked behind her. "Keep up Bea!" Her maid servant scurried up.

With one look at the crowd milling outside the alehouse, Mistress Jourdemayne decided to cross the road and brave the mud and offal, blood and muck of the roadway by the slaughter pens.

"Oh ma'am, you can't mean to go that way?" said Master Newbold, in horror.

"Which would you sooner brave, William? Muck underfoot or the muck of those drunken men?"

She was right. A scuffle had started on the ground outside the alehouse and three young men were being evicted from the building. Swearing, cursing and fighting, they jostled amongst the drinkers who had gathered on the patch of earth outside.

Rosalie put Bea in front of her and dashed to the other side of their cart driven on by Fulk.

"Quickly...come."

Suddenly there seemed to be more men. Men everywhere. Dashing, rushing.

Bea was pushed against the cart and Rosalie was jostled against Master Newbold.

"Here...here! Here we are!" shouted a voice and several apprentices, by the look of them came running up the roadway.

Master Lorimer, the cutler, had exited his shop and threw up his hands in horror at the scene before him.

"Oh! Lock up the shop Will," he said to his apprentice, "It's the gang of Green Man drinkers who come to set Urban Whitelock free from the lockup. I'd heard they would."

Mistress Jourdemayne watched as the revellers, brandishing sticks and various tools came rushing up the side of the town cross and past the cutler's shop. In two shakes of a lamb's tail, Master Cutler and his boy had closed the flap of his window and bolted it.

But not before Rosalie had inquired of him what he thought was happening.

"Whitelock is a notorious housebreaker and thief, madam," said the cutler haphazardly throwing his wares inside the shop. "Master Barbflet, the town reeve, has arrested him and he's in the lockup awaiting trial."

"Oh..."

"And they are determined to set him free."

"Why? Do they not wish to see justice done?"

She received no answer for the man's door banged and she heard the inner bolt go down.

"Mistress…" yelled Fulk, trying to calm the frenzied cart horse, Jacob, "Jump up. Jump up…to safety here."

Bea was there before her and quickly clambered up onto the cart bed with the package of wool. She fought off a couple of lads who tried to relieve them of their purchases, with a brass pot bought that morning. It made contact with at least one head if the 'dong' noise was anything to go by.

However, Rosalie was spun round and dizzied by a couple of apprentices, fullers by the look of them, catching hold of her for fun.

They jogged past banging on the cutler's door for a lark and ran on.

Now several other men came up behind her. She lifted to her toes to try to see if she could find Master Newbold but he was not to be seen.

She laid about her pushing the men away and trying to clear herself a space, until one of them grabbed her hands.

He smelled of chickens and had but two teeth in his jaw.

"Oh, here's a fine fighting chick!"

She bit his wrist.

He slapped her but she rose again and lifted her knee.

It found its mark and he went down in the crowd of legs, yelling obscenities.

She turned round and round. She could not even see the cart now. On she was pushed, past the town cross and its crumbling stone base of steps. Around the corner past the doctor's house to the building which housed the lockup.

Here the press of men was greatest.

She managed to push her way to the edge of the road to lean against a house wall breathless and shaking. She saw one of the town guards who was responsible for looking after the prisoner go down with a bloody wound to his forehead. Of the other town guard, there was no sight.

Another woman had become entangled in the rioting men. She too was stuck in the rabble but this lady had no strength to pull herself free, for Rosalie could see that she was elderly, bare headed and grey of hair.

Her anger at these men lent her strength.

"How dare you attack a defenceless old woman!' she yelled and waded into the surging crowd.

Kicking and punching as hard as she could, she managed to reach the poor old woman just before she went down under the feet of a braying donkey which had suddenly appeared in the middle of the mob.

The donkey kicked out and one man went flying. This cleared a small space and Rosalie was able to grab the woman by the waist and drag her backwards to the relative safety of the house wall.

The door of the lockup splintered and a victorious cheer went up.

Rosalie saw a man lifted on the shoulders of the throng. He was good looking, about twenty with a smart smile which turned to laughter as he was borne away down The Marsh.

The man who owned the donkey came up and dragged the protesting beast out of the way down Oxford Street.

The tail end of the stream of men staggered drunkenly after the man borne aloft by his rescuers.

The two guards were being attended by one or two townsmen who had been brave enough to come out from their businesses to see what all the fuss was about.

Rosalie turned to her old woman. But she had gone. In her place was the two toothed villain of earlier. He grinned. A blast of foetid air assailed her nose.

"Think you can get the better of Thomas Two Tooth do you?' She could just catch what he'd said, for his speech was slushy and indistinct.

He caught her by the headdress and the hair beneath and dragged her close to him, pushing her along the roadside and into the dark alley to St. Mary's Church, close by.

She fought as best she could but he managed to capture her and marched her up to the church door.

"Help!" she cried.

Rosalie looked round for help but there was no one here. She shouted "Father Torold!"

There was no answering bass voice. A grubby hand was clamped on her mouth.

The man had now got the church door open and he pushed her inside slamming the outer door with vehemence.

"Ever done it in a church, mistress widow lady?"

"Done what?"

Rosalie backed away.

"You surely cannot mean to harm me here in church! You would be damned by God."

"I'm damned anyway. What's one more damning? I'm always in trouble."

Rosalie ran up the nave. "Is there anyone here?"

She heard a door open and close quietly but she saw no one. It was very dark in the church. No light was visible on the altar but the sanctuary light winked red at her in its lamp of brass.

With trembling fingers she took out her eating knife which was suspended from her belt in a small leather scabbard and waved it at the man.

"Come on then. Let's see how brave you are?"

The man laughed.

"That little thing?"

"I know where to stick it!"

"Oh ma'am," said Thomas Two Tooth, "So do I!"

"Pah!"

"You can't do nothing with that little thing but with this...I can do damage." He fiddled with his tunic, reached into his disgustingly filthy braies and pulled out his member.

Rosalie didn't flinch.

"Pah! That little thing! Come on then. I've seen bigger pizzles on an ant!"

The man launched at her angrily. This time she did flinch.

But he didn't reach her. Down onto his head came a large wooden candlestick. The sort which lies either side of the altar and which house huge candles on feast days.

His eyes rolled up in his head and his body lolled forward and fell face down.

Rosalie held her breath and dropped to her knees.

Gentle hands lifted her up.

"Madam… here sit."

Rosalie, shaking with relief, sat on a chair placed by the sanctuary light.

"It is the Frith chair but Father Torold will not mind, I'm sure."

Rosalie rewound her head cloth. "Thank you."

"Wait while I find something to bind him."

In the recesses of her mind, Rosalie was sure she'd heard the voice before.

Feet tapped away on the tiles of the church.

Her mouth was dry and her face full of anxious perspiration. She wiped her forehead with the remainder of the cloth which hung down her breast and looked around.

Now she could see a little better in the darkness having got her night eyes, as they say.

Not quite at her feet was the obnoxious Tom the Tooth. He did not stir.

She leaned over him and braved the stench of chickens.

'What can you do to him to get even?' asked her little devil.

"Rosalie Jourdemayne, you are in a church!"

'Well..what?'

She looked over her shoulder to make sure her rescuer was not on his way back and with the little knife which was still in her hand, she cut the strings of the purse which the man wore at his side on his belt.

There were quite a few coins in it.

She hurried to the altar, genuflected and poured the stream of coins onto it.

"Thank you Lord," she said quietly. Then she threw the purse into the dark recesses of the body of the church and sat once more, her heart hammering, her mouth twitching with a nervous laughter.

Her rescuer returned.

"I have found a cord... this will do to bind him. That was an attempted rape and a breech of the King's peace. I'll make sure he's delivered to the town authorities."

"Sir Hugh?"

"Aye..." His face lost its seriousness and took on its usual jovial demeanour.

"Mistress Jourdemayne. Oh. I did not know it was you!"

"It is very dark in here."

"It is."

"I thought I saw you in the street. It *was* you who helped Old Mother Hensett from the danger of the crowd?"

"I did but she disappeared." Rosalie grasped his sleeve. "Is she alright?"

"Aye. I bundled her into the Doctor's door. He'll look after her."

He finished tying up his prisoner.

"I thought I saw this piece of offal drag a lady to the church door and followed a way behind. I had no idea it was you."

"Well. I must thank you for your help. You saved me from having to stick the man and possibly..."

"He was intent on rape."

"Yes..." she giggled..."he was."

"Are you sufficiently recovered to walk out?"

"I am a little shaky but I must go and find my maidservant and my steward not to mention my cart and purchases.'

"I saw a cart on the corner of Oxford Street. Might that be yours?"

"Fulk was driving."

"Your young lad?"

"Yes."

"I didn't see your man, Master Newbold was it?"

"Yes and Bea."

"Ah yes."

Into Rosalie's mind came the story of Bea's friend and the seduction by this man, Sir Hugh.

Rosalie stood and wavered a little,

"Ooh."

"You are dizzy. Lean on me."

'It seems you have no choice,' said the little voice in her head, 'he has hold of you as firmly as Two Toothed Tom...or whatever his name was.'

It was true, he had her in a firm embrace.

"Sir Hugh, you are hurting me."

"Oh...madam. I am sorry. I simply do not know my own strength."

She could feel the muscles of his arms against her own. His taut chest was against her side.

"Please sir. I can stand."

He let go and marched to the door.

"You will wish to lay a charge against this stinking townsman?"

"Must I go to such lengths?"

"I heard him say that he's been in trouble before. Would you wish another woman to endure what you have had to experience?"

"Then I must report him."

"I am your witness madam." He bowed low.

'He really is good looking isn't he?' mused her devilish voice. 'Such lovely manners and ways of speech. And those eyes..."

"Thank you."

The door was opened, a rush of air pulsed through it as they met the outside. Rosalie staggered against him.

Her face lifted to his. He stooped. And he kissed her lips.

CHAPTER TEN ~ CUTWYTHY FARM AND A REVELATION

It was not possible to talk about making her vow that day. She became quite shaky as she made her way out of the church and found Fulk in a panic running up and down the street by the market cross.

"I just sent Bea to look for you, ma'am."

"Well, here I am."

"You alright?"

"I am a little shaken but…"

"She has had a terrible experience, young Fulk. Get her up on the cart and take her home. I have a felony to report and a felon to detain."

"You did not kill the man, Sir Hugh?" said Rosalie at a whisper… "Did you…?"

"Ah no. His head is harder than that. He'll have a terrible headache when he wakes at last. That's all."

He seemed so nonchalant about it.

'Well, I suppose, he's killing people all the time. That's what knights do…isn't it?' said her devil. 'I expect you could get quite blase about it.'

"Where is Master Newbold?"

"In the back of the cart. He took quite a tumble but he's alright. I managed to pick him up and put him in there," said Fulk.

Rosalie ran to the tail of the cart.

"William..oh, William."

William Newbold struggled to an elbow. "Madam, did you manage to get to the church?"

"In a manner of speaking, yes. But no. I didn't get to speak to Father Torold."

There was a huge bruise on William's head.

"What happened to you?"

"I was caught up in the fracas and someone took a swing at me."

"Oh!"

"And so I retaliated and before I knew it, I was on the earth with stars in my head."

"Oh William. I am so sorry for dragging you into this."

"Oh no ma'am. Please. I haven't had so much fun since 1174."

"What happened in 1174?"

"Well I…"

Then Bea returned.

"I have been looking for you everywhere."

"In the cart Bea. We are going down to the town reeve's house with Sir Hugh."

But Sir Hugh had gone.

"SIR HUGH!?"

"Without Sir Hugh today I might be lying defiled in St. Mary's."

"I beg your pardon?"

"He saved me…"

"Did he try to defile you...the… pig… Where is he? I'll slice his…"

"He has gone on ahead to give an account of the attack and then he will return for his prisoner. Or maybe he has taken him down to the town reeve...I don't know in which order…" Rosalie felt the beginnings of a headache and was feeling light headed and just a little bit warm when she spoke about Sir Hugh.

*****

It seemed a much longer journey home than it had been an outward trip. Rosalie felt tired and somehow dirtied. And she was worried about William.

He kept burbling on about some event which he had attended in 1174, thirty years ago. Neither Rosalie or Bea could fathom it, except that William, a young man then, had really enjoyed himself for he chuckled and giggled like a girl now and again.

Eventually they turned the corner of the farm hedge.

A few chickens dashed about the yard as the cart trundled in but no one was there to welcome them.

"No Master Hayward?"

"He was going to check on things with the sheep and see what he could do with that apple tree," said Bea. "He'll be on the farm somewhere."

"Fulk, get the cart stowed. Bring the purchases to the hall."

"Aye ma'am."

Rosalie and Bea managed to get a grinning Master Newbold from the back of the cart. It was almost as if he had imbibed a great deal of alcohol, he was so merry. But they both knew that was highly unlikely.

They stowed him safely in his room and retired to their bedroom to chew over the day's events and check their purchases.

Rosalie took up the brass pot she had bought.

"Dented."

"It made contact with an idiot apprentice's head, that's what."

"Hmmm."

"But the wool is unharmed."

"Thank you Lord."

"So are you going to tell me what happened in the church?" said Bea. "Between you and Sir Hugh."

"Nothing happened between Sir Hugh and me."

"But... Why did he have to go down to the town reeve then?"

"To report a crime."

Rosalie could see that Bea was not going to give in.

"So what did Sir Hugh do?"

Rosalie combed her own hair with a bone comb and took her time with it, pulling the teeth through her blonde locks with precision.

"He saved me from being raped, that's what he did."

"Noooo!"

She told the tale about Two Toothed Tom and as she told it, she became just a little bit...uncomfortable.

She thought back to the church and particularly to the purse which he had hanging from his belt.

How much money had she tipped onto the altar of St. Mary's?

There were silver pennies, half pennies and a few quarter pennies. She thought the whole thing might have amounted to a shilling. Twelve pence!

Tom the Tooth was not an artisan, nor a skilled workman. He was a simple labourer, she thought. Being familiar with the wages of her own labourers, she puzzled over how much money he'd had in his purse. Why was he walking about town with so much money on him?

"I think that my attacker must have been a thief or a cut purse, Bea."

"Why's that?"

"He had a whole shilling in his purse."

"Twelve pence? Where would he get that kind of money save he stole it ma'am?"

"I have no idea. Anyway...it's not our problem now. He's locked up in Master Barbflet's big barn, until he can be dealt with."

"He'll be there a long while. The court only sat last week. That's when Whitelock was tried. He was waiting to go off to Winchester."

"I can't say that I can be sorry for Tom Two Tooth, sitting in that cold and draughty barn on short rations."

"Maybe you should tell the town reeve that he had all that money too."

"Ah no. If I do that, then I will have to admit to robbing him myself!"

"You didn't rob him. You gave it to the church."

Rosalie shrugged. "I'll leave it." But it still left a strange feeling in the back of her mind. And there was also something her attacker had said. How did he know she was a widow? He didn't know her.

Master Hayward came into the yard before midday for his dinner.

"I have dealt with the apple tree in the orchard," he said, ever practical. "And I have logged it. You should have some nice scented apple logs for the winter, ma'am, for the fire here."

"Is everything well on the farm, Master Hayward?"

"Aye mistress, considering."

"Do you know if anyone else was struck by the lightning? Master Godechepe's lands for example?"

Hayward looked out through the window. "I heard that before we had ever had our misfortunes with the lightning, a farmhouse on the western border of his lands was struck and burned to the ground.

"No! How awful. Do we know who lived in it?"

"Master Godechepe's sister, I believe."

"Oh no! I have met...nay not formally met, but seen the lady. I hope that she was not hurt?"

"It seems she has lost almost everything," said Hayward sadly, "but yes, she was saved. I hear she is now staying with her brother."

"I cannot imagine how awful it is to lose everything to fire. Even that which is not consumed by flames will be ruined by smoke."

"She has little more than that in which she is dressed, I'm told."

"Oh...I think that we must pay a visit, Hayward. We must help where we can."

"What do you mean to do mistress?"

"Visit Master Godechepe's house and see what we might do to alleviate the poor lady's suffering. I am about to take a vow of celibacy and one of the things I must do is think about others. It's not just a matter of eschewing carnal relations; it's about doing good works."

"You wish to go now?"

"Will you accompany us? Bea and I will find some items of clothing we no longer need and I'm sure we can find some other things."

"Would it not be better to send a lad over there to ascertain, ma'am, just what is needed, if anything?"

"I think that we need to act quickly. Once you start to overthink about these things, the impetus is lost and nothing is done."

"I will ask Fulk to harness the small cart. I will ride beside it on Filbert," said Ancelin reluctantly.

"I would be grateful for your aid. I have never been to that part of the county before."

"We shall take the road past West Woods, madam. It's by far the most direct route for a cart."

The cart was loaded with items for which Bea and Rosalie had no further use and they set off just before dinner hoping to make Master Godechepe's farm in the middle of the afternoon. The girls did not feel the need for food, though they took with them some bread and cheese to tide them over.

The countryside here was a little different from their own downland with small fields laid out haphazardly to sheep and crops and it seemed odd without cattle.

West Wood loomed dark and large on their left hand side and the girls were glad when they were past it.

It was a lonely place. They met no one on the road and Rosalie began to wonder if the storm had driven folk away, for there was no one in the fields; no shepherd, nor anyone tilling the small plots here and there around an isolated cott.

At last they drew close to Cutwythy Farm where Master Godechepe had a substantial house, which had just been re-thatched, she noticed.

Rosalie looked round eager to see what kind of place this man had. All seemed tidy and organised. There were several large barns, no doubt full to the brim at this season with produce and folds crowded with sheep newly brought in from the downs, for counting and culling. Amongst them Rosalie noted some black sheep. Now they were a novelty, she thought.

Prosperous. It all looked prosperous.

Master Godechepe was crossing his yard as their cart trundled round the farm hedge. His face grew startled and then merry as he realised whom the cart contained.

"Mistress Jourdemayne. This is a surprise."

"Oh Master Godechepe," said Rosalie from the cart seat. 'We hope that we do not inconvenience you with our arrival."

"Not at all dear lady."

He held up his hand to help her down, but Master Hayward was there first.

"We hear that there has been a disaster and have come to offer our help."

The man's face grew sad. "Aye. It's a terrible thing."

He took her elbow and steered her to the house door.

"All lost."

"No lives I hope?"

"Alas...whilst my sister Eleanor was rescued, her maid was not. She died of her burns this morning."

"Oh that is terrible."

"Poor woman. My sister is quite distraught."

"Oh I'm sure."

"Might I ask if the weather affected you personally adversely?" asked Henry.

"Nothing but a couple of trees struck by lightning and set on fire. But Master Hayward managed to contain the flames and so we have not suffered unduly."

"I am pleased to hear it." Godechepe smiled at Hayward.

"Come, come in, I will introduce you to my dear sister."

Eleanor Godechepe, for she had never married and still carried her maiden name, was a fine woman of almost forty, with silver pale hair, barely concealed by a white linen coif and veil, and skin as pale as milk.

There was no doubt, even at her age, she was a good looking woman with long elegant fingers and a small waist.

"Mistress Godechepe we are so sorry to hear of your loss."

The woman's eyes filled with tears. "Yes. Thank you. Adelina had been with me many years. I will feel her loss keenly."

"We are told that everything contained in your house is perished…"

"The house was my brother's but we had made it our own," said Eleanor. "He is such a generous man."

"We have brought with us some gifts of clothes and other things which we hope will go some way to helping you out of your misfortune," said Rosalie.

"That is most kind," said Henry Godechepe. "Did I not tell you Nell that we had such kind and charitable neighbours."

"You did brother. Thank you." The woman dabbed her eyes with a small square of linen. "It is more than I could hope for."

"What happened Master Godechepe?" asked Hayward, "That your house is burned?"

"The thatch was struck by lightning, we believe. The storm was so fierce."

Cider was fetched for the men and a pressed apple juice for the ladies. Master Hayward hung around the door and leaned on the wall, refusing a seat, for there were only a few in the hall and so many to be seated.

Eleanor seemed to quickly forget her misfortune and entered into chatter with Rosalie, wishing to know all about Forceleap Farm and its famous cattle.

With a quick look at Master Hayward, Rosalie launched into an explanation of how their cattle were so very different from other breeds and waxed lyrical about their beauty.

"They are slightly larger than the normal breed of cow. The Templars, who breed them up in the north of England, have paid attention to their strength and suitability as draught animals. They are as good if not better than the oxen which you see about everywhere."

"And the beef, sister mine, is far superior, I'm told, to ordinary beef," said Henry, smiling.

After a while it was obvious that Eleanor Godechepe was tiring of talking about cattle. Rosalie knew that *she* could go on all day.

The silence dragged on for Rosalie did not wish to bore the lady.

"I am afraid that I have no beautiful clothes like the cotte you were to the celebration at Master Ivo's but, until you can obtain your own...."

"My brother's generosity, Mistress Jourdemayne. He bought the silk and linen material for that excellent cotte. And now it is no more." The woman lowered her head and it seemed as if she would cry but did not.

"I do not know what I should do without my dear Henry."

"He is indeed generous, mistress Eleanor, I know it."

Rosalie caught the expression on Hayward's face from the corner of her eye. Quizzical? Surprised? Disappointed perhaps? She could not quite tell.

What she could tell, was that he was fascinated by the poor woman Eleanor Godechepe, for his eyes lingered on her a little too long, as they swept over the party in the room. He had not spoken since they'd arrived except to ask after the storm damage.

'She is a handsome woman and a handsome woman in distress,' said her little voice, 'why should he not be interested?'

"When you are feeling better, perhaps you would do us the honour of coming to Forceleap Farm to dine with us?"

"We should like that very much, shouldn't we Nell?"

"I think we should," she smiled.

"And now we must take up no more of your time."

"Must you go so soon," said Henry

"We must if we are to be back for supper and home before dark."

Rosalie stood and Bea made for the outer door. Master Hayward still lounged against the wall. He wasn't exactly staring at the woman Eleanor Godechepe, but he had not much taken his eyes from her.

"Master Hayward, shall we make our way home. Mistress Eleanor looks fatigued. Perhaps she needs some rest," said Rosalie more curtly than she intended.

"Madam." Ancelin bowed and exited the farmhouse, his face unreadable.

"Well!' said Rosalie's little devil. 'That was interesting.'

*****

It was several days before Rosalie had the leisure to go back into the town, intending this time to speak to Father Torold, come Hell or high water.

This time, she took Master Hayward with her and rode pillion on his horse, Filbert. They dismounted at the town cross and Ancelin took hold of the reins to steady the horse.

"I will go into the church and find Father Torold. If you can wait here for me, Master Hayward."

Hayward looked towards the lock-up, the door of which was now mended.

"Is that where your attacker is being held?"

"I was told by Sir Hugh that he was held in Master Barbflet's large barn which can easily be secured but they might have transferred him here now they have mended it."

Hayward was curious. "You go. I want to see if he's here. I want to get a look at him."

Rosalie made her way up the alleyway to the church door. She dithered on the step, as her little voice said 'This is most unpleasant Rosalie Jourdemayne. Too soon. You have come back too soon.'

"Nonsense." She squared her shoulders and put out her hand to the ring which opened the church door.

Suddenly out from the inkiness of the interior a great black beast with flapping wings enveloped her as she stepped inside.

"Oh! Madam, I am so sorry."

Father Torold, his dark cloak billowing in the draught of the door, put out two hands to prevent her from falling.

"Ah...yes...father..."Her heart dropped back down to its usual resting place. She swallowed hard. "I have come to see you."

"See *me*? Well, I'm afraid..." said his rich bass voice, "I am called out urgently madam. Please go into the church to wait for me should you wish." He lifted the tools of his trade; a bottle of holy water and the oils needed to anoint the dying. "I am called to give extreme unction on the Marsh."

'Oh!' said her little devil 'that sounds very painful.'

"How long will you be?"

His voice floated back to her as he ran through the alleyway and onto the street by the High Cross. "Oh, a little while, I expect."

Rosalie looked into the body of the church. The darkness pressed in. She saw herself lying on the floor, weeping and Two Toothed Tom standing over her exultant.

'Don't go in. Not alone,' said her little voice.

"No, I shall wait for him...here."

And then she thought better of it and tripped back down the alleyway into the light and tumult of the marketplace.

Master Hayward was on tip toe staring through the tiny blank window in the lock-up door, shielding his eyes for better vision in the light of the day. The door was splinter new with metal bars and shone out bright in the sunlight.

"Master Hayward?"

"There is no one in there." He turned. "You look...upset. What has happened?"

"Ah it's nothing...I just have to wait a while for the priest. He has gone to minister to the dying."

"Where has he gone?"

"To the Marsh, he told me."

Hayward laughed out loud. "Then he will be some time. The Marsh is the worst part of town, a den of depravity and degradation. If a confession is required he will be hours!"

Rosalie sat down disconsolately on the steps of the High Cross.

"Then I will wait."

Master Hayward sat beside her.

They stared at the bustle of the marketplace.

"Ma'am?"

"Yes?"

"You are absolutely sure you want to go through with this vow?"

"Ancelin!..That's him!"

"What?"

"That's the man who attacked me."

"It can't be. He's locked up...somewhere."

Rosalie shot up like she'd sat on a thistle. "It's him, I tell you. There cannot be two who look like him in the town."

"Show me."

She pointed and ran across the road to peer around the corner of the glass maker's house.

"It's him. He's going up the hill."

Hayward rapidly reached for a hold of the horse's reins and walked him gently across the road.

"Then we follow."

"Why isn't he locked up?" asked Rosalie absolutely perplexed.

"I don't know. You say that he had admitted to other felonies in your hearing?"

"And in that of Sir Hugh."

Rosalie took hold of his arm. "And...and something else. I might just have relieved the man of his purse when he was out cold on the floor of the church. Perhaps. Maybe."

"You did what?" They walked up the hill, keeping to the shadows of the buildings.

"He had a purse full of money. I think there might have been as much as a shilling in it. I emptied it out on the altar and left it there."

"Oh..."

"I wanted him to pay for his foulness. So much money. Do you think that he had also been thieving?"

"It's a distinct possibility."

"So that begs the question, why is he running free?"

The man sauntered up the road totally confident and crossed into

Silver Street. Hayward and Mistress Jourdemayne followed.

Here there were fewer people. A couple of the Jewish community were outside their houses, talking. They nodded politely as they passed.

Reaching The Green, they watched as their quarry crossed the road yet again and disappeared down an alleyway between two houses.

"Do we follow?"

"We have come thus far," said Hayward.

He tied Filbert to a bush. "Come."

A frisson of excitement fizzed through Rosalie's body. She had never done anything like this before. She was enjoying the feeling but a little part of her was worried.

'What if it gets dangerous?' said her devil.

"I have Master Hayward."

'He is a farm manager, not a knight. He carries no sword.'

Her voices came to an abrupt halt as they travelled the narrow alleyway side by side.

Master Hayward pushed her behind him and put his fingers to his lips.

Rosalie was not to be denied. She dropped to her knees and peered around him, holding onto the back of his belt for stability.

He looked down at her and she thought she saw a small smile flicker on the edge of his mouth, as she peered up at him. "What is he doing?" she whispered.

"Waiting."

"What for?"

Hayward hissed back "If I knew that...perhaps I would intervene."

They waited. And waited. The man with two teeth shuffled his feet. He leaned against a wall. He picked his nose.

Then he slid down and rested on his haunches, leaning on the wall.

Rosalie got up from the ground. "What is he doing now?"

"Waiting. Patiently," said Hayward pointedly.

From the other end of the alleyway which debouched onto Barn Street, came a whistling man.

The gloomy roadway here was only a matter of a few feet wide; only wide enough for two people to pass carefully. The second man came up nonchalantly.

The overhanging buildings above them blocked out much of the light. Rosalie could see that the man who had entered the alleyway at the far end was wearing a sword. A long one. Apart from that he was a black shape.

"Well...? I don't have all day," said a voice.

"I done what you wanted. Now for the rest of my money. The thieving little bitch stole what you gave me."

"Did she now?"

"And why did you have to 'it me so 'ard."

"Because you, you stupid fool, were about to do something I had *not* asked you to do. I had to stop you."

"Aw, I could'a had some fun."

"No...you couldn't. Frighten, I said. Not rape!"

"Well I frightened her good and proper and now I want my money."

There was a tinkling sound as coins changed hands.

"Now get out of my sight. And stay away from the town reeve...if he catches any wind of this..."

"Aw don't worry. You won't say. I won't say. And Mistress nose in the air..."

"CHEEK!" said Rosalie's little devil.

"Won't say nowt."

"No. I managed to convince her to let me handle the non existent report to the authorities."

"Be seein'ya. Sir."

Rosalie and Master Hayward had to scuttle very quickly back through the alleyway and onto the Green to avoid being seen by the man who exited the narrow lane.

But he was close on their heels with a long tread. Master Hayward grabbed Rosalie by the waist, turned her to the wall of a barn and put his head down to hers.

"Quiet. Don't move."

Both hands on his breast, she waited until the man had passed. A shiver flew through her which she was unable to identify. Then the anger surfaced.

"The twisted tongued, conniving, base born liar!" said Rosalie to cover her embarrassment.

Master Hayward let her go.

"I apologise. But it was all that I could think to do to avoid being recognised."

She watched as the man strode on down the road and into Oxford Street.

Hayward sighed. "Sir Hugh has many questions to answer."

"He'll answer them. I will be furious when I see him next."

"He planned your abduction by that degenerate."

"That is why he had so much money on him. But why?"

"So that he could worm his way into your affections. There is no better way to woo a lady, some might say, than to save her honour. She will be eternally grateful."

Rosalie recalled the kiss which Sir Hugh had given her. It had come from nowhere and she'd had no way of avoiding it.

She almost spat out into the roadway as she remembered the feeling of his lips touching hers.

*****

They walked slowly back to the high cross. A quick look in the church and in the little cottage close by, where Father Torold lived, showed that the priest had not yet returned.

"Do we wait ma'am?"

"No Ancelin. I have had enough for today."

"We should go down to the town reeve at the mill and report what we know. It can't go unpunished."

"Sir Hugh of Yatesbury is a respected knight of the realm, Master

Hayward. Our word will not stand against his."

"Master Barbflet, the town reeve, is a fair man. He'll listen."

"No. I cannot accuse one of my neighbours of...well...whatever I would be accusing him of."

Ancelin sighed. "If the man turns up at Forceleap Farm, make sure you are not alone with him. Call for me, wherever I am."

Rosalie looked up at his honest face. A visage she hadn't really, truly looked at before.

A straight nose in a rectangular face with a slight cleft in the chin; a tanned face but such good skin with none of the wrinkles she had seen on men who work outdoors. Dark auburn brown hair with a slight wave thrust back from his forehead.

Her heart gave a little wriggle.

"I will," she said.

Bea was pacing the hall when they reached home at last.

"Whatever is the matter Bea?"

"Oh Mistress, I'm so glad you're back. It's Master Newbold."

"What about him?" asked Rosalie, throwing off her cloak.

Bea wrung her hands in front of her. "He is most unwell."

"What's the matter?"

"He hasn't really been well since...you know...the day we came back from town but today, he is refusing to rise from his bed and seems delirious."

Ancelin had come in quickly after Rosalie; with one look at his mistress, he turned tail.

They heard his voice echoing through the screens passage,

"I'll be off back into town and I'll fetch the doctor."

CHAPTER ELEVEN ~ THE PASSING

Rosalie rushed across the passage and pushed the door to Master Newbold's room. A quick glance outside showed that a wind had risen and that it was tossing the tops of the trees along the Forceleap approach road.

Her steward was lying on his back in his shirt on a disordered bed. The man had been so hot that the pillow was wet.

"Bea… clean linen! Now. We must make Master Newbold comfortable.

She leaned and took his hand.

"William. Tell me. What is wrong?"

William's eyes opened. Those cheerful blue eyes which had chivvied her through thirteen years of pain and anguish. The expressive lips which had been able to speak words which had made her smile, if not laugh, when the rest of the world was against her.

"William. It's me, Rosalie." It was as if he didn't recognise her.

"Oh… ma'am."

He tried to pick up the blanket and pull it up to cover him but failed. She pulled it up for him.

"Do you hurt somewhere?"

"Oh my head hurts, it's true but it's nothing. I am so tired."

"Then you shall sleep, sleep as long as you wish. Master Ancelin has gone for the doctor in Marlborough. We shall have you as right as the adamant in no time."

William's lips creased into a smile.

"Dear Ancelin. What would Forceleap do without him?"

"What would I and Forceleap do without *you* my dear William." A single tear tracked down her cheek.

"Now, now," said her embarrassed steward. "I'll have no tears."

Rosalie smiled against her own anguish and brushed it away.

Bea came into the room with clean linen and together they managed to get Master Newbold into a fresh bed and a new shirt, with as much dignity as they could muster.

The day was moving on fast to afternoon and no one had eaten. But no one felt like eating. Master Newbold was fed water from a tiny cup and thanked her profusely for her help, in a sort of awkward way.

"You have given me so much help over the years, William. If this is how I can repay you…"

"Ah no ma'am, it is my job to help. To run the house. And I have been amply rewarded. It is not your job to feed water to an old man."

"Then I do it out of love for you."

Now William became even more ill at ease.

"No, ma'am."

"You have been the best father to me these many years, better than was my own father."

He smiled then and closed his eyes. "I never had a daughter…"

It was close to vespers when Ancelin Hayward came rushing back into the farmyard.

"The doctor follows me. He has been very busy in the town but he will come presently. And I took the liberty of calling in at Preshute, for the priest."

"Good. I fear…"

"Fear what, madam?"

"I fear that William is beyond our help…but…"

"No. That cannot be true. You know what a clever doctor Doctor

Johannes is… he will…"

"It's almost as if he is resigned to leave us."

Ancelin sat down wearily at the hall table.

"Then we can do nothing but wait and pray."

And this is what they did. Together at the hall table.

Rosalie relieved Bea later that afternoon and sat by Master William's bed until the darkness was descending. She lit a candle.

His breathing was steady but there were no deep breaths as if he could not fill his lungs.

Rosalie stared out of the window. It was odd how the whole view had changed with the removal of the old lime tree. It had been there as long as she had been at Forceleap farm. And so had William.

She found his eyes looking at her.

"I am not afraid to die," he said suddenly.

She took his hand again quickly. "No one should be afraid to die, William. It is but a soft breath, passing from one life to another. A better life."

"This life has been good."

"This life *is* good and will be, for you, again. I promise."

"You cannot make that promise," he said smiling weakly. She could not argue with him.

"The doctor will be here soon," she said.

"If God wishes to take me then there is no one will prevent him. Not even Doctor Johannes."

"We will get you better," said Rosalie swallowing down the lump in her throat.

He almost laughed then and would have done so had he the strength for it.

"Aye…I will be striding about this farm again…"He ran out of breath and took another. "I feel better knowing that you are sitting here with me."

"I will sit here..I will not leave."

He closed his eyes and said. "I was never quite like the rest of you…"

"What do you mean William?"

"Like Master Roger, and Master Ancelin and you."

"Oh?"

"Having grand intentions, improving things, making plans."

"Those things which you have done, you have done well, William. There is no doubt," she said.

"Oh...I am a little man. I never saw myself as being anything great. I am nothing much. I simply...serve."

Now Rosalie could not prevent the tears from falling.

"I am not a great man..."

"Why should you wish to be, William?"

He laughed quietly and it cost him.

"I never thought to leave Forceleap Farm."

"You will not leave it," sobbed Rosalie. "You will be here forever."

He patted her hand. "I love Forceleap. I never wanted to go anywhere else, though if I had, I might have risen to greater things."

"Oh William...like what?"

"I might have been steward to a great man...left a mark."

"Would you truly liked to have done that?"

His blue eyes, now no longer twinkling and a little dulled searched her face. "No. Not really. I have the best mistress."

She brushed away several tears from her cheeks and wiped her hand over her running nose.

"I would never have left *you*," he said.

"Then do not leave me now."

"Madam, the doctor has been sighted riding up the Manton road," It was Bea hovering in the doorway. She went to the window and closed the shutters against the stiff wind now blowing.

"Thank you Bea. We are ready to receive him."

William squeezed her hand "I will never leave you."

"Oh William. "

"I just go on ahead..."

"Oh William. I will miss you."

"And I will see you again one day. Though the waiting will be very hard."

"I will miss you...but come...why are we talking thus...you are going nowhere. The doctor will be here in a moment."

"Ancelin..where is Ancelin."

"In the hall, I believe."

Now he began to be a little anxious.

"I want...him...him. Here."

"Bea...fetch Master Hayward."

"Aye ma'am."

Ancelin came hastily into the room.

"William, my friend, how are you?"

"Leaving I think."

Ancelin tossed a quick concerned look at Rosalie.

"No. Not possible. You have too much to do, Master Steward."

"When Master Roger was alive, I had a great deal to do."

"And you did it wonderfully well, my friend," said Ancelin.

"But now. Now the two of you can run Forceleap Farm together. There is no need for me."

"You taught me well, William," said Rosalie, "but I still rely on you greatly."

"You are not like Roger who couldn't reckon two barley beans together."

"He couldn't?"

"Not well. And his writing…ugh."

Rosalie was quite surprised at this for she thought her husband had been literate and numerate."

"He wasn't good. But he muddled through. With help."

"Oh. I…thought…"

"But you. You are as sharp as a pin."

She smiled. "As I say I have a good teacher."

"And Ancelin is a good teacher too."

Master Hayward came nearer. "Rest old friend. You are tiring yourself with speaking."

"No, no I need to say something." He swallowed as if he was having difficulty getting his mouth to speak words and Rosalie gave him water again.

"I have made my will...such as it is. It lies in that coffer."

"Oh William...there is no need..." began Rosalie.

"And I made my peace with God at Corpus Christi."

"You need have no worry about that. The priest is on his way," said Master Hayward.

William nodded and then seemed to lapse into a fitful sleep.

"Shall I stay or go to greet the doctor?" whispered Ancelin, his face as white as a tanned man's might be.

"No stay here. Bea will go."

And so he stayed.

They heard the doctor's horse clop around the farm hedge.

William opened his eyes and at the same moment, the shutter which Bea had latched not moments before, blew open with a bang and the gale came in, blowing out the candle.

Ancelin leapt to secure it again. He heard the words.

"Marry her, Ancelin. I will not leave until you do."

He looked back at his old friend.

William's eyes were fixed on him, twinkling and blue and as lively as they had been just last week.

The farm manager gave an infinitesimal nod.

There was a hissing sound and William breathed out.

With a sob, Rosalie closed William's eyes.

The doctor entered the room.

"I am sorry Dr. Johannes," said Ancelin, his voice breaking, "You are just a moment too late."

*****

The wind buffeted the farm all evening. Rosalie could not be convinced to leave the room of her dead steward, indeed, she had climbed onto the bed beside him and circled her arms around him until she had no more tears to cry.

Then she sat in a chair and stared at his slack jawed face until Bea came in and brought her some warmed ale.

"Ma'am, take this."

"Thank you Bea." Rosalie wiped her eyes, red and swollen and stood up. Crossing herself, she said, "He was but a relatively young man. Fifty or so. What can have taken him off so quickly?"

"Master Ancelin has been talking to the doctor. He seems to think the knock on the head which he received the other day might have set up some disease."

"Oh...then I am responsible, for if he had not come with me..." she wailed.

"No madam, it was an accident. Nothing more."

Rosalie flounced from the room angry with herself and went into the hall where Ancelin Hayward sat staring into the fire.

"Are you still here Master Hayward? Have you no home to go to?"

"I have a home but just at the moment, I do not feel I want to go to it."

She stared at him. She had thought him a strong man beyond tears but he'd obviously been crying.

'That does not signify weakness, but humanity,' said her little voice.

"Then stay here tonight. I must say, I do not wish to be alone either."

The wind rushed around the old farmhouse setting up bangings and creakings and Rosalie jumped. She had a headache with crying, her face was puffy and there was a stone lodged in her belly. Her heart ached and the pain would not go away. Visions of Master Newbold came unbidden into her mind. The first day she had seen him as a seventeen year old maid and his kindness to her. The day that she had been given Dyamant as a puppy by a grudging husband, as a Twelfth Night gift. She was sure that had been William's doing.

Oh! Dyamant. The dog had been very fond of Master Newbold.

"Ancelin? We should let Dyamant see Master Newbold's body for she was fond of him and I do not think we should keep the fact that he is...gone...from her."

"He wasn't her master but he might as well have been. Yes, we should do it."

Dyamant was snoozing in the solar with Bea who was sniffling in a corner and sewing a new shift by candlelight. Dyamant lifted her head and gave Bea a nudge as if to say, 'Why are you crying?'

"We shall take Dyamant in to Master Newbold, Bea," said Rosalie, "She should see the body so that she knows he is gone."

Bea nodded but did not look up.

Rosalie took Dyamant under her arm and lifted the hem of her dress to walk down the stairs. The dog wriggled and squirmed and Rosalie was forced to set her down.

Dyamant ran to the steward's door.

"She knows," said Ancelin.

"Yes, it seems like it."

It was now fully dark and Rosalie took up an oil lamp which she had lit in the hall from the embers of the fire. Dyamant looked up to her, willing her to open the door and Rosalie pushed it. The dog ran in.

Up onto the bed went Dyamant and sat looking at the shrouded figure under it's linen sheet. Rosalie pulled back the cover.

Dyamant licked the face of her steward but three times and whined.

"He is gone Dyamant. We shall see him no more."

The dog sniffed around a little while and then sat and stared at the body.

"Make your farewells and go back to the hall."

Dyamant jumped from the bed and sat staring into the corner of the room. Rosalie shone her lamp there, but she could see nothing. The little dog tilted her head this way and that as if someone was speaking to her and she wished to catch every word they'd said.

"Come now Dyamant," said Rosalie, pulling the linen sheet over Master Newbold's head once more. "Time to go."

The dog would not move.

"I cannot leave you in here."

Rosalie turned for the door. The light flickered over the room, lighting up the few sticks of furniture; the chest, a small table, a writing slope.

Her tears came unbidden again. She set down her lamp and, lifting the lid of the coffer, found the document that was Master Newbold's will.

"Come Dyamant. Let's leave Master Newbold to his rest."

She turned once more, the dog preceding her from the room and as she swivelled to close the door, she swore she could see Master Newbold standing by the window, in full daylight...just as she had seen him that very first day thirteen years ago.

A siffling wind passed. "Welcome to Forceleap Farm," said his warm baritone voice.

*****

"No! It can't be," said Ancelin Hayward, as they pored over the last will and testament of William Newbold, by candlelight that evening.

'In the name of God, Amen. On 21st January 1205, I, William Newbold of the parish of St. George's of Preshute set out my testament in the following manner. First, I commend my soul to Almighty God, the glorious Virgin Mary, and all the saints, and my body to be buried in the cemetery of St. George's Preshute. I bequeath 2shillings 4pence to the high altar of that church, in recompense for any forgotten tithes. I bequeath 6pence to the parish fund of the same. I wish to have a priest for 12 years in St. George's church to sing for my soul, for which I leave monies. I have no issue and no relatives and so for the residue of all my goods and monies, I leave them to the disposition of Master Ancelin Hayward of Forceleap Farm. In testimony to which, I have set my seal to this present testament. Drawn up on the date mentioned above.'

"He never said anything to me," said Ancelin in a shocked voice. Not a word."

"The monies are lodged with the Jews on Silver Street in the town it seems," said Rosalie, something big coming into her throat and an uprising to her eyes.

"I did not think he was such a wealthy man," said Hayward.

"He was a gentleman with a little land of his own and some standing in the county, I believe before he was ever steward to my husband. You know that this is often the case with the lesser folk. Stewards are often drawn from the county's elite. Second sons and that sort."

"I didn't know," said Ancelin.

"No one could have guessed it. He spent little money. He must have saved all his wages from Forceleap, all his life."

"I have not nearly that much…"

"Do I not pay you enough?"

"Aye…enough for my wants but."

"You rent a property and that costs you…Master Newbold lived here at Forceleap."

"Aye…I suppose that is it."

They sat in silence for a moment.

"You are now a man of means, Ancelin," said Rosalie, smiling shyly.

"Aye…I suppose I am."

"And I think you too should live here at Forceleap… if that is what you'd want that is."

"Do you wish it?"

"If you can bear to take on Master Newbold's old room."

"Aye…I can bear it. I think."

"I think you love Forceleap as much as dear William did."

Ancelin Hayward forced his face into a sad smile. "I do."

*****

The first visitor to arrive after the death of William Newbold, was

Master Dankworth.

"Oh madam. Two such misfortunes in such a short time," was his first utterance before he had ever bowed his way in.

He had no idea how the latter misfortune, as he called it, was the more painful to her.

"Thank you Master Dankworth. We shall miss Master Newbold greatly."

"It is more than a body can bear."

"Forceleap Farm will not be the same without him but I know that he would wish us to carry on and..."

"You can be at no loss to understand, Mistress Jourdemayne, to comprehend the reason for my journey here."

Rosalie scrutinised his face. "Indeed, sir, I am unaware, apart from the desire to commiserate upon the death of my steward...."

"Madam, you know that I worship and adore you..."

"Master Dankworth...please...now is not..."

"You are now without a male advisor. Without a man ...a man who cared for you...I know, as a father cares for his child. I offer myself in his place as an arm on which to lean."

"Master Dankworth, this is most improper at this time." Rosalie put the hall table between them.

"Oh, madam, know that I am not to be trifled with." Rosalie could see that he was working himself up to something.

"I have never sought to trifle with you, sir."

"Then the rumour that I hear is untrue?"

Rosalie's brow furrowed. "Rumour?"

"That you will soon be formally betrothed to Sir Hugo of Yatesbury."

Rosalie was shocked and the shock showed on her face.

"Ah.. I see that your astonishment means that this is a scandalous falsification."

"Indeed sir, it is."

"And yet the rumour is abroad and you have not yet contradicted it."

Rosalie sat down heavily. "I had no idea that the rumour *was* abroad."

"For some days now. Tell me and tell me truthfully. Has Sir Hugh made you an offer of marriage?"

"No sir, he has not. Not recently. And if he did, he would be most forcefully rebuffed."

Master Dankworth now tried a different tack. "I knew that it could not be true. He is a man of...indifferent morals. I did not think you would be so taken in."

"He did tell me that his late mother, almost upon her deathbed, made him promise that he would marry and marry quickly."

"Indifferent morals and shallow feelings."

"That is my reading of him too, sir."

"Will you make me a promise that you will not become engaged to him?"

Rosalie was now thoroughly fed up of the man's attentions.

"What is it to you? You have no control over me. You are not a male relation. What I do or do not do, is surely irrelevant to you."

The man spluttered.

"I am fully determined to act in a manner, which will make up my happiness, without reference to you, or indeed, to any person so utterly unconnected with me."

Dankworth spluttered some more.

A voice rode over Dankworth's next utterance.

"You are wrong, Master Dankworth. Mistress Jourdemayne is not without male protection. She still has me."

Slowly Dankworth turned to the door behind him. Ancelin Hayward stood, his fingers in his belt, his booted feet set slightly apart.

"And I have her best interests and those of Forceleap Farm at heart."

"Hayward!"

"Sir."

The man looked from one to the other.

"With all due respect. You are a farm manager. What do you think you can do? You are not a gentleman farmer with property. Do you not consider that such a connection with you must disgrace the lady in the eyes of everybody?"

"There Master Dankworth, I must correct you," said Rosalie suddenly. "Master Hayward is now a man of property and fortune, for he is the beneficiary of the will of my dear steward Master Newbold. Everything that was William's is now his. I believe that makes him your equal, sir."

Dankworth addressed Ancelin directly.

"You are determined to ruin Mistress Jourdemayne in the opinion of all her friends, and make her the contempt of the county."

"On the contrary, sir. I will protect her reputation, her livelihood and her person with my life."

Dankworth's eyes narrowed.

"And now, if you do not mind, we both have work to do. We have lost a dear friend and a fellow worker. There is much to do."

"Forceleap Farm will go to the devil. Mark my words."

"You are entitled to your opinion, sir," said Rosalie. "However erroneous."

Master Dankworth stretched his fingers and bunched his fist two or three times.

"Good day to you."

He stormed out.

Rosalie began to shake.

"How dare he?"

Ancelin poured her a cup of water.

"I think he does actually have your best interests at heart, he just doesn't know quite how to voice it."

"No, I mean Sir Hugh. How dare he put it about that I am to be engaged to him. How *dare* he."

"Ignore it."

"How can I?"

"It's probably the result of Sir Hugh's little deception. He feels that you will soon fall into his arms."

"It is, Master Dankworth says, "all over town.""

"Then we must issue a rebuttal."

"How?"

"Leave it with me...two can play at rumours."

*****

And then it was the turn of Master Godechepe, bringing with him, his sister Eleanor.

"We have not come to dinner as you kindly offered a while ago ...no, no. We are just here to express our heartfelt sadness at the passing of such a fine gentleman as Master Newbold, "said Henry. "And will not stay long."

"And our sincere condolences at your loss," added Mistress Godechepe.

"Thank you. Both of you."

"If there is anything we can do."

"But you have your own troubles. Though it is very kind of you," said Rosalie, waving them to a seat.

"We are coping. Master Hayward has been of inestimable assistance. Without him, I should certainly have foundered."

The man himself then walked through the door.

"Oh, forgive me. I did not know that you had visitors, ma'am." He was about to turn around but Rosalie called him back.

"No, Ancelin, do stay. Master and Mistress Godechepe have been so kind in coming all this way to bring us their condolences."

"Most kind," said Ancelin in a voice devoid of any feeling.

Once more Rosalie felt that there was some strange emotion between her manager and the woman Eleanor.

"The storm was fearful was it not? Was Master Newbold distressed by it, Mistress Jourdemayne? Was this why he fell ill?" asked Eleanor.

"No, he sustained a wound upon his head in the riot in the town the other day when he accompanied me to Marlborough and, sadly this left him with some injury...which." Rosalie could not keep the tears from her voice.

"Thunder and lightning, Mistress...*Godechepe*..." Rosalie noticed how he paused upon the name, "Was never anything that William feared," said Ancelin Hayward.

"No, no of course not," said Henry. "You were in town when the man Whitelock was broken from his prison?"

"We were."

"Well, he had gone into Savernake Forest, so I hear, to live the life of an outlaw. Good luck to him."

"I would hope that the warden will chase him out or recapture him," said Rosalie earnestly.

"Oh I have no doubt. The Lord Belvoir will not tolerate such reprobates in his domain," said Henry.

"I wish that the same could be said for another felon who seems to have escaped justice."

Ancelin cleared his throat and took the attention away from Rosalie's utterance.

"You are ahead with your autumn tasks, Master Godechepe? "

"Aye we are on course, Master Hayward, for a successful year end. Despite the awful beginning."

"And you, Master Hayward? "asked Eleanor.

Rosalie answered. "We begin the culling of cattle soon and those we have chosen to breed and have had out to the bull will be cared for by our stockmen over the winter."

Eleanor seemed a little disconcerted by Rosalie's answer.

'Perhaps she does not like the fact of a woman being involved in stock management?' thought Rosalie'

'More like she doesn't like the fact you know all about cows being put to bulls!' said her little devil.

Rosalie watched this woman carefully as Master Hayward talked about the cattle with Master Godechepe. Eleanor looked around the hall, noticing everything. She fiddled with her fingers and the rings upon them. Finally she looked up at Hayward as he came to the end of his question and answer. Not once did she look at Rosalie.

'She likes him. She does,' said Rosalie to herself.

And then she found herself watching Ancelin. "And he...by the way he looks at her so intently, likes her.'

A stab of...something started up around her heart and ended up in her stomach.

She wasn't jealous. How could she be?

The conversation came to an end, the drinks were consumed and preparations were made to leave.

As he handed his sister up to his cart, Master Godechepe turned to Rosalie.

"Oh...I nearly forgot to say. I hear that congratulations are in order. You are to be married?"

"I am afraid this is a mere rumour and I assure you it is not true at all."

The man let out a huge sigh. "There you are sister," said Henry. "I *told* you that Rosalie would not be so foolish."

"Indeed that would be foolish," said Mistress Godechepe, "We had heard that you had accepted Sir Hugh..."

"No, I most certainly have not and I cannot imagine where the rumour has originated."

Henry Godechepe put a hand to the place where his heart rested. "Oh that is a relief."

He bent, took Rosalie's hand and kissed it. "It means that there is still a chance that you might accept a proposal from me?"

Rosalie was astonished into silence.

But her little devil filled the gap. 'Oh no. Not another one. Ah but this one is rich and a nice man with nice manners. And would make a good job of looking after you.'

She answered it immediately. "I do not need to be looked after."

"I think you know, sir, that I am intending to take a vow of celibacy."

"Are you still resolved upon it?"

"I am."

"It's just that it has been some time since you spoke of it and I thought perhaps you had changed your mind, since you had not yet achieved it."

"I have not changed my mind but...circumstances have...intervened to prevent my carrying it through. I shall do it as soon as I can, at St. Mary's church in town."

"Oh no...dear lady please...reconsider."

"My brother has never in his entire life been so smitten, Mistress Jourdemayne, " said Eleanor Godechepe. "I promise you no woman has ever captured his heart. But you...you are different."

Rosalie felt overwhelmed. "Oh Master Godechepe, I am flattered but..."

"Say please that, at the very least, you will think about it," said Henry. "And not rush into this vow too soon."

Ancelin Hayward watched from a distance. He cannot have failed to understand what was being said. But his eyes were on Eleanor, devouring her as if she might disappear in a puff of smoke.

Rosalie suddenly felt let down. She had no idea why. And she had no idea why she said,

"Sir, your confession leaves me speechless. I had no notion you felt this way about me..."

"From the moment I met you madam."

Rosalie ran her hand across her forehead. "Please leave me to think about it. I cannot possibly give you an answer now."

"I know. I know. It was most inappropriate of me to speak of it... at such a time."

"Today my thoughts are not my own, sir. A man I loved deeply as a father has left me unexpectedly. I must be allowed time to grieve."

"And so you shall. You shall have all the time you wish. Have I your permission to call again soon and..."

"You may do as you wish, sir."

The man beamed as if he had been given the world.

"Then I will wait."

*****

Rosalie and Bea were sorting apples picked from the orchard ready for pressing the next day when they heard the clop of a horse's hooves upon the cobbles of the yard.

"If that is Sir Hugh, I have no wish to see him," said Rosalie.

"Yes ma'am," said Bea wiping her hands down her sacking apron.

"No wait! Where is Master Hayward?"

"He is in the slaughter pens supervising the…"

"Peek around that corner and tell me if this is Sir Hugh, Bea. If it is, I will see him and I will have Master Hayward with me."

Bea cautiously peered around the edge of the building. "Ah no ma'am, 'tis not that particular knight. It is the other one."

"Sir Maurice FitzAlan?"

"Yes. He is dropping from his saddle now."

Rosalie heaved a sigh of relief. "Then we shall have no confrontation and have not the need for Master Hayward.."

Sir Maurice was looking around a little lost when Rosalie followed by Bea skirted the corner of the apple store which housed the cider press.

"Have you come to help us press the apples for cider, Sir Maurice?" said Rosalie nonchalantly. "We have a good crop this year." She smiled warmly at him.

The man bowed.

"Madam, if you are in need of help then I am happy to oblige."

"Ah no. I jest with you, sir. Do come in and take some cider with us."

Seated at the hall table, the man complimented her on the quality of her cider.

"Our Forceleap apples are famous for it. Though we scarcely have enough and I was thinking of planting further trees…"

"Extending your orchard? That is a capital idea, madam."

Bea and Rosalie exchanged glances.

"So what brings you to us on such a lovely morning, Sir Maurice?"

"Oh...nothing much. I simply came to ask if what I have heard is true; that poor Master Newbold is no more?"

Rosalie immediately lost all jollity. "You hear correctly. He died on Monday last and will be interred at Preshute on Friday." As soon as she thought of this event, a lump came into her throat and a prickling began at the back of her eye.

"I am so sorry to hear it. I am so very sorry for your loss." Then he realised that Rosalie had become upset.

"Oh madam, I did not mean to upset you," he said with a horrified expression. "It's just that the man and I, Master Newbold I mean came from the same area of Wiltshire..."

"Melksham?"

"That's right. And so we had much in common... him being a second son as am I."

"I knew that his birthplace was in the north of the county but did not know exactly where."

Sir Maurice went on to tell Rosalie that he and Master Newbold had conversed often after church at Preshute and that he was hoping to be able to attend his funeral.

"I have no right to prevent you from attending. Please, you will be welcome."

"Thank you."

"I hear that you suffered in the violent storm."

"A little damage to trees, nothing terrible."

Then there was a silence.

The man was looking at her with an adoring eye but was saying nothing.

'For a knight with an important job at the castle,' said her little devil, 'He is surprisingly modest and shy.'

"Unlike the other specimen of knighthood I know," said Rosalie.

"I beg your pardon, madam?"

"Nothing, Sir Maurice."

Once again they'd stumbled to a halt.

"I suppose you have come to ask me if I have yet made my vow of celibacy, sir knight? she said, thinking to forestall the next awkward question.

"Ah no...I knew that you had not yet achieved your goal. Master Newbold told me."

The mention of dear William set up another spasm in Rosalie's already wounded heart and she gave a slight sob.

"But you are a resolute woman and will no doubt secure that particular ambition soon."

His limpid blue eyes dwelt on her unhappy face. "Madam are you quite alright?"

Bea stepped forward to give her mistress succour but was too late; Rosalie burst into tears.

"I am so sorry Sir Maurice. The wound is raw as yet," she said. "I cannot quite believe he is gone."

"Neither can I," said the knight, "I was talking to him only last Sunday at church...He was quite well then..."

They then had to tell the man about the wound which William had sustained.

"Ah, that makes sense to me. I have had experience of such wounds proving fatal after a while..."He realised what he'd said as Rosalie's face creased again.

"Oh here I go again. I am so sorry for upsetting you."

The man stood, "I am not good at sensitive things, my poor lady, I am much more used to the gruff and bluff men of the castle. Please forgive me."

"You are a good man, Sir Maurice," said Rosalie. "And I thank you for coming today."

"Even though I have upset you?" His expression made him look like a small boy.

Much against her better judgement she took the man's hand and squeezed it.

"It is not you who has upset me, sir. It is the death of my steward, a man I loved like a father."

Suddenly she was clasped to his bosom and was crying into his shoulder.

Bea hovered on one leg wondering what to do but the moment did not last long. Rosalie tore herself away. "Oh do forgive me."

But not before Master Hayward had come in at the door of the hall and caught sight of the embrace.

CHAPTER TWELVE ~ GRIEF, ACCIDENT AND GOSSIP

Business of the farm engaged Rosalie for some days after the visits and at last the day of Master Newbold's funeral arrived.

Rosalie dressed with care in a dark cotte of blue and her beautiful fine oval linen veil with the added embellishment of a crown of gathered and stiffened linen. Over all, she swung her dark blue cloak of wool, lined with pale blue linen.

The cart rolled up to the door of the church, with Fulk driving as usual, and Master Hayward riding alongside on Filbert.

Many of the farm workers had trailed after the cart upon which their mistress was seated, for she had given permission for any who wished it, to attend the funeral.

The little church would be packed.

The weather was dull, not cold but grey and miserable; miserable enough for a funeral.

Rosalie Jourdemayne swept through the small porch and into the body of the church, wanting to be as small and insignificant as she could. So many neighbours and friends of Master Newbold's were watching her. She walked on demurely, her face down, to the front of the church and stood with her head bent. Crossing herself and genuflecting to the altar, she made her way to the left hand side, where waited Master Hayward and Bea and a few of the senior men of

Forceleap Farm.

The priest entered and the Latin began.

Rosalie was unaware of the words the priest spoke, even though she was quite able to translate and understand them. It was all over quickly and the coffin was carried to the graveyard where several of the congregation stood about with long faces. Others blended into the trees further out, not wishing to count themselves amongst the higher folk of the area.

Rosalie scanned the trees to the edge of the graveyard. Dark yews and turning oaks, their leaves, yellow, rust and red giving the only colour to such a dull day.

But just as the coffin was lowered into the earth, a shaft of sunlight pierced the clouds overhead and the graveyard as a whole was bathed in an amber glow. Rosalie looked up at the rays of Heaven and as she did so caught a movement of something to the hedge by the gate.

She stared.

Master Hayward looked to her quickly; she had gone very pale.

"Mistress Jourdemayne?" he asked solicitously watching her wide eyes as she stared into the distance. He followed her gaze.

Everyone else was engaged upon the lowering of the coffin and the words of the priest; no one else saw the tall, shadowy figure in a cabbage green cotte who, still and silent, loitered by the gate.

Ancelin narrowed his eyes and with a deal of concern in his face he turned to Rosalie.

"Do you see him, ma'am?"

She whispered, "I do. I see him."

Her eyes fully filled with tears for the first time that day, "He said he would not leave me…"

When Ancelin looked back, the figure had gone.

Coins were handed over and the requisite thanks given.

People began to turn away, to make for home or to go back to Forceleap for the funeral reception.

Master and Mistress Godechepe, who had stood at the back of the church, turned to their cart, saying that they would be delighted to come back to the farm. Sir Maurice gently took Rosalie's elbow and said that as much as he would love to enjoy the pleasure of Forceleap Farm once more, he had to get back to his duties at the castle. Rosalie nodded distractedly.

She noticed that Master Dankworth was not present at the funeral. 'Good,' said her little voice, 'then you do not have to suffer his interminable sycophancy.'

However, sadly, there was one person there whom Rosalie had no desire to see. He strode across the wet grass, his rust red split cotte flapping around his knees; his gold yellow belt gleaming in the sunlight.

He bowed.

"Mistress Jourdemayne."

"Sir Hugh."

"Please accept my apologies for not calling upon you before. I have been from the county on business these past few days."

"I did not expect you to call."

"I did not know your steward well but he seemed to me to be a fine fellow. I am sorry he has quitted this world."

"Not as sorry as I am, Sir Hugh," said Rosalie coldly.

The man tossed his golden locks and fingered his short cropped beard. "I am glad to meet you here...for"

"Oh?"

"I have something very important to say."

"Oh! Is this about the man who made an attack upon me, sir, in the church?"

Sir Hugh placed one hand upon his waist.

"Ah...that villain."

"What became of him? I should very much like to know."

Sir Hugh scratched the side of his nose. 'He is about to lie,' said her little voice.

"He was taken up by the town reeve and shut in the lockup, I hear. He has been in and out of trouble for years. My testimony will convict him and I suspect he will hang."

"Hang?"

"One less low and unsavoury creature to plague the world...eh?"

"Where there is one gone, another will take his place."

Sir Hugh smiled a reproving grin. "Now madam, you are somewhat cynical."

"Some might call me..realistic, Sir Hugh."

Rosalie felt the presence of Master Hayward creeping forward through the grass behind her.

Sir Hugh gave a cursory glance around. "Might we perhaps take a turn around the graveyard, madam...alone?"

"Ah no, sir. This event should not be turned into a stroll for pleasure."

"Then perhaps we should go into the porch?"

Rosalie turned and threaded her way across the dewy grass, to the church porch. She looked up at the stonework and swivelled in front of the door.

"What is it you wish to say?"

Sir Hugh did not realise that Hayward had followed them at a discreet distance and was listening.

"It must be deeply distressing for you, mistress, to lose such a vital member of your household," he said.

"He was more than a member of the household, sir. He was a beloved friend."

Sir Hugh's eyebrows rose.

"Friend you say?"

"Yes, a valued member almost as if he were family."

"I see. One must, do you not think, hold *family* in high esteem. One should always appreciate the value of blood and ...connection."

"I value friendship, and honesty more."

"As you should...as you should. But madam, Master Newbold was in your employ; he was not and could not be family," said a seemingly shocked knight of the realm.

"He was as good to me as a father, sir. I would have nothing said against him.'

"Oh I would say nothing. Except that I could detect no exceptional manners or accomplishment in the man."

"You did not know him. Say no more."

Sir Hugh fiddled with his sword belt. "Well...I suspect you are greatly in need of good company now."

"I am in need of *no* company at this very moment," said Rosalie.

"Oh come, come. Good company is hard to find. And when it *is* found..."

"Are you telling me sir, that you, on account of your breeding, manners and knightly education are good company?"

"Do you not think so, Mistress Jourdemayne?"

"Your esteem for rank and connection, Sir Hugh it seems, is far greater than mine."

The man laughed out loud.

"Oh no surely, mistress. You surely wish to make...*good connections.*"

"I wish to make no connections, sir."

The man heaved his body round in a gesture of disbelief. "Oh not *that* again. This vow of celibacy, which you have not yet made."

"No matter what you say, no matter what little plots you have hatched..."

"Plots?"

"I will make that vow. And yes. Plots. You are discovered, sir."

The knight threw up his hands, "You really are the most infuriating woman."

"I will not marry you. And it is despicable that you have cast about the rumour that you and I are betrothed."

"The kiss we exchanged, madam, in the church..."

"That kiss was as a result of a moment of fear and then gratitude. It had no meaning beyond the moment at all. You took advantage of my vulnerable state."

"No meaning? You ungrateful woman...I saved you from the ignominy of rape!"

"A rape which *you* had set up yourself!" Her voice rose in pitch and people still standing about in the graveyard looked over to them.

"Don't think that I have not uncovered what you did. You expected me to fall into your arms, and incidentally Forceleap Farm too, with indebtedness and respect."

"I... I can explain."

Rosalie pushed past the man in disgust and made for the sunlight beyond the porch.

Sir Hugh was not giving up easily.

"Rosalie, you cannot simply leave me like this..."

"I can. I will."

"But Rosalie, I am on fire for you. Please."

She turned and her face was furious.

"Sir, were you in actuality on fire, I would not even allow my dog to urinate upon you. Good day."

And with that rejoinder, she marched up the gravel path.

*****

Ancelin stood in full view of Sir Hugh and stared at the man malevolently.

"I would be extremely grateful, sir, if you would not visit my mistress again at Forceleap Farm. She has no wish to see you ever again."

"That is not for you to say."

"She has instructed me to say it. We both witnessed your disgusting payment to that man in the church and should it become necessary, *I* will find him, *I* will pay him and induce him to tell the truth of what you did, to the authorities."

Sir Hugh spluttered incoherently.

"And what then your good family name, your connections, breeding and rank?"

He turned with a swish of his green cotte and took Rosalie's elbow and walked her to the cart.

"Did I do well? she asked.

"You did very well," smiled Ancelin.

*****

"What is the matter, what has happened?" cried Rosalie as she ran beside the men carrying a body.

"He slipped in the barn and a beast trod on him, ma'am," said Warin Logge. "I suspect a broken arm."

"Take him into the hall. I will look at him."

They struggled into the building with the hurt man moaning between them.

'It is Thomas Cotterill, oh no. He is not a young man, he will not mend quickly,' said Rosalie's little voice inside her head.

Warin Logge made the man comfortable on the hall bench. "Aw ma'am, don't worry, he's as a toadskin, tough as they come. He'll mend."

"Let me see."

It was obvious the man's forearm was broken.

"Fetch Master Ancelin."

"Aye ma'am."

"Well he won't be much use now," said one of the men."That's the end of his arm."

"Don't talk like that," said Rosalie and she chivvied the men from the hall. "That helps no one."

The man Thomas was moaning in pain and Rosalie sent Bea for some willow bark for the man to chew on. She knew that this was effective as a pain reliever and always kept some in the house.

Ancelin Hayward came running into the hall a little later.

"Logge here told me what happened? Is there anything I can do?"

Rosalie had been waiting for him and whilst she waited she had looked carefully at the man's arm.

"There is no damage to the skin, just bruises. The break seems to me to be a clean one in one of the long bones."

"You have felt the bone?"

"I have. Master Cotterill has been most brave and allowed me to examine him," she smiled.

"Must it be took off?" said Logge who had come back in with Master Hayward.

"Oh...no..not that!" cried the poor patient. "Not that...anything but that!" a sweat breaking out on his forehead.

"No. We must, I think, pull the bone back into place and..."

"How? How can that be done?" asked Ancelin.

Rosalie squared her shoulders. "When I was a young woman, I once saw a break very similar to this."

"Was that the sailor man who broke his wrist, ma'am?" said Bea.

"It was." She looked at Master Cotterill and smiled sweetly, "And I can say that that sailor was not the brave man you are, Thomas."

The man had been shaking in shock but at Rosalie's words, he sat up with a determined look on his face.

"Get him to a chair," she said. And roll up the shirt sleeve as high as you can."

"What do you intend?" asked Hayward.

Rosalie, feigning a confidence she did not really possess, said,

"I saw the doctor at the time, put back the bones of the man's wrist and bind them in place."

Ancelin stared at her. "You think you can do this?"

"With your help and the grace of God. I am willing to try."

Cotterill was now shaking again.

"Thomas, will you allow me to try to mend your arm by putting the bone back into place? I can think of no other remedy. I cannot promise that it will work. I cannot promise that once the bone knits...if it does, that you will not carry the result of the break for the rest of your life but it will at least save your arm from further damage."

Thomas Cotterill, chewed again on his willow bark flake.

"Aw ma'am, I gotta put myself into your 'ands and God's. The pain is mortal bad and I don't want them to take off my arm...no..my old 'eart would never survive that."

Rosalie nodded. "Will you hold the man's arm as straight as you can, Ancelin? Grip it...here. And keep it as still as you can."

Thomas closed his eyes.

"The pain will be severe for a moment, Thomas, I think, but you may bite on something if you wish."

"Ah no mistress...just get on with it. I can bear the pain."

"Ancelin, are you ready?"

Bea settled the man's shoulders into her bosom. "Lean on me, Thomas," she said.

Logge knelt down in front of the patient and took the man's legs to immobilise him further and to prevent him from wriggling.

Ancelin took hold of the man's arm and his fingers closed around Thomas' wrist. The break was halfway up the arm forearm.

"Now all of us together we hold tight."

Rosalie's slight fingers took hold of Master Cotterill's hairy arm with one hand either side of the break.

"On my count, Ancelin, I wish you to pull the man's arm straight. A straight and as hard as you can. One, two, three."

Grimacing with the effort of fighting against Thomas' natural desire to draw

back, Ancelin pulled.

Rosalie pushed the bone, which she could feel grating under her fingers.

"Now let go."

Cotterill let out a huge cry and subsided into sobs.

Her gentle fingers probed the wound and Ancelin once more took Thomas' hand but now with no vehemence in the grip.

"Is it done.?"

"The bone is back in place. Now it must be bound so that it has a chance to knit. It must not be bent. It must be kept straight."

Bea relinquished the sobbing Thomas and ran for linen to bind the arm.

"There will be much bruising but that is something you must bear."

Thomas sniffled and wiped his nose and eyes with his sleeve.

"By all that's 'Oly and virtuous ma'am, you are a good woman. I commend me to God now, for you 'ave done your part."

"Can you get home?"

"I can take him in the cart." said Warin Logge.

"Where does he live, Warin?"

"At the bottom of Long Deadmans, ma'am."

"Me wife is there and…" began Cotterill.

"Then take him home and explain to his wife what has happened and what should happen. And remember it must be kept still and straight."

Thomas managed to grab Rosalie's hand with his good hand as she passed him and he kissed it.

"God bless you Mistress Jourdemayne. Even if it don't work, I will always remember your kindness."

She smiled and patted his shoulder. "Plenty of ale or cider, Thomas. That will dull the pain."

"Oh aye ma'am. That I can take!"

Whilst she was sorting some willow bark preparation for Thomas to take home, Ancelin Hayward came up behind her.

"That was very capable, mistress Rosalie. Did you really see this done a while ago?"

"Yes I did and the success of it stayed with me so that I remembered what to do."

Bea came up with the bandages.

"We must find a piece of wood which will keep the arm straight and then bind it up."

Warin went off to complete that task.

Ancelin hunkered down beside the very pale patient and gave him a cup of cider.

"You are lucky we have such a calm and composed woman in Mistress Jourdemayne, Thomas. There are not many who would know what to do, let alone be able to do it without fainting or flinching."

"There is nothing remarkable about what I did. And I cannot see a fellow man in pain and ruined for the rest of his life without me trying to do something."

"God bless you ma'am," said Thomas again.

Logge returned with the piece of wood and together Ancelin and Rosalie bound up the arm.

"I will come to you, Thomas in a few days and see how you are. Long Deadman's Field is not so far for me to walk from here."

"My wife and me will be pleased to see you, mistress."

"How about work, mistress?" asked Warin Logge. "Ol' Thomas won't be able to...."

"He must not work. He must keep as still as he can. I forbid you to work Thomas, do you hear?"

"Aye ma'am but what are we to do for money?"

"You will be paid as if you were doing a full day's work, Thomas. I will see to it that the money comes to you. And food so that you need not work your field."

"For how long…"

"As long as it takes your arm to mend."

They all looked round at each other. "That is most generous, mistress," said Ancelin.

"And if I fail and the arm is useless, then we shall think again about what you might do, Thomas."

Thomas had now drunk two full beakers of cider and was a little tipsy.

"Lord above! You are not a good woman; you are an angel," he said and was immediately embarrassed by his utterance.

*****

The day of the dinner invitation drew close. Master and Eleanor Godechepe were coming to dine as promised.

Rosalie and Bea bustled about the house making everything spic and span and then turned their attentions to what they might eat.

"Master Godechepe is very interested in our beef, Bea, so that is what we shall give him."

Bea grinned mischievously, "You're going out of your way to do the best for the man, ma'am. You sure you don't have a reason?"

"They have been very kind to me, Bea, " said Rosalie, "Why should I not wish to please them?"

"Not that you *like* Master Godechepe, then?"

"I like him, yes. But only as a friend."

"You're not goin'ta marry him then?"

"Bea get on with your cutting. I want that parsley really fine."

"Yes ma'am."

A little later, Rosalie took out the glass cup which Master Godechepe had given her and looked at it carefully.

She was still of the opinion that she could not keep it. But, oh how lovely it felt in the hand and what a delight it was to the eye. She put it on the table before her and, her head upon her hand, she stared into the depths of the colours dreamily.

Had it really come all the way from the lands which Christ had trodden? Sunshine radiated from every glint and glimmer. Yes, she could well believe it did hail from such a far distant and heated place.

She was leaning on her folded arms on the table, staring at it, when Ancelin Hayward came into the hall and paused in the doorway, watching.

"Master Cotterill sends his regards, ma'am."

Rosalie jumped.

"Oh forgive me, I did not mean to startle you."

"You have been down to Long Deadmans?"

"Aye, I have this morning. He is still in some pain as you would imagine but..." Ancelin almost laughed though the subject matter did not really warrant it. "He is most amused that he can waggle his fingers without too much pain."

"That is good to hear."

He came into the room. "What have you there?"

Rosalie reached for the felted cloth in which the little cup had rested.

"It is a gift from Master Henry Godechepe...a costly gift and most beauteous. I am almost afraid to handle it."

Ancelin's face took on a hard look. "They come to dinner today, do they not?"

"They do."

"I will be off to my house then. There are still a few things I wish to collect from there. I'll take the small cart."

"Oh Ancelin," Rosalie stood and took a step towards him. "I had hoped that you would join us for dinner."

"Dinner?"

"I have Henry and Eleanor Godechepe, and me; Bea will serve and so I have an uneven number. That will never do. It is most unlucky."

"Oh," said Ancelin with a disappointed air. "Then I would be pleased to attend to make up the numbers." He bowed and left.

'Well, what's the matter with him?' asked Rosalie's little devil. 'Wasn't he pleased to be asked? He is a gentleman now.'

Rosalie watched the man walk across the yard with a downcast air. "I cannot imagine what is wrong with him," she said and she went inside to wrap up the little cup for the last time.

*****

Dinner was taken at the fifth hour of the day before the sun was at its highest.

Master Godechepe regaled them with stories of the days when he imported wine from France and Germania.

"Oh sister mine, you're right. The very worst part of it all was the sea journey there and back."

"Oh Master Godechepe, why is that?" said Rosalie.

"The food madam, it was inedible. Unlike your fine fare. Very fine if

I might compliment you."

"Thank you, sir."

"Oh, we had cooks and suchlike on the ships, we weren't complete barbarians but oh dear, they were not of the highest quality."

Ancelin sharing a plate with Mistress Godechepe, picked up a piece of beef.

"Two or three days of inconvenience, sir. Surely that is as long as it took you to come and go from Kent to France."

"And a day or so, sometimes longer for the negotiations."

"Ah yes. But then you were on dry land, albeit foreign."

"Where I prefer to be," said Henry, good naturedly.

"What made you leave Kent, sir? asked Hayward. "To become a sheep farmer here?"

"Well...I had made my fortune - there is money in wine - and I hankered after a simpler life and tedium was, frankly setting in with the journeying to and fro. And I am getting no younger."

"But, you had no experience of farming?"

"I had a small piece of land upon which I had sheep in the county of Kent. Naturally I did not work it myself but my men were good. I brought them with me here, those who would follow."

"And you brought your sister, Mistress Eleanor from Kent too?" Ancelin's eyes sparkled.

"I did. She was happy to come to Wiltshire."

"And yet she has not the same accent as you, sir?" said Rosalie. "You are a Kentish man, are you not?"

"I am and my voice betrays it," said Henry taking a sip of his wine.

"And yet Mistress Godechepe has the accent of Devizes of Wiltshire, sir," added Ancelin quickly. "I have noted it, since that is my home town."

Godechepe did not flinch but Rosalie watched as Eleanor's face coloured.

"I think that is because before she came to live on my land, she resided in that fair town for a while, did you not, my dear?"

"I did and I have such an ear that it took me no time at all to copy the local speech."

"Ah…"

"But then, I did not like the town and decided to come closer to Henry."

"I see."

Ancelin speared another piece of beef from the serving plate. "And you have never been a married man, sir?"

Henry laughed. "No, never. I have never found a woman I wanted *to* marry. Until now." Henry gazed longingly at Rosalie who tried to change the subject quickly.

"It is not…"

"So you were unmarried when you lived in Kent?" went on Ancelin Hayward.

"Before I came here in 1201, I was without a wife, yes."

Rosalie gave Hayward a scouring look. She almost wanted to kick him under the table but he was not close enough.

"Can we not talk of marriage please. You know it is a subject upon which my heart does not like to dwell."

"You are still determined in your making of a vow, then?" said Henry. "Am I not to hope…never to think…"

"As much as I like and respect you, Master Godechepe…"

"Henry…please."

"I will not marry."

"This is final?"

"It is. I go to the church on Friday to arrange it with the priest."

"Then I must resign myself to a broken heart, madam." Henry looked downcast.

"You will restrict yourself to works of charity and helping those less fortunate than yourself?"

"When I take this vow, I will be conscious of that obligation, yes."

"Well you have made a good start it seems," said Eleanor Godechepe. "We heard that you performed a life saving act upon a man on the farm the other day. That was brave and selfless of you."

"I did what any other woman would have done for a fellow being who was suffering."

"Oh no! said Eleanor, "I would not have had the first idea how to help. It was fortuitous you were here."

"You are without doubt," said Henry, "The most remarkable woman. Is it any wonder you have taken my heart like no other."

"Oh, I am sure there must be a lady somewhere who will take your heart," said Rosalie.

"Never. I am through with wooing."

"You have no desire to return to wine, sir?" asked Ancelin.

"They were great days when I brought wine over from France, from Burgundy, Anjou, Bordeaux but no, a man reaches a certain age and he has a desire to settle down, find a wife, put down roots and maybe have some children."

"Ah, there you and I would never be suited, sir," said Rosalie bravely.

"Oh…?"

"I have no desire for children."

"You do not?" said Eleanor. "Why, begging your pardon, is that not most unwomanly. Do not all married women desire children?"

"Not this one."

"You have none madam?" asked Ancelin pointedly, of Mistress Godechepe.

This time, Rosalie did find his foot under the table and ground her toes into his shoe.

Eleanor looked down but did not reply. Henry bowled on with,

"I am sure if you were to find the right man…"

"No, sir. I am determined."

"Surely you wish to have someone upon which to settle Forceleap Farm, after you are gone, do you not?"

"No, sir. I do not. Not particularly."

"A son to follow you, to take on Forceleap?"

"No sir. And if you are to speak like this about me, then I must declare this subject utterly closed or dinner will be over."

Ancelin cleared his throat.

"I am sure Master Godechepe does not mean…"

"No, no more."

The rest of the dinner was accomplished in a frosty atmosphere.

As the Godechepes were about to leave, Rosalie, standing on the step of the hall brought out the felt wrapped parcel.

"Master Godechepe. Please accept this, your gift to me, back again. As much as the item pleases me, I must refuse it."

"But, my dear, it was given in friendship. I do not need for you to .."

"Please take it. I cannot accept it."

The man's hand came out reluctantly to receive it from her.

"I see."

"Goodbye and thank you for coming. We have enjoyed your company."

They rode away at last.

Rosalie turned to Ancelin. "Why on earth were you so discourteous to them?"

"I was not discourteous."

"All those questions? They were almost *accusations*. I thought that you admired Mistress Godechepe."

Ancelin bit his lip. "I cannot tell you. It is not important... now."

*****

"Ah now mistress, sit yourself down. Why, all my melancholy thoughts 'ave flown with your appearance," said Thomas Cotterill grinning from his seat by the fire.

"Melancholy, Thomas. Why should you be sad?" said Rosalie, taking off her gloves and finding herself a small stool. The house had two rooms only, with a central fire and very little furniture.

She looked around. "You are cosy here in your little cott. And you have your wife...to nurse you. You shall not want for money, I promise."

"Aye, my Maudie is the best of women. And you are the most generous lady."

The wife of Thomas Cotterill bobbed a curtsey.

"She won't let me get a mooning about and bein' maudlin."

"I am glad to hear it."

Rosalie pointed to his dirty bandage. "And the arm, how is it?"

"I can wriggle my fingers so I suppose, it ain't all broke. I got you to thank for that."

"I hope you are staying put and giving it a chance to mend as I advised."

"'E is ma'am. Though 'e gets quite a sore head with boredom."

"Oh, I is. But...but..." laughed Thomas. "It always ends with us laughing out, don't it Maudie?"

"Laughter is very good for pain, Thomas," said Rosalie, smiling.

"Aye. Maudie brings me all the gossip of the countryside and we laugh about it over our ale at night."

"Gossip?"

"Oh aye. She keeps her ears and eyes open and brings me all the tales of the doin's in the wider world."

"I 'ave a sister as works at Master Dankworth's and we 'ave a daughter at a house in town. Not to mention my brother who works for Farmer Godechepe," said Maud.

"For Master Godechepe?"

"'E is a shepherd there...but for 'ow much longer we don't know."

"Has he plans to move on?"

"Plans? Bless me...my brother never made plans in 'is whole life. No. It might be that 'e becomes laid aside."

Rosalie was about to ask why, when Thomas, stirring himself said. "Now Maud brought me news last night, that Farmer Godechepe was at Forceleap in the day."

"How did she hear this?" said Rosalie and the little voice inside her head took in a breath to complain that, again, her private business was not so private.

"We do know that Farmer Godechepe admires you greatly," said Maud with a wink..

"How did you hear that?"

"Oh you cannot keep a bit 'o news from gaddin' about the countryside," Thomas touched his nose. "You got it from ol' Mother Angel, my love, didn't you?"

"Well I must have you know that Master Godechepe may think highly of me but I am not reciprocal in my feelings...I do not feel the same way about him. He has declared his affection but I am not about to accept it."

The two rustics looked at each other and Thomas winked.

"We are very pleased to 'ear it. *Oh we are.*"

"Oh? Oh why is that?"

Mistress Cottterill then found herself a stool and sat by Rosalie. She took up a stick and poked at the fire.

"We don't like to tell tales."

"Tales?" said Rosalie. 'And yet they'll repeat gossip with impunity,' said her little devil.

"We only tell tales what we know to be true and as yet we don't know it's absolutely true...but..."

"Yes." Rosalie found herself leaning forward in impatience.

"Farmer Godechepe ain't as rich as 'e makes out."

"Oh?"

"'E's got debts in the town and to the Jewish men. And like I say, 'e might be laying off soon."

"Oh that is very sad. And most sad for the men who work for him."

"Now, Maudie, didn't I say that Mistress Jourdemayne was the finest lady in Wiltshire. She thinks of others...always of others," said Thomas.

"Aye Tom, you did."

"How did this misfortune come about? Do you know?"

The two exchanged a glance.

"Well, first it were the winter."

"We all suffered there," said Rosalie. "It delayed our planting by months and we had to feed the cattle... Our sheep had to be rescued from the snow on the downs and folded..."

"Aye, but you have a care for your beasts...and you 'ave a good manager."

"You mean to say that Master Godechepe did not look after his ewes? Even in all that bad weather."

"'E ain't a farmer is 'e? 'E's a merchant."

"I see."

"And I 'ave 'eard..." said Maud

"Yes?"

"That he spends money what he 'asn't got. On that woman of 'is... and..."

"Woman?"

"Say no more Maudie," said Thomas Cotterill, suddenly serious. "The mistress don't want to 'ear about that."

"Why don't I want to hear."

Again the knowing look.

"Well you *like* the man. And it would pain you to know..."

"I do not like the man...that much," said Rosalie with irritation.

"Well just let us say that all is not what it seems up there at Cutwythy Farm."

"Oh Thomas, you cannot leave me hanging like this," said Rosalie. "Whatever do you mean?"

Thomas took a large swig of his cider pot and shook his head. "I daren't say any more."

"Why not?"

"I don't wanna spoil Master 'Ayward's story."

"Story?"

"Aye 'e was 'ere yesterday. And 'e was asking advice."

"Advice, Thomas...of you?"

"Aye. He was sort of pullin' things together and 'e came to us to... well, put it together."

"Master Hayward did?"

"Aye. A finer man never lived."

"You ask 'im, when you get 'ome, Mistress Jourdemayne. 'E knows it all."

Rosalie worried at the inside of her cheek all the way home.

"What *did* Ancelin know? Why did he not tell her what he *did* know?"

She marched into the hall and bellowed for Bea who came running from the kitchen,

"Ma'am?"

"Where is Master Hayward?"

"Ah, he's gone to East Kennet to his cott to fetch back the rest of his things."

"When will he return."

"I don't know as he will tonight."

"Thank you."

Now Rosalie had to worry the inside of her mouth further as she waited for Ancelin to return.

CHAPTER THIRTEEN ~ THE TRUTH

It was Friday.

Ancelin did not return the next morning either. Rosalie decided to go to the town alone and speak to Father Torold.

Rosalie had Filbert saddled and with Bea riding pillion, she jogged into town. As Bea had predicted Master Hayward had not returned the previous night. Nor did he turn up the next morning.

Father Torold was drinking his morning ale in his little cott when Rosalie scratched on the door and called out.

"Father Torold. It's Rosalie Jourdemayne."

"Ah...come in...come in." The jovial priest made her comfortable in his small home.

"You are wanting to make a vow of celibacy, I think? Do I remember correctly?"

"That is correct. I know that it is unusual for women as young as I am to do it but, I am determined."

As she said that, for the very first time a little disquiet invaded her heart. But she didn't listen to it.

Father Torold nodded. "I understand your willingness to become a vowess, Mistress Jourdemayne. A lady such as yourself; one with much property and wealth, might seek to avoid remarriage to protect her state of independence. Of course, the state of celibacy with the dignity it affords, is a capital opportunity for spiritual development in this world and eternal happiness in the next."

"I have realised this."

Torold looked at her closely.

"I would also become a vowess because I wish to escape the ever present and overwhelming pressure, to remarry."

"Who is pressurising you?"

"Oh Sir Priest, you have no idea how many suitors I have fended off this past month or so," said Rosalie seriously. "I am greatly perturbed in spirit. Threats, plots and evil persuasions have become daily worries. And I even fear for my life."

'Do you?' said her little devil.

"No not quite,but that might be the next thing," she answered in her head.

"Men seek to annexe Forceleap Farm, father, for with *me* comes the farm and that is their real reason for pursuing me, even though I reject every advance."

"You are saying that your vow would be a means of ensuring your personal safety?"

"I...yes...I am. Heavens knows what will happen next."

Rosalie then went on to tell Father Torold about the flood, the fire in the orchard and her almost rape though she did not give any names.

"You poor woman."

"And so you see why I feel so vulnerable."

"It is not a thing to be done lightly but I can see that you have thought about it deeply. Once made the vow can only be rescinded by an appeal to the Pontiff. To break a vow is a serious crime."

"I know it."

"We cannot do it immediately. We need to contact the bishop and he must come, or you must go to him, in order to make your vow before him.

"Oh..I had no idea."

"Then he will bestow upon you a ring, a mantle and often, a veil.

You will then promise to live stably in the chaste life you profess and devote your life to good works."

"And Forceleap Farm?"

"Indeed."

"Then we must contact the bishop. Do you think I will be able to convince him of the seriousness of my intention?"

"It will take some time but, yes. I will do that for you. And as far as your intention is concerned...Many women who make the vow are wealthy. Indeed it is a desirable state, for no one has responsibility for you. The bishop I am sure will view you favourably."

Rosalie sighed with relief and grasped the hands of Father Torold.

"Oh thank you...thank you," she said. "I feel better already."

*****

The autumn had run on in a series of warm and sunny days, punctuated by grey skies and cool winds. The swallows left the barns for...wherever they went. The little flycatchers who'd nested in the ivy were seen no more. Everyone began to think about Christmas, for Michaelmas had come and gone.

It seemed to Rosalie that Master Hayward avoided her and one day, after her trip to St. Mary's, she caught him coming over the orchard field with a rake over his shoulder.

"Ancelin. Are you avoiding me?"

"Certainly not, ma'am."

"Then come and take dinner with me, there is something I wish to ask you."

Reluctantly, it seemed to Rosalie, he downed tools, washed his hands and came into the hall.

"Ancelin...I am convinced that you are staying away from the farmhouse. You have not used your room for two days."

"I have been exceedingly busy."

"Well now you must be unbusy and answer me a question."

"If I can."

"I have been told by Master and Mistress Cotterill that you know something about Master Godechepe. They seem convinced that you are biding your time to tell me something."

Ancelin sat at the table and looked at the food laid out. His appetite had gone completely.

"Ma'am...I hardly know where to begin."

"Thomas seemed to think that there was some...irregularity in Master Godechepe's affairs."

Ancelin leaned forward and looked down at his hard worked hands.

"You like the man. It would not be right for me to...I cannot..."

"*You* seem to hold an affection for *Mistress* Godechepe. I have seen you..."

Hayward looked up quickly. "Nothing could be further from the truth."

Rosalie shuffled to the edge of her seat to be closer to him.

"If you have an affection for her, then you must tell me."

"Why must I tell you?"

Rosalie's little devil said… 'He has you now!'

"Because I want to know."

"I can tell you now truthfully that I have *no* affection for Mistress Godechepe."

"Then why do you look at her like a lovelorn boy?" Rosalie's nostrils flared with...what was it? Anger? Indignation? Jealousy?

Ancelin threw back his head and laughed. He laughed so hard it made the rafters of the hall ring.

"Lovelorn?"

"Well perhaps that is not quite the right word. But you must admit that whenever you see her you are struck dumb and can do nothing but stare and on one occasion in particular, insult her, through nerves, I have supposed."

Ancelin was still laughing.

"Nerves? You think I am nervous around her?"

"Well...yes. There is certainly something going on."

Ancelin sliding up the bench, came one seat nearer.

"I hold no affection for the woman. I know where she comes from...I know who she is."

"She is Master Godechepe's sister from Kent," said Rosalie, confused. "Isn't she?"

"She most certainly is not."

"Then...who?"

"She is his *mistress* and has been for the four years he has lived in the area - perhaps before." Ancelin sat back. "She has never been to Kent."

"But..."

"The man Godechepe is a liar. The woman who poses as Eleanor Godechepe is the widow of a sempster in Devizes. Her name is Eleanor Fabricant. She is no more his virgin sister than I am a knight of the realm."

"Why the subterfuge?"

Ancelin looked a little worried now.

"I cannot prove it but...I suspect the woman lives with him as his wife, when away from prying eyes. They are not married. He will not marry her, for what benefit to him would there be? "

"Benefit? The widow of a sempster must surely have some marriage piece or..."

"She is penniless. Her husband left her nothing. All she has is her good looks with..."

"Oh you admit then, that you think she is good looking?"

He did not answer. "Her good looks with which she managed to snare Master Godechepe."

"But surely he knows that..."

Hayward laughed again. "He knows...of course he knows. He passes her off as his sister so that he is free to move amongst the wealthy ladies of Wiltshire in search of a wife. She is very useful in making introductions. It is easier to trust a man who is close to his sister, is it not?"

"A wife but that is..."

"Do not think that he will slough her off when you are wed. When he is married, he will carry on as normal with his mistress with all the added benefit of a legal wife. And Forceleap Farm to boot."

"Never. I have never considered him for a husband."

Rosalie's brow furrowed.

She heard Bea telling her in her head, to stop it or if the wind blew she would stick like it. She straightened out her expression.

"How do you know all this?"

"I knew the woman in Devizes when I was a young man. As I say, that was when she was married to a sempster living on the market place. Fabricant drank; everyone knew it. One night he was discovered dead in a pool of his own vomit and Eleanor became a widow."

"And then she took up with Master Godechepe?"

"I suppose that's true for I then went to Swinedun for work and finally came here to Forceleap and lost all my contact with my home town and its gossip."

"And that is why you knew she spoke as a Devizes woman?"

"She did not recognise *me*. But I knew her. *Eventually*."

"That is why you have been staring at her...?"

"Trying to place her. To work out where I'd seen her before. It was only the other day that it dawned on me. She was never as exquisitely dressed nor had the manners of a fine lady when she lived in Devizes."

"What does Master Cotterill know?" asked Rosalie.

"He has heard from his brother-in-law that the farm is in trouble. The man Godechepe is the sort who leaves debts wherever he goes. That is why he is looking for a wealthy widow to marry?"

"And I am a wealthy widow...Oh Ancelin!" Rosalie covered her face with her hands. "Was I so taken in?"

"We all were until the other day."

Ancelin took Rosalie's hands. "But now we are one step ahead."

"You are certain that Henry Godechepe is not a man of fortune?"

"Mistress Cotterill had cause to be talking to Madame Angel..."

"The old woman who lives close by Cutwythy Farm?"

"And she overheard Master Godechepe and his farm manager arguing."

"Arguing? You and I never argue."

"In the overheard conversation it was declared that Godechepe was in need of yet another loan."

"But the man is rich. He sold his wine business…"

"He was. But he is now in great want of money."

"And he pays his attentions to me because…"

"He wants Forceleap and your money."

Rosalie was utterly appalled.

"Sir Hugo…Master Godechepe, Master Dankworth… all villains."

"Ah, Master Dankworth, I think, cannot be set in the same box as the other two."

"But you said…"

"I did tell you that really, he has your best interests at heart…and I think he does. He is just over zealous."

"But the damming of the streams?"

"Not Master Dankworth I think, after all."

Rosalie thought back to the day when she had spoken to Ralph Dankworth about the floods. His face had been very open with not a trace of mendacity.

"If not him, then…"

"Godechepe?"

"The fire in the orchard?"

"A metal groom set to catch the lightning. Did you notice that Godechepe's house had been recently thatched. It occurred to me that the metal groom may have come from there."

"And the stealing of Dyamant?"

"I told you and William that there had never been a sheepfold upon the down where Godechepe said he found Dyamant. I believe he simply abducted her and then when he saw us searching, turned up with her."

"To make me grateful to him?"

"And you *were* grateful."

"But not grateful enough to marry him."

Part of Rosalie was very angry indeed. Part of her felt used and vulnerable.

She stood abruptly.

"He has sought to intimidate me, to fool me, to ruin me."

Tears sprang to her eyes but these were tears of frustration and anger.

"Well...I have organised with Father Torold that I will make my vow as soon as the bishop can be made aware I wish to do it. Then no one... NO one will be able to trick me into becoming a wife."

"Rosalie. Please." Ancelin stood up to be level with her. "Do not do this thing."

"Whyever not?"

"Because I could not bear it."

Rosalie looked at him deeply. He backed away to the door.

"Ancelin?"

He backed into Bea coming in from the yard.

"Mistress, it's Sir Maurice again. He's come from the castle."

Then Ancelin did something he had never before done. He tugged on his forelock as a villein might do to his lord. As if she was his liege lady.

"Mistress Rosalie," he said. And he was gone through the door.

Rosalie followed him quickly but he was striding across the yard, passing Sir Maurice FitzAlan.

"Good day, Hayward."

"Good day, Sir Maurice."

Rosalie looked through the courtyard hedge, up into the orchard. All was quiet there, all work done.

A shadowy figure in a cabbage green cotte stepped from behind one of the trees. It drifted in sight.

"William!" she called out.

Ancelin looked back at her, then following her gaze; he too turned to look at the figure.

It hovered in their sight for just a few moments, shivering as a scene does when the weather is extremely warm and heat haze makes play with things, and then it was gone.

Ancelin looked back at Rosalie. And then he too disappeared.

*****

Rosalie smiled at Sir Maurice FitzAlan. "You are most welcome, sir. Will you take some refreshment?"

"Ah no...thank you. Do not trouble yourself. I will not be here long."

"Your duties at the castle draw you away?"

"Indeed."

"Then sit please, for a short while and tell me how things are in the town."

"Ha, ha, Mistress Jourdemayne. I am not the person to ask about the town. I rarely go there."

"I did not see you at Preshute church last Sunday, for worship?"

"No, I attended St. Peter's. I was on duty."

Sir Maurice laid his hand upon his sword hilt.

'It really is a very fine weapon,' said her little voice. 'He really is a striking example of manliness.' Rosalie's eyes ranged over the man. 'And very handsome.'

"Sir...you seem a little discomfited?"

"I worshipped at St. Peter's and it was there, after the service, that I heard a very...a very...worrying and upsetting thing."

"You did?"

Sir Maurice licked his lips. "I heard that you had accepted a proposal to marry Sir Hugo of Yatesbury but that once you had plighted your troth, the villain gave you up. Rejected you. Wickedly abandoned you..."

"Oh!"

"Is this true? I must say that, from what I know about the man, this is not out of character and you have probably had a lucky escape..."

"No, sir. I have never plighted myself to Sir Hugh. It was a foul rumour put about by him, in order that he get his hands on Forceleap Farm. He has always had a desire to...in his own words, marry Pennyhooks to Forceleap."

Now it was Sir Maurice's turn to say "Oh."

"He did try to coerce me...forcefully, I must say but, Sir Maurice, I resisted, as I would resist any man."

Maurice looked down at his feet.

"So you were not jilted?"

"No. I was never betrothed to him in the first place." Rosalie wondered where Sir Maurice had obtained this information. And then she remembered her manager saying that rumours could be spread by more than one man. 'Ancelin,' she thought. 'It's him!'

The man let out a huge sigh. "Then, I am content." He suddenly looked a little sheepish. "If it were true I *was* intending to go and teach the man a lesson and rescue your honour ma'am. Now I shall be content to speak ill of him at every opportunity I get."

"Speak ill of him?"

"We rarely move in the same circles but when we do, I shall not be kind."

"Please do not risk injury or your good name on account of poor Rosalie Jourdemayne," she said smiling sweetly at him.

"Madam I was willing to lay down my life for your reputation. My good name is as nothing..."

"Oh Sir Maurice. I am very grateful and flattered that you think so highly of me."

"Ma'am, I am a man of few words. I have not the silver tongue of other men. I live amongst gruff soldiers nearly every day of my life. I have no sisters and so no feminine influence in my life. I cannot help but be totally captivated by your charm, intelligence, beauty and goodness of heart. There I have said it. Madam, I love you with all my heart."

Rosalie sat back on her chair.

"Oh, Sir Maurice. That is very sweet of you.."

"But I know, yes, I know, that you would never accept me as a husband. I have no position. I am a second son with no fortune, no land save that which I *might* be able to gain in the service of my Lord and King. I can offer you nothing."

"Except your heart," she said playfully.

"Yes, ma'am, my heart. But that will not be enough for a lady as wonderful as you. There is no doubt that you have penetrated my soul. I live half in agony, half in anticipation, unjustifiable, I know. I know that you can not marry me. I know that you are set upon this vow you will make. I just could not let you do it not knowing that there is one man who would marry and love you to the world's end if he could. But you must know that I could never be a farmer...I am a soldier through and through. And so...it would not be a good match..."

There was then a pause in which Sir Maurice became quite embarrassed.

"Oh sir. That was a fine speech. And there is no doubt to me that it is from the heart. But, Sir Maurice, I do not love you. I admire you, yes. I do not love you. I am sorry. I do not. And I will not marry where I do not love."

"No. I know that. But I had to tell you."

She took his hand. "We can be friends?"

"Aye, we can be friends," he said cheerily and smiled on a sigh. "Then I am content."

She led him to the outer door.

"You will always be welcome at Forceleap Farm," she said, "Why I never had a brother...you will be welcome as a brother sir. And that relationship allows this..."

And she gave him a quick peck on the cheek.

Ancelin Hayward came around the corner of the hay barn just as Rosalie lifted her lips to Maurice's cheek and his heart sank to his boots.

CHAPTER FOURTEEN
THE FORCELEAP

Rosalie festered for the rest of the morning. How dare Henry Godechepe play with her in such a way. Then she began to doubt what had been said and thought, worrying her lip, what if this is an untruth? What if this is gossip put about by malicious people wishing to impugn Master Godechepe.

No, Ancelin would never be so taken in. Surely.

But in the next moment she had resolved to go to Cutwythy Farm and have a frank discussion with Master Henry Godechepe. She would have it from his lips. Only then would she believe the story. She had no doubt that if Henry was guilty as charged, that she would find him out by a word, a deed or a look.

Fulk saddled Filbert again and Rosalie trotted off across the downs, her anger building with every mile. The wind had risen and there were a few drops of rain but Mistress Jourdemayne was not to be defeated by a few drops of rain.

As the roofs of Cutwythy Farm came into view, her anger abated a little and she rehearsed what she would say in her head.

If Master Godechepe was a gentleman, he would admit his folly and accept her chastisement. If not...well we would see.

Rosalie did not smile as she was helped down from her horse by the groom. She looked around.

"Where is your master?"

"At this hour, mistress, in the house."

She marched unannounced into the hall.

Mistress Godechepe, or should she call her, Fabricant for she was a widow and must take the name of her true husband, was sitting at the table. Henry Godechepe had her hand in his own and he was kissing the palm. The gesture was eloquent.

"Master Godechepe!" said Rosalie harshly.

"Madam!" Henry recovered quickly. "We didn't know that you were coming to see us. We would have welcomed you at the door."

The woman Fabricant drew back her hand and adjusted her head dress. Rosalie noted that today she was wearing the barbette and crown she had worn when she'd attended the festivity in Marlborough. And a new blue wool cotte with bands of embroidery at the cuff and neck.

"My sister and I are just celebrating some good news."

"Oh?"

"Yes. Our house by Pewsey Down is to be rebuilt. Eleanor can once again have her own home."

"I am surprised that you can find the funds to rebuild when you are so deep in debt, sir."

Henry did not flinch. "I beg your pardon. Debt? Where have you heard this calumny?"

"It is not true?"

"Not at all."

Rosalie noticed that Mistress Fabricant was not the dissembler her lover was and was distinctly ill at ease.

"Then the other rumours I have heard will not be true either?"

"And those are, said Henry solicitously, coming to take her elbow and removing her cloak.

"That your sister here is not a blood relative at all. That she is the widow of a sempster of Devizes."

"Where have you heard such utter nonsense?"

"From a reputable source, I think." Rosalie refused to sit.

Henry and Eleanor exchanged a glance.

"And that your sole purpose in paying me attention was so that you could relieve me of my fortune and my farm."

"No madam. You are misinformed. I pay court to you because I love you. Do I not Eleanor?"

"Oh Henry, you speak of no one else. If it were not so utterly heartfelt, you should become tedious."

"There now, sit down please. And take some refreshment."

"No. I will say what I came to say and then you and I will part ways and never meet again...unless we must be thrown together at church or some other place."

"I can only say that someone has been feeding you complete lies. Why as I say, only today I have settled funds upon a builder to rebuild the cottage at Pewsey Edge."

"And I hope those poor builders will be paid."

"Madam, are you calling me a liar?"

"I suppose you have managed to secure the loan you have been seeking. Probably from the Jews in town."

"I have no dealings with the Jews in town. That, madam is beneath me. Do not speak so, Rosalie."

"I will thank you to call me Mistress Jourdemayne from now on."

Henry looked shocked. "Would you toss away a good friendship for the sake of town gossip, madam?"

"I do not believe gossip. Your face belies the truth of it. I have come to see your guilt for myself."

Again the look passed between the two occupants of Cutwythy Farm.

"I can assure you there is no truth in any of it."

"And furthermore that you are about to lay off some of your workforce. What do you say to that?

"Whom am I about to lay off?"

"A man named William Herd, I believe, a shepherd for one."

"Aw that lazy, foul mouthed idiot! Yes. I am laying him off at the end of the season. He is a good for nothing slugabed."

"And no other men?"

"Those with whom I am dissatisfied will be laid off without doubt. Further shepherds can be had two a penny from the hiring fair."

"What price loyalty, sir?"

"You are lucky. Your men have been with you a long time. I am new here. I must…"

"You are not spoken well of, sir, amongst the workers of the area."

"Then let folk speak ill!" Henry Godechepe's face convulsed with anger. "I have heard enough of this rubbish."

Rosalie watched him. She was now convinced by his angry outburst that she had caught a raw spot.

"I see, sir, that this, more than any of my other accusations, has upset your normal sanguine disposition. "I am inclined to believe the gossip."

"Believe what you like, Rosalie, but never doubt that I love you."

Mistress Fabricant, as Rosalie now liked to call her in her head, gave Henry a strange look.

"By your expression, madam," said Rosalie, "The tone of that declaration is not something you want to hear."

"I cannot know what you mean," replied Eleanor.

"That the man loves another woman. You believe it don't you? It must be very disconcerting for you. How often has he declared the same to you, Mistress Fabricant."

The woman took in a shocked breath.

"How does it feel to be tossed aside? Ah but then, you are not his wife, are you?"

Eleanor jumped up. "You foul mouthed harpy!" she cried.

Henry moved behind Rosalie.

"I see there is no changing your mind."

"Admit it and I will leave and say not a word to anyone."

"I would like to think that true."

"My word is my bond," said Rosalie with venom in her voice. "I am about to make the vow of celibacy I spoke of. The bishop has been informed and it will happen soon. Then I can be wife to none. My word will be my oath. It always is."

"Ah...that is ...unfortunate," said Henry.

"What?"

"Eleanor, Parchment and pen."

"Yes Henry." Eleanor scurried off at his authoritarian word.

The door behind Rosalie was suddenly closed and locked. Henry strode to the only other door in the hall and stood before it until Eleanor returned. Then it too was locked.

"Open that door," said Rosalie, her chin coming up. "I will not be confined here."

"You will be confined, madam, until you set your name to a document of my devising..."

"Document? What document?"

"One allowing me the honour of becoming your husband at last, and master of Forceleap Farm."

"Never. Do not be foolish. I cannot write. Whatever makes you think..."

"Oh Rosalie, I know you can write. You are the most accomplished woman I know."

"Never!"

"Then you will not leave this house - alive."

"Don't be stupid Henry," said Rosalie trying to placate him. "You would commit murder over a few furlongs of land?"

"Sit!" he bellowed and Rosalie, recalling her years of training at the hands of her bully husband, sat. Sadly.

"Now I will dictate and you will write."

"I will not."

Under her sleeve a knife nicked her left arm. "Take off your wimple."

"What?"

"Take it off..." Henry Godechepe snatched at the wimple which Rosalie wore under her chin and tore off the pins securing it to her brow band. He tossed it onto the table.

"How dare you!" Rosalie's hands instinctively came up to her damaged neck.

"That's right, protect your neck...for there will be a knife at it soon."

"It won't be the first time," said Rosalie bravely but Henry wasn't listening.

"Now write..." The knife came closer and pricked her throat.

"The date is..."

Rosalie swept the room with her eyes. Eleanor stood petrified, by the door like a rabbit before a weasel.

'You could reach that other door and take the key,' said her little voice. 'You just need to distract him.'

"And how do I do that?"

Rosalie wrote the date upon the parchment.

"Now, I Rosalie Jourdemayne..." went on Henry. "Write it..."

'The pin in your headdress...it's one of your larger bronze ones. Take the pin!'

Rosalie's left hand strayed to the wimple thrown casually onto the table top as she wrote.

"...by the Grace of God..."

Her fingers closed on the pin and whilst Godechepe stared up to the rafters, forming the next sentence, she took the pin slowly into her palm.

"Mistress of Forceleap Farm. To all those that this present letter shall hear or see..."

Suddenly she leapt up and forward - let the knife prick her, she had had worse - and picked up the inkwell.

She threw the contents into the eyes of Henry Godechepe and turning the pin rapidly in her hand she thrust its sharpened end into his face.

She ran with a quick look back. Eleanor was still motionless by the inner door and Godechepe had his hands to his face.

With fumbling fingers, Rosalie turned the key in the lock and she was free, running across the farmyard with quick steps. She stooped to pick up the hem of her dress and ran for all she was worth for open country.

*****

She had no idea where she was but that did not seem to matter. She needed to find cover, any cover. She scanned the downs. No trees. If she could make it to that little spinney in the distance, there might be a way of reaching a road or a cottage.

She ran on until a stitch in her side made her stop. She dared not look back but, sadly could not control her head. She twisted. Far in the distance was Master Godechepe, his hand to his cheek, stumbling after her.

The wind had now picked up but thankfully it was behind her and lent her speed.

'Run Rosalie, run,' said the voice in her head.

"I *am* running!" she replied out loud as her breath came in short snatches.

Her hair was working its way free from her crespinette.

'Do not leave it behind. If you make the trees, he will know where you have gone if it drops to the ground.' For once her little devil was being helpful.

She snatched it from her head and her blonde waves cascaded out across her shoulders. Shoving the handmade twisted item down the breast of her cotte, she ran on.

The trees closed around her.

She looked back. Godechepe had recovered his poise and was following steadily.

'Left or right? Left or right?' said her devil.

"Right. The trees are denser."

'You will not make such progress...'

But Rosalie was already threading her way through the trees at a pace.

She laughed at herself. "Ha! I am as nimble as I was when I was a girl!"

Four steps further on and she stumbled to a halt, catching hold of a tree for support.

'You may be nimble but you are no longer young,' said her voice.

Launching herself from the tree she ran on, breaking out at the top of a hill. She scoured the horizon, her heart thumping in her breast.

There a few furlongs away was a dip in the ground. "Maybe I could hide in there?"

'As long as he doesn't see you travel across the open ground - you could.' Her voice was being sensible.

Rosalie ran down the slope, missing her footing now and again. A pain started up in her breastbone... "Oh just a little further." The rain which had hitherto been just a few half-hearted drops now decided to come down with seriousness. She was soaked in moments.

Rosalie had to stop to catch her breath. She chanced a look behind. Godechepe was not there.

'He must have gone left when you turned right,' said her voice.

"Yes, let's hope it."

She found herself counting the steps to the dip in the ground.

"Fifty, fifty five...sixty." And she was there in the hollow. She threw herself down and panting like a hare, she turned on her back. "He cannot see me here."

After a while, when she had regained her breath, she risked a look over the top of the dip. Taking back her wayward hair, she tucked it behind her ears.

Godechepe was quartering the ground around the spinney. She could see his sky blue cotte, stained with ink and his black splattered face where the ink had marked him. But at this distance not the blood which had poured from the wound in his cheek.

'You need a weapon,' said the little voice in her ear.

Rosalie scouted round for a branch...anything she might use. There was nothing.

'More trees up ahead,' said her voice. 'Where there are trees there are fallen branches.'

Rosalie scrambled up and tumbling further down the slope, she made for the trees a furlong ahead. But before she could reach the safety of the wood, she met an unscalable obstacle.

A fence eight foot high reared up before her.

"No! A deer fence!"

'The fence will carry on,' said the voice in her head. 'Either side'

"Yes but there is no way I can scale it."

'But if you carry on, you may come to a deer leap and then you can be away!'

Taking her bundled and soaked cotte in her hands, she stepped out along the fence as fast as she could.

Yards and yards and yards of fence stretched out beside her.

'Keep going.'

"My strength is failing me." Her bad ankle gave a twinge.

'No it's not. Keep going. Eventually you will come to a dip.'

Feeling just a little miffed with her voice she ploughed on light headed.

Again she counted.

"One hundred and sixty five. One hundred and sixty six..."

On one hundred and ninety she looked back. Godechepe was following.

"Oh will it never end?"

Her hose was now down round her sodden ankles, having worked their way there with running.

"Oh!" she cried in frustration.

"Two hundred and...oh."

There by her side was a dip in the fence. Yes! She could easily scale it.

She scrambled to its platform and looked down. It was then that her poorly ankle chose to remind her that it had had enough of the exercise and she fell against the fence.

"Argh!"

Stumbling and hopping, she stood on the top of the bank. The wind gusted and she held onto the fence for safety.

The drop was prodigious.

A ditch on the other side, designed to stop the deer from leaping over the fence was three feet deep and lined with chalk stones and flints in places, as large as a fist. The bank upon which she stood made the deer leap at least twelve feet.

It would not be a soft landing.

She had dithered too long. Nonchalantly coming up behind her, Godechepe was grinning.

"I'll give you this mistress - you can run!" The knife was still in his hand.

"I will not do as you ask so you might as well leave me here," said Rosalie with a sneer. "You will have to kill me."

Godechepe took a step forward.

"After what you have done to me… it would be a pleasure," he said breathing hard.

Rosalie backed further onto the turf platform upon which the fence was erected.

The wind buffeted her dress to and fro and her hair tangled over her face. She grasped it back.

'OH…' said her little voice. 'Is this where we die then…?'

"If you come any nearer I will grasp you and take you with me down the slope," said Rosalie through clenched teeth.

"You..you are nothing. A slip of a thing. Try it!"

He came closer and now he was halfway up the inner slope of the deer leap, his knife extended.

Rosalie took out her own knife.

Henry Godechepe scoffed. "That will be as nothing."

"I did damage with a veil pin. I can mark you with this too."

He laughed then and his voice was taken away on the wind. She looked at him carefully. This was not the man she had known. Not the mild mannered, kind, farmer. This was a devil. 'However did you think that Master Dankworth's eyes were devilish?' asked her voice.

The eyes before her were indeed devilish. Henry had an expression she had never seen before. Sheer greed and hate.

She backed further through to the small lowering of the fence.

"I will jump!"

"Please do. It will save me from having to push you."

Into Rosalie's memory came a conversation about the deer leaps, which she and Henry had shared at the gathering in Marlborough. 'He was a very different man then,' said her devil.

And she remembered the story she had told him. About the widow who had thrown herself from a deer leap in anguish over the death of her husband.

"Yes, that is what they'll say of me," she said to herself. "When they find my broken body on the stones beneath."

"I see that you remember the story you told me."

'How does he know what I am thinking?' said Rosalie to her inner voice.

"I am not afraid to die."

She looked up and over her shoulder to the rain speckled down and recognised her own land in its dips and furrows, banks and knolls. Oh so close and yet so far.

"And yet you do not need to die," said Godechepe coming yet closer. "You need only to consent to marry me."

Rosalie took a deep breath. "I was married once to a man who beat me, scarred me, subjected me to terrible torments of the mind and body. For thirteen years. You think I want to repeat that?"

"I would be a *good* husband. You can have the freedom you obviously desire. Within reason."

"Whilst you play at brother and sister with your mistress! Never!"

"Then I have no choice." He came closer, his breath was almost on her cheek. "I cannot allow you to live and tell the tale."

"I told you, I am not afraid of dying. My only regret is that I did not listen to my heart when it told me that the best man that ever lived was right under my nose…"

Godechepe looked puzzled. Rosalie could see the wound she had inflicted on him with her large bronze pin. It would scar his handsome face forever. Good.

"A man ten times your worth, nay a hundred. Oh Ancelin," said Rosalie to herself.

She looked down at the stones of the ditch behind her. Would it hurt when she hit the bottom? Would she lie wounded until she died or would she break her neck instantly?

A buffet of wind took hold of her sodden cotte and she teetered on the edge of the precipice. She was cold. So cold.

"Oh Ancelin, I wish I had told you that I love you," she said.

'Maybe he will hear it carried in the wind,' said her little voice growing fainter.

Henry Godechepe grabbed Rosalie by the waist and forced her over the lip of the fence. Her feet scrabbled upon the chalky surface. A gust of wind stronger than hitherto took hold of them both. She put out her two hands and felt for the palisade of the fence, straining against the bulk of Master Godechepe as he pushed.

Then just as she managed to turn a little, the knife he held came out and nicked her wrist. She let go.

She was falling, falling and then she ceased to fall.

Strong arms came out to reach for her. Hands closed around her shoulders and pulled her back. Arms wound themselves around her and hugged her close.

"Rosalie."

She opened her eyes, for she had closed them against the looming ground which she had been sure she would hit.

"Ancelin?"

Ancelin Hayward turned her from the drop and stood close, holding her wet body against his equally wet cotte.

"What?"

She stumbled a little, not understanding what had happened and he held her close so that her ankle would not give way.

"He is gone," he said.

"Gone?"

"The forceleap has taken him. That and the wind."

Rosalie focussed at last on the bottom of the ditch. There was Godechepe; his blue cotte soaked; his face scarred by blood and ink, rapidly fading in the rain and his eyes staring to the windy heavens.

"Is he...?"

"He looks it, but I must scramble down and find out."

Although Rosalie was very shaky she too said that she would clamber down.

"Although...just for a moment, hold me tight. I thought I would never see you again."

Ancelin's strong arms came around her again and they leaned against the parapet.

The wind buffeted around them but together they resisted it.

Ancelin rested his chin upon the crown of her soaked blonde head.

"I thought I had lost you."

"No. No…" She lifted her face so that he might kiss her wet lips very gently. Once. "No. You have found me."

*****

Gradually Ancelin hand by hand, foot by foot climbed down the almost sheer slope. The clay and flint, chalk and earth bank was pitted here and there and it was possible for a man to clamber down. Not so a woman with a bad ankle.

"You will not make it safely. Stay there and I will climb up again."

Hayward stared at Godechepe and crossed himself.

"He *is* dead," he shouted up, against the wind which took away his voice. "I will have to get a party out to recover his body."

Placing his booted feet on the bank once more, Ancelin made short work of the incline and stumbled over the ridge of the short fence.

"We shall have to walk back to Cutwythy Farm. Can you manage it?"

"Eleanor is there. My horse is there..."

She looked at him, his hair plastered to his head, his wet clothes clinging to him, his face full of worry and concern.

"I cannot walk back to Forceleap."

"Then you shall ride and I will lead you."

"No, we shall both ride."

He smiled then, a sincere smile, one with affection in it.

"How did you know? How did you find me?"

"I quizzed Fulk. He told me you had gone out on Filbert with a determined look on your face. In the light of what I'd told you earlier, I wondered if you had gone to confront the man Godechepe and so I saddled Goliath and followed.

"You were not far behind."

"I arrived as you were running across the downs and I saw Henry Godechepe follow you, a knife in his hand. I knew I had to trail him."

"Thank heavens you did. I would now be lying at the bottom of a bank, dead or dying, giving truth to the legend of the Forceleap."

He took hold of her once more.

"I knew...I know what you would do."

A little recovered, Rosalie said, looking up at him, "You do *not*, sir." Her voice was playful and cheery.

"I knew."

"Because I am headstrong and...what was it?"

"Stubborn. Headstrong and stubborn and wilful and totally infuriating and lovely."

Her little voice was about to say something and she shushed it quickly.

"But you are all those things and that is why I love you."

"Oh Ancelin. Why have you not said so before?"

"Because...because...I did not feel that you would look at me. I am an employee. I am nothing. I could not declare my love. Besides, you had other suitors. I did not know which one you favoured."

"Oh Ancelin, you silly fool. I favoured *you*."

"I am a fool. And you are a stubborn and headstrong and wilful woman but you are MY stubborn and headstrong and wilful woman. Will you do me the honour of accepting my proposal of marriage?"

"Master Hayward. You are a silly fool, but you are MY silly fool. And I would be honoured to become your wife."

They kissed then, to cement the bargain on the top of the Forceleap palisade with the wind and the rain buffeting around them and a few curious sheep for witnesses.

*****

"I do hope the priest of St. Mary's has not yet been in contact with the bishop," said Rosalie, the next day. "I will feel such a fool that I will have to tell him that, far from making a vow of celibacy, I am now to be married."

"Then just write a letter telling him that. Do not mention the vow," said Ancelin.

"Hmmm .I expect he has not had the time."

"Let us hope so. Might you notify him that we think that November is a good time for a marriage?"

"He can have no objection," said Rosalie. The time of harvest was past and the time for planting had not yet arrived. It was a good time, for the animals had been slaughtered for food, so freshly butchered beef, mutton, pork, and other meats were to be available for the wedding feast.

"I will write to him straight away and get Fulk to take it into town."

She took up her stick and hobbled out of the hall.

Ancelin followed, a grim look on his face.

"How is the ankle today?"

"Painful but bearable."

"You must rest it as much as possible, if you are not to limp up to the church porch on our wedding day," he laughed.

"Oh Ancelin!"

Hayward looked out of the door. "How could the weather be so very different today?"

Bright sunshine and a thin high cloud was visible over the hedge of the farmyard.

Rosalie took out her writing equipment. Roger's writing equipment.. ah Roger. What would he make of all this?

Ancelin's face clouded.

"Rosalie?"

Yes.?"

"Come here."

"I beg your pardon?"

"Here..come here a moment."

"What?"

He took her in his left arm and pointed out through the gate to the rise of the orchard.

"Look."

She took in a startled breath.

"William."

There in the bright sunlight was a tall man in a cabbage green cotte; a man with a small dark beard and twinkling blue eyes.

"Oh William."

The figure smiled and turned and walked away, fading as he walked. It took a great deal of will power for Rosalie not to follow.

"It is done and he is content," said Ancelin Hayward.

Rosalie looked at him oddly and then gave into an urge to kiss him.

She reached up and placed her mouth on his.

For the very last time, for she never heard it again, her little voice said,

'Well, Rosalie Jourdemayne. How lucky you are. I can tell you, there will be no reason...no reason at all to *ever* dispose of THIS husband.'

❧ FIN ❦

GLOSSARY

Anchorite - A religious recluse.

Angevin - Kings Henry 2nd, Richard 1st & John. All holding land in Angers, France.

Beat the Bounds - Mark parish boundaries by walking round them and striking certain points with rods.

Betrothal - Formal engagement to be married.

Clunch - Soft limestone capable of being easily worked.

Cods - Genitals

Coffin - Pastry case.

Cordwainer - Shoemaker.

Corpus Christi - Feast day commemorating the institution of the Eucharist, observed on the Thursday after Trinity Sunday.

Cotte - Coat, a long simple garment worn by both sexes.

Crespinette - Hairnet.

Cutler - A man who makes small tools and cutlery.

Distaff - Tool for hand spinning.

Extreme unction - (In the Roman Catholic Church) a former name for the sacrament of anointing of the sick, especially when administered to the dying.

Filet - A headband.

Fold - A wattle fenced pen or enclosure in a field where livestock, especially sheep, can be kept.

Furlong - Old measurement, an eighth of a mile, 220 yards.

Frith stool/chair - a seat, chair, or place of peace. Also OE frithstól, a place of sanctuary or safekeeping.

Gnomon - The projecting piece on a sundial that shows the time by the position of its shadow.

Groom - A thatching tool.

Hogling - Old name for piglet.

Kirtle - Cotte, bliaut or dress for a woman.

Leaks like a toad - When threatened toads secrete an unpleasant substance from behind their ears.

Leat - An open watercourse conducting water to a mill or stream.

Lime mortar - Cement made with lime.

Mass dial - A scratched or engraved sundial on a church wall telling the times of worship.

Melusine - A woman of legend, like a mermaid.

Mercer - Purveyor of cloth and other goods.

Oxbow cut offs - A U-Shaped lake that forms when a wide meander of a river is cut off, creating a free-standing body of water.

Roan - A horse coat colour pattern characterized by an even mixture of colored and white hairs on the body, while the head and "points"—lower legs, mane and tail—are mostly solid-colored.

Rouncey - A workhorse.

Roundelay - A circle dance.

St. Swithun - According to tradition, if it rains on Saint Swithun's day (15th July) on his feast day it will continue to do so for forty days.

Sarsens - Sandstone blocks found in quantity in Wiltshire.

Sharbat - Sherbert.

Shift - Under petticoat.

Sweetmeats - Sweets made with honey or rarely sugar, at this time.

Tally Sticks - An ancient memory aid device used to record and document numbers, quantities, or even messages.

Templar - The Poor Fellow-Soldiers of Christ and of the Temple of Solomon, also known as the Order of Solomon's Temple, the Knights Templar or simply the Templars, were a Catholic military order founded in 1119.

Town reeve - Mayor.

Vow of celibacy - A voluntary vow of sexual abstinence. In some cases, it can also be a promise to remain unmarried.

Wimple - A linen garment which runs under the chin and to which is pinned a veil.

AUTHOR'S NOTE

This novel grew out of my Savernake series; murder mystery novels set in the early 13th century. I wanted to write a 'romance' set as close as I could to Savernake Forest in Wiltshire, but not actually in it. If you know the area, you will be able to place the names but they aren't all exactly where I say. I have taken a few liberties with the geography.

but they aren't all exactly where I say. I have taken a few liberties with the geography.

The real Forceleap Farm is near Charlton, close to Banbury (Oxfordshire) in Northamptonshire. As I say in the book, it originated as Four Leas Farm but Forceleap is much more evocative and trips from the tongue.

Fields in the Middle Ages were often named. Many retain these names today. Long Deadman's is a field in Charlton aforementioned, close to the real Forceleap Farm - one wonders how it got its name.

Deer leaps were just as I describe them in the text, though the real Forceleap Farm has never had any.

Between these covers you will encounter some characters you already know from the Savernake Novels. Johannes the doctor in town; Sir Maurice FitzAlan, a captain of the guard at the castle and Father Torold, in particular.

There was an anchorite at Preshute church. Records show that King John gave a stipend to an Alice of Preshute for quite some time.

Thanks must go to The Newbottle Estate who own the real Forceleap Farm and who allowed me to use the name. They too farm Longhorn cattle, as they are now known.

Thanks also go to The English Longhorn Cattle Society for their help. In the past these cattle were known as Long Horned as they were not a distinct breed, even though the Templars did indeed breed and keep them in Wiltshire and on their other properties in the north of England.

The county boundaries have changed since the thirteenth century, indeed in my lifetime. Wantage was once in Berkshire and it is now in Oxfordshire.

The vow of celibacy was a common occurrence in the Middle Ages. Women and men would make the vow for a variety of reasons. The vow didn't mean that they had to lock themselves away, as they would have done if they had taken monastic vows and entered a convent. They could continue to work, run businesses and live with family as long as they refrained from conjugal relations.

Widows were actively encouraged to make vows for it safeguarded them from exploitation. As I say in the text, the church was happier for them to profess chastity than remarry. The rite is as I describe though it varied a little from diocese to diocese.

The song which Rosalie sings is a 13th century one called Mirie it is. Here's a translation.

Mirie it is while sumer y-last
With fugheles song,
Oc nu necheth windes blast
And weder strong.
Ej! Ej! what this nicht is long,
And ich with wel michel wrong
Soregh and murne and fast.

Merry it is while summer lasts,
With birds in song;
But now there threatens windy blasts
And tempests strong.
Ah, but the night is long,
And I, being done such wrong,
Sorrow and mourn and fast.

Thank you to Charlie Farrow (my publisher) who suggested a while ago that I write a romance. I never thought about doing it, indeed I thought it 'wasn't my thing' until I started it. It was researched and written in four weeks! The fastest I have ever written anything!

Susanna M. Newstead August 2020

About the Author

Susanna, like Rosalie has known the area around Marlborough all her life. After a period at the University of Wales studying Speech Therapy, she returned to Wiltshire and then moved to Hampshire to work, not so very far away. Susanna developed an interest in English history, particularly that of the 12th and 13th centuries, early in life and began to write about it in her twenties. She now lives in Northamptonshire with her husband and two small wire haired fox terriers called Delphi and Tabor. Forty years of writing Mediaeval murder mystery, she has now written her first romance. The first of many we hope.

ALSO BY SUSANNA M. NEWSTEAD

THE SAVERNAKE MEDIEVAL MURDER MYSTERIES

Belvoir's Promise
She Moved Through the Fair
Down by the Salley Gardens
I Will Give my Love an Apple
Black is the Colour of my True Love's Hair
Long Lankyn
One Misty Moisty Morning
The Unquiet Grave
The Lark in the Morning
A Parcel of Rogues
Bushes & Briars

Please visit her website for further information
https://susannamnewstead.co.uk/